SPRINGTIME
OF THE
Song

Also by Phyllis Clark Nichols

THE FAMILY PORTRAIT SERIES
The Christmas Portrait – Book One
The Birthday Portrait – Book Two
The Christmas Portrait Surprise – Book Three

THE ROCKWATER SUITE
Return of the Song – Book One
Freedom of the Song – Book Two
Ransom for a Song – Book Three
Christmas Wedding Song – Book Four
Searching for the Song – Book Five

CHRISTMAS BOOKS
Christmas at Grey Sage
Silent Night, Holy Night
Breath for the Soul: Self-care Steps to Wellness
Co-authored with Dr. Jan E. Patterson

NOW AVAILABLE IN AUDIO BOOKS –
Read by Phyllis Clark Nichols
The Christmas Portrait
The Birthday Portrait
Return of the Song
Freedom of the Song
Ransom for a Song
Christmas at Grey Sage
Silent Night, Holy Night

SPRINGTIME
OF THE
Song

The ROCKWATER Suite

—

Book Six

Phyllis Clark Nichols

 Southern Stories Publishing

Dedication

For my Bill,
who makes even a stormy, winter day seem like springtime.

Chapter One

---◆---

Two or One

Tuesday, September 14, 2010, at Rockwater

Caroline was lost somewhere between the melodic line of "Some Enchanted Evening" and the memory of her studio back in Moss Point. Her fingers never faltered as she almost whisper-like sang the last phrase. With the resolving chord still reverberating through the halls, she sat silently at the piano and closed her eyes. It had been an enchanted evening her first visit to Rockwater, meeting Roderick, and playing this piano for the first time since her parents had sold it when she graduated high school. This Hazelton Brothers grand piano, hers since childhood, had been home for her, that place where she could always return and know what to do. She needed home right now.

She breathed in the warmth of the late-afternoon sun streaming through the loggia windows. As her fingers silently traced the piano keyboard, she recalled the slant of the afternoon autumn light through the bay window in Moss Point when her studio had pulsated with music and the comings and goings of her students. She was remembering them one by one when there came an abrupt knock on the front door. No ringing bell, just a constant clobbering that she feared might take the door off its hinges.

Lilah and Celia, Roderick's assistant, had already left for the day, and Roderick was in his office. She rushed to the pounding urgency at the door. The yellow delivery truck caught her eye in the side glass panel before she opened the door to an unfamiliar face. The regular delivery man would have known to deliver to the back entrance.

"Ma'am, I'm new on this delivery route, and I'm sorry to say I could not find your doorbell. I apologize for knocking so hard, but I thought I heard some music inside a few moments ago and didn't know if you could hear me." He raised the hand holding the package. "I have a delivery for a Mr. Roderick Adair, and I will need a signature."

Caroline stepped closer. "Of course. I am Mrs. Adair, and I'll be happy to take the package." Announcing she was Mrs. Adair was still unfamiliar to her.

He extended his clipboard for her signature, and she signed her name. *I am Mrs. Roderick Adair. I am no longer Caroline Carlisle, the music teacher.*

When she returned his clipboard, the man handed her the large, padded envelope he held.

"I do understand about the doorbell," she said. "It's not in plain sight." She pointed to the bell on the side stone wall and watched a slight pink spread across his cheeks. "If you'll be making regular deliveries in the future, we'd be grateful if you would follow the driveway to the back where the office is located. You can't miss that entrance, and someone will be there to receive your packages. And if Lilah's here, you'll probably leave with a bag of home-baked cookies."

"Yes, ma'am. I'll remember that. The regular driver has taken ill, and I'm just filling in. Not that I wish him any harm, but his route is better than the city routes any day.

This is a mighty beautiful place you have here, and I do hope to stick around long enough to make another few deliveries to sample those cookies." He tipped his cap. "You have a fine evening, ma'am." He turned, stumbled slightly, and walked away to the truck.

"Thank you." She closed the door and turned the lock. The package felt like a full ream of paper, and she didn't recognize the return address.

Better get this to Roderick in case he's waiting on it.

She hummed as she turned, her bell-like voice singing the last line of "Some Enchanted Evening" echoing as she walked through the loggia and down the hallway to the kitchen and out to the office wing. She was about to push the door open to Roderick's office when she heard him speaking.

"No, Caroline has no knowledge of any of this."

Surprised, she paused during the following silence and waited.

The baritone voice that had mesmerized her almost three years ago with their first phone conversation now puzzled and frightened her with its unfamiliar, angry tone. "Yes, I will tell her when she needs to know, but right now she has no need to know."

Caroline stood in the hallway outside the door, listening intently for the next words. Nothing. Quietly stepping away from the office door, she cradled the package with both arms as though she were trying to hang on to something she suddenly and unexpectedly felt slipping away. She trudged the hallway back to the kitchen.

———•———

Late Tuesday afternoon at Moss Point

Angel returned her clean paint brushes to the jar on the counter and sat down in the chintz-covered chair to admire her work, another still life of roses. Only these American Beauties were arranged in the 1905 Johnson Brothers Antique English Victorian porcelain bowl and pitcher purchased by Sam's mother on a trip to England. This painting would be her anniversary gift for Caroline and Roderick. And one day the bowl and pitcher would be Caroline's too. Another few afternoons of detail work, and the painting would be off to the frame shop. She and Sam would take this to Rockwater at Christmas, which happened to be Caroline's first wedding anniversary.

Although Angel relished every moment spent in her studio, she missed Caroline and the music that had been made here for the seven years Caroline called this Twin Oaks studio home. But all that had changed now. Caroline was married to Roderick, the man who'd captured her heart and brought her music back. Once again, the cottage was Angel's art studio and a guest cottage for Roderick and Caroline when they visited.

Angel remembered the afternoons she and Sam would sit on their back porch up at the main house to listen to the music wafting from the studio windows and through the garden. A bit melancholy, she picked up the phone from the table next to the chair and called Caroline. She was about to hang up when someone answered.

"Hello." The voice was somber.

"Caroline? Is that you?"

Angel heard her take a deep breath. "Why, yes ma'am, it is."

"Oh, good. For just a moment, you didn't sound like yourself. You all right, sweet girl?"

With only slight hesitation, Caroline responded. "Of course. Why on earth wouldn't I be all right? I've just been trotting from one end of this house to the other answering the door and delivering the mail. All this running makes me breathless and makes me long for a simple studio."

"You mean like the one I'm sittin' in right now? I've been here all afternoon dabbin' and swipin' paint on this canvas, but I was missin' your music and rememberin' how you had a revolvin' door of boys and girls showin' up every afternoon for their piano lessons. Those were good days, Caroline—at least good days for ol' Sam and me."

"And for me. I miss those days so much, Angel. I'm finding with fall coming that I long for the days of lining up my schedule and interviewing new students. But my life is different and filled with other activities now. I even made a batch of peanut-butter cookies this morning like I used to do."

Angel heard the longing in Caroline's voice and propped her feet on the hassock and got comfortable for a chat. "I suppose you're settlin' down from all your travels and then that marvelous Guatemalan Children's Choir you hosted. Everyone safely back at home now?"

"Yes, finally, but the house is so quiet. I'm glad you and Sam could be here for the concert. The children stayed for a few more days after you left, and of course that meant Sarah and George and little Rosita were here with us. We had a couple of fun events out here at Rockwater, and we took the girls to Lexington for an outing and to a real Kentucky horse farm."

"I can only imagine the joy and excitement of those sweet girls."

"Oh, yes. And everywhere we went, they were treated like royalty. I spoke with Sister Gabby a couple of days ago, and they're getting back to their normal routines at the orphanage but asking when they can return to America."

"Well, tell me. You might imagine Sam is dyin' to know. Were the fundraisin' activities successful?"

"Yes. The children were well received in every venue. We raised enough money to pay all the expenses of their trip with almost forty-five thousand dollars left over to continue to fund the girls' educations and the work of the choir."

"Well, slap my Aunt Susie, that's just fabulous. And what about Lydia? Did she decide to move in with the two of you? Never have I met anyone like that woman. She really seemed to be enjoyin' herself."

"You know if Lydia hadn't started the African Children's Choir, then there'd probably be no Guatemalan Children's Choir. She has been my strong guide, and yes, she stayed for a whole week after the children left. Lots of walks and talks, and she finally got Roderick back on a horse."

Angel giggled. "Ah, yes. I remember her sayin' she came to Kentucky to sample the bourbon and to ride horses."

"Well, she did plenty of the bourbon sipping. That woman is fearless in every way. Comfortable in her skin no matter where she is. She got in a couple of rides with Roderick. Said it was better than a camel. Roderick and I are planning to ride when he has time. He seems to be so busy these days, catching up on all the things he didn't get done when the choir was here."

"Yes, judges and business moguls always are busy—busy minds and always plannin'."

"I wish I knew more about his business. It seems that in the last nine months, we've been traveling or planning something all the time, and I've had so little time to even think about his work. I'm looking forward to a quiet fall and getting ready for the holidays. Maybe that will give me more time to learn about his business."

Angel sighed. "And why would you want to do that, girl? Leave Roderick to his own business, and you get back to yours."

"You sound like Lydia."

"Well listen to her if you won't listen to me. You've had enough change in your life. Do what you're really good at and what makes you happy. We're all expectin' some spectacular new work from you. You just be you, and let Roderick do what Roderick does."

"It's just that he's always been so interested in the things that interest me and in the people that I love. I think it's time for me to do the same for him."

Angel sat up in her chair. "I can tell you've been givin' this some thought. Who am I to tell you what to do? You'll figure it out, and if you don't, Roderick will help you."

"Yes, I hope he will."

Angel caught the uncertainty in her voice. "For sure. For sure he will, if that's what you want to do. Well, I was just missin' your voice, but I need to get myself back up the lane to the house. You know the judge. He'll be rattlin' the plates and sittin' at the table with his fork in one hand and his knife in another, waitin' on his supper. Lucky for me, Hattie left a fresh chicken pot pie ready to stick in the oven. Wish you were here to put your feet under our table, girl, but there'd be one lovelorn, lonely man under a Kentucky moon tonight if that were so. Love you, and we'll talk again soon."

"Love you too. Goodbye Angel. You always know when to call. And give Sam a squeeze for me."

"You can count on my givin' Sam a squeeze. You just remember how much we love you. Bye for now."

Angel laid the phone down, sighed, and pondered the conversation before she started her walk home.

———•———

Later Tuesday afternoon at Rockwater

Roderick entered the kitchen and saw Caroline leaning into the open refrigerator. "Are you just cooling off, or could you be looking for picnic fixings?"

"Just looking." Caroline stood and closed the door. "Does this mean you're finished for the day, or are you just coming out for air?"

He walked to her and put his arms around her scant waist. "For air. You're my air." He held her close and buried his face in her sable curls. He felt the familiar caress of her child-sized hand against his cheek. He took that hand, kissed it, and backed away. "I probably need a shave. I think I started work this morning without a clean shave, and I'm here to tell you that my wife does not like stubble."

"She must be highly demanding." Caroline smiled. "Yes, you've been busy all day. I've hardly seen you. I suppose you've had a lot of catching up to do. You were so attentive and generous with your time when Sister Gabby and the Guatemalan girls were here, and then a week with Lydia. Are you catching up, or are you working on another big deal? I've noticed you've been on the phone so much and glued to your computer."

Before he could answer, she turned to the kitchen counter and picked up the package. "Oh, and this was delivered a few minutes ago. Feels like five pounds of paper, and probably means more work."

Roderick picked up the package and looked at the return address. "Well, you'd be right about that. But it won't be done tonight. You didn't happen to see any picnic fixings in the fridge, did you? I mean, if it's not too much trouble, I'd like to hike up to Blue Hole and stick my feet in the water and clear my head. Just a few more days and the chill in the air will mean no more feet in the spring water until springtime. What do you say?"

He was relieved to see the real smile, not the forced one from earlier, along with her raised eyebrow and the familiar wink.

"I'll even help with the picnic. But we need to hurry—only about an hour and a half of good daylight left." He watched happiness spread across Caroline's face.

Her answer was the two steps she took to the refrigerator. She opened the door and started handing items to Roderick. "I'll get our food ready. Would you get our light jackets and a towel? And maybe a flashlight just in case."

He loved that she was a just-in-case kind of woman.

Within a few minutes, sandwiches, cheese, fruit, a bottle of wine, and some of her fresh-baked cookies were ready for packing. Roderick started stuffing the towel and flashlight into the bottom of the backpack. "Now why didn't I think of a picnic backpack? I could have made another industry out of that idea. I guess it's because I didn't know much about picnics until your first visit to Rockwater. But this picnic backpack was a perfect birthday gift. Only you would have thought of such."

Caroline wiped the counter. "If you're holding on to a basket, you can't hold my hand. You're not the easiest fellow to buy gifts for, and don't be surprised if your next gift has wheels. I've been thinking we need a couple of bicycles."

"Bicycles on a horse farm? I'd be the laughingstock of Lexington. What's wrong with a horse or just a long walk?"

"Of course, you're riding again. I must get used to that thought. But maybe I could use a few lessons before we take the horseback ride to Blue Hole. That's not exactly like riding in the arena. Did . . . ?"

Roderick slipped his arms through the backpack straps,

and before she could voice her question, he answered, "Yes, I have the flashlight." He chuckled. "We're getting more like Sam and Angel, an old married couple finishing each other's sentences. I knew you'd ask." He helped her with her jacket. "We'd better start making tracks."

Hand in hand, they strode out the kitchen door and started down the path to Blue Hole.

———•———

They sat side by side on the boulder with their legs dangling above the topaz water ten feet below them. Caroline was mesmerized by the late-afternoon light reflecting on the glassy surface, completely undisturbed by the bubbling deeper blue depths of the spring. It was no wonder this was called Blue Hole. "Did you give up on the idea of putting your feet in this water?"

"I think I did. No climbing down just yet. I'd rather not move. This seems right on the edge of perfection."

"Just on the edge?"

"Of course, these peanut-butter cookies are perfection. Between the smell of them in the oven this morning and your piano playing, I almost sent Celia to the barn for a piece of rope to tie myself to my office chair. Do you remember how Odysseus was tied to the mast of his ship as he sailed by the island and wanted to hear the sirens sing? He didn't want to be lured to his death by such temptresses and their music."

"I don't recall ever having been labeled a temptress. Maybe I should play the piano more often. It's just that it's been a while since I've had the time to sit and play. And honestly, I suppose I've been somewhat nostalgic today. This is the time of year when I started a new season of teaching—new students, new schedules, new music, but always peanut-butter cookies. I have no students, so I made cookies."

"Glad you did. Sounds like you're missing your students?" She felt the gentle stroke of his finger on the back of her hand.

"Perhaps. I did enjoy teaching. Teaching brings instant gratification, even with the frustration. Not many jobs allow you to experience that."

"Truer words have never been spoken. I guess you've been—no, *we've* been—so busy the last several months with travels and then the children's choir that we haven't given much thought as to how you'd like to spend your time once our lives settle down."

She chortled a bit. "You mean settling down to being old married people?"

"Not exactly. It's just that you've had so much change in the last couple of years. All the work you did with Bella, marrying me, moving away from everyone and everything that was familiar to you." He paused. "Oh, and in the middle of all that, you were kidnapped, and that became one of life's hitching posts for both of us."

Caroline had a sudden shiver just remembering the shed in Guatemala and the mudslide that had nearly buried her and Lydia. "I don't want to cast a shadow on a perfectly lovely picnic with that kind of talk, and I do not want that event to be what my life hinges on—before and after I was kidnapped. Besides, life's all about change. Change is the constant, is it not?"

"How I love the way you think." Roderick paused. "I suppose I've been selfish and a bit presumptuous thinking you'd be happy as just my wife, making Rockwater your home, and then traveling with me. As my wise and noble sister chastened me last week before she and George left, I must remember that you've been an independent woman, and you may have desires that would include something other than just being Mrs. Roderick Adair."

Surprise bled across Caroline's face. "You and Sarah talked about how I should be spending my time? And what would make me happy?"

"I guess we did. Sarah was just reminding me that your big event with the choir was done and that a woman like you needed things to do besides be at my beck and call."

"Did you come to any decision about what I should be doing?"

"Couldn't even pay me to make that decision. Sarah figures you'll get involved in the documentary that's being done on Bella and that you might want to pursue your music again. But no, any decision you make about how you spend your time would be yours and yours alone."

Caroline seized her opportunity. "Well, you'd be entirely wrong about that." She lifted her legs and turned her body to face him. "Roderick, you know this we're-married-now thing? It means we don't make decisions alone. We do life together. We are one now."

"One?"

"Yes. Two became one. I don't cease being who I am, and neither do you, but we make our life-altering decisions together. I can't even think about deciding how to spend my time without discussing it with you. Would you want me to do that? Just make my own decision and prance in and tell you what I'm planning to do?"

He stammered. "Hmm, that might not go down so easy, but if it meant you'd be happy, I would adjust. I do trust your judgment."

She realized this conversation was not getting her what she desired. She wanted to know what he was keeping from her, and she preferred coaxing rather than asking. "But trust goes both ways. If I made the decision without including you, doesn't that show a bit of mistrust of you on my part? At the least, it would expose my own self-centeredness."

"I'm trying to understand your position, Caroline. But knowing how much you love me, I cannot imagine you'd make a decision that wouldn't be best for both of us. I would assume that you considered my feelings in your decision."

Caroline took a deep breath and turned back with her legs dangling from the boulder. "Well, you'd be absolutely correct about that. I guess we're coming from two different places. After all you are the business mogul whose job it is to make decisions, sometimes swiftly and often alone, and I've grown up in a rather sheltered environment where I've included those I'm closest to in all my significant decision-making."

"Excellent insight. Should have thought of that myself." He took her hand and held it to his lips. "With your analytical mind, you'd be a formidable businesswoman."

Ah, this is my opportunity. "Speaking of that, I have made a couple of decisions."

Roderick laughed. "You mean all by yourself?"

"I am serious, and yes, all by myself." She hesitated.

"I'm waiting."

"I need to go to Durham for a few days. They're starting the documentary on Bella, and the producer would like me to be there. And frankly, I think Gretchen would be more comfortable as well."

"Just say when, and I'll tell Albert to file a flight plan, and I'll make arrangements to be there for a couple of days. Not sure I'll be able to stay for a whole week. I have a couple of senators coming from Washington for a meeting."

"Thank you. I'll give Gretchen a call tomorrow for more details. Do I need to be here for your meeting with the senators?"

"No. That's not necessary. Okay, that's one decision. But you said you made a couple of decisions."

"Yes. I want to know more about your business. I was telling Angel this afternoon that ever since we've known each other, you've always expressed such interest in my life and what was claiming my time, whether it was Bella or the Guatemalan Children's Choir or my music. I've been grateful for all your attention, but I think it's time to turn the tables. I'd like to get more involved in your affairs, at least become more knowledgeable so that I can speak intelligently with you and others about them and under-stand your pressures and stresses."

"But, dear Caroline, why would anyone so gifted as you be interested in Adair Enterprises? No one can do what you do musically, and my business would be a waste of your time. And besides, my business is constantly changing."

She stood up and dusted off the seat of her jeans. "Is that a 'No, I don't want you involved in my business' kind of answer?"

He joined her on his feet. "No. That's not what I meant. If you truly want to know more or get involved, then yes. But . . ." He stammered again.

Caroline put her hands in her jacket pocket. "But what?" She watched the deep crease between his eyes become even deeper.

"Well, it would take some time to educate you, and honestly, right now is not the best time for me to do that. But it won't be long before things will settle, and I'll involve you."

Her spirit wilted and her curiosity heightened, she knelt and started putting away the remains of the picnic. "I see. Guess we'd better get back home before we need the flashlight."

Springtime of the Song

In the smoldering light of dusk, they quietly ambled the familiar path from Blue Hole back to Rockwater. Without thinking and as naturally as breathing, Caroline hummed the melodic line of "Some Enchanted Evening" as she walked, holding tightly to Roderick's hand.

Chapter Two

---◆---

Shadows

Tuesday afternoon, September 14, in Durham, North Carolina

Gretchen strolled through the Duke University Gardens on the way home from her bakery. Although Sam had taught her to drive and guided her through the purchase of a car before she left Moss Point and moved to Durham, she still preferred walking to and from the bakery. Thirty years of walking where she needed to go in Moss Point was an ingrained habit that she had no interest in breaking. Normally she was home earlier, and Karina stayed later to close the bakery. But today, Karina had left at noon to take Bella to her music lesson at the university.

The breeze was cool—not chilling, just cool—and the yellowing leaves whispered autumn's approach. The angle of the afternoon sun cast shadows across her path as she meandered the longer walk home. Having lived in Durham long enough to see all the changing seasons, she counted it a blessing to walk through the gardens almost daily. Each season was accompanied by its own beauty and palette of colors. So much of her time was spent baking, ordering supplies, planning, and thinking of the future, but the serene paths gave her time alone to be mindful, fully present with the beauty of the gardens, like a child pursuing wonder.

The phone rang as she walked through her cottage door. She dropped her bag in the desk chair and pulled the scarf from around her neck—the silk scarf Peter had given her.

Karina's voice was hurried. "Hi, Mammá. Just checking in. Hope you didn't mind closing the bakery today. Bella has finished her lesson, but I would really like to take her shopping for a new dress. She needs something special for the documentary."

"But Karina, there is no need for you to do that. I can take her shopping later this week."

"I know you could, Mammá, but I'd really like to do it, with your approval. And I think you should go shopping for yourself later this week. With the documentary, and with Peter's upcoming visit, you could use a few new things for yourself. Maybe we can make a list of things this evening."

Gretchen could not muzzle her smile as she listened to her daughter. "Make a list? I must think about that. If buying a new dress for Bella is something that would bring you pleasure, then yes. But at least come by the cottage and allow me to give you some money."

"You know how you taught me about the joy of giving? Then allow me this joy, Mammá. I've never had the opportunity to buy Bella anything. I promise to choose something that would be most appropriate for a young girl her age, and I'm thinking maybe blue or green. Bella's developing her own style lately, and her choice always seems to be blue, just like you. I promise not to disappoint you. She's getting impatient. I need to go. We will be home in a while."

"My sweet daughter, you will make a good choice. Of

that I am certain. Enjoy yourselves. Bye for now."

After years of misery married to Ernesto, and so many of those years apart from Karina after she ran away, leaving Gretchen to raise Bella as her own daughter, Gretchen had finally found freedom. Ernesto had died, but not before he made his peace with her, and Karina had returned—truly returned—in every way. And Bella, who had lived like a caged bird, was free. Free to be seen and have her music heard. No longer were peace and kindness rationed.

Since Gretchen had raised both Karina and Bella, she thought of them and treated them as sisters. But on occasion lately, she'd sensed Karina's assuming her rightful role as Bella's mother. Gretchen lived in gratitude they were learning to be family. Karina was studying music at the university and helping run the bakery, and the university was studying Bella, a rare musical savant.

Gretchen picked up her scarf, caressing it as she folded it perfectly and put it on the shelf next to the front door. It had been Peter's parting gift to her last spring at the airport in Vienna, and now he would be coming from Austria to visit her and to meet Karina in a few days. She had hoped to find her family when she returned to her homeland after three decades, but finding Peter again had been the rare blessing she'd never dared to hope or pray for.

Although it saddened her to think he had spent all those years alone, it pleased her in an odd way that he had never married. Relief had come for both of them when Gretchen explained why she'd abandoned him and her family, leaving them to wonder if she was dead or alive more than thirty years ago. Finally, she had told Peter the truth about his brother's assault of her, and he'd had the answers to the question that had plagued him all his adult life.

The phone rang again. She stepped to the desk to answer. "Hello." Silence. "Hello?"

More silence and then a faint voice speaking as if to someone else, "It is Gretchen," before an abrupt click.

She put the phone down and felt her face grow pale. Second time this week. The silence sent a shiver down her spine, reminding her of the calls from Ernesto's partners after he went to jail. He had warned her they would come for her if they did not get their money.

She had been relieved to move away from Moss Point when Duke University offered to educate Bella. She had hoped the move might dissuade Ernesto's friends, but Bella had been in the news so often that Gretchen knew it would not be difficult for them to find her. Her past had many shadows, and no matter the peace and happiness she had now, the shadows never vanished.

———•———

Tuesday evening, Hotel zur Post, in Melk, Austria

Peter sat in the hotel dining room, nervously stirring his coffee as he awaited Iris Brandhof. The clerk at the front desk had directed him to the hotel dining room to wait for her. She had called several times over the last few weeks, always inquiring about Gretchen and Bella and when they would be returning to Austria. His standard answer was that he had no knowledge of their return or if they would ever return.

But Iris's call Monday afternoon and her penetrating questions about Gretchen and Nicolai, his brother, had summoned him back to Melk. She had hinted that that were things Peter needed to know. He had not forgotten his experience years ago with her and his wayward brother, and he knew how determined and manipulative she could be.

Peter had visited Nicolai only once in the early days of

his imprisonment years ago, and there had been no contact since Nicolai's release and no reconciliation. Peter had moved from Melk years ago to a new life away from the drama created by his brother and Iris, and returning now only brought memories that were better left entombed.

Needing no more caffeine to add to his agitated spirit, he pushed his cup of coffee away and sat back in the chair. He looked at his watch, wishing he had not agreed to meet Iris at the hotel. It was her office, her turf, not his, and her lateness was her way of indicating that she was in control.

I shall give her five more minutes, and then I leave.

As he waited, his thoughts turned to Gretchen and his upcoming trip to see her and how he wanted to resolve these issues with Iris before he left for America.

He looked at his watch again. *Six minutes. I shall wait no longer.* He rose from his chair, left money on the table for his cup of coffee, and started toward the door.

Nonchalantly, Iris entered the dining room and confronted him. "I do hope you were not leaving."

"Yes. I was leaving, Iris. You are late." He looked squarely into her face. "And truly, I think you have nothing to say that would be of interest to me."

"And I suppose that is why you would come all the way from Linz? Because you have no interest in what I have to tell you?" She started to walk toward the table where Peter had been sitting. "Come, Peter, I have knowledge that you must learn."

Peter followed her, and they took seats across from each other. Peter spoke first. "Then you must speak hurriedly, for I am taking the six-thirty train back to Linz."

"Perhaps you might wish stay after you hear what I have to tell you. The hotel has lovely accommodations, and I could arrange for a room for you."

"I have no need to remain in Melk. My life is in Linz

now. A most happy life, I might add." He watched the lines grow deeper in Iris's brow and the muscles in her soured face tighten.

"Yes, Peter. You have lived well, quite well, while your own brother languished in prison for crimes he did not commit."

He fought his desire to tell her exactly how well he had lived since moving from Melk, but there was nothing to be gained by goading her. "Iris, I have never understood why you maintained Peter's innocence with the evidence against him. He was tried, convicted, and has served his time. In my heart, I have forgiven him because he is my brother, but thoughts of what he did to those young women still haunt me. I have no understanding of your belief in his innocence. My only hope is that he is a different man now."

"Nicolai could never have done those things. He loved me, and those horrible girls were jealous because they could not have him. They accused him falsely. He spent years in prison because of their lies."

"I have heard nothing from him since his release a few years ago. But you stood by him all those years, even when you were married to the elderly Mr. Brandhof. If my brother loved you, why did he not join you in Melk after his release from prison? As a young widow, you were free."

"I did not bring you here today, Peter, to speak of those things in Nicolai's past. I will tell you what I have learned of Gretchen and her past."

The tightness in Peter's chest quickened his breath. "Gretchen? And why are you so interested in Gretchen. She is living her life thousands of miles away."

Iris's lips curled as she said, "You may recall Gretchen's disappearance was a front-page news story for weeks after she went missing. And there are those reporters who are still interested in her story now that she has reappeared as though from the dead."

Iris's smugness caused his anger to rise like molten lava, but he had determined on the train ride to Melk there would be no eruption. He would not give her the satisfaction. He knew nothing good would come of it. "And why is it, Iris, that there are those interested in Gretchen now after all these years? And who is it who has spurred this interest?" He shook his head and pushed his chair from the table.

"Gretchen's daughter's performance at the anniversary celebration at the church last spring revived the interest. Front-page news with pictures. You must admit Gretchen's past is fascinating and mysterious. A reporter I spoke with certainly thought so. Are you aware that Gretchen disappeared to marry an American soldier who turned out to be a criminal? He is dead now. And do you know that Gretchen's daughter, Bella, is a rare musical savant and is famous in the United States? She performs in public places, and they are about to film a documentary of her."

He would never empower Iris with his knowledge of Gretchen's story and how much of what she had concocted was based on lies. "I still cannot understand why this would be of any interest to you or to a reporter in Austria."

"Because there is more to Gretchen's story than we know. Even in my feeble research on the internet, I was able to learn many things about her life. About her husband who was imprisoned. I know that she lives in Durham, North Carolina, with both her daughters. But a skilled investigator could find out so much more from public records, especially if he went to North Carolina." Iris sat on the edge of her chair and motioned for the waiter. "Would you like a fresh cup of coffee, Peter?"

"I think not. I shall not be here long enough to drink it." He had become more than tired of the smirk on her face.

"Then you may watch me drink mine, because I have more to tell you." She stared at him directly as she said, "Gretchen abandoned you, allowed you to think she was dead for over thirty years. Are you not interested in learning why? And would you not like to hold her accountable for abandoning you and her family the way she did?"

He was resolute. "No, I would not. Why would I ever wish to do that? My life is complete, and it is not my task to judge. I have no need to make trouble for anyone, especially Gretchen, a woman who lives thousands of miles away. Perhaps she has had enough trouble of her own. Let her live in peace, Iris."

"Never. Not until I have some peace. There are missing pieces to this story that I or some reporters are willing to dig for. Look what Gretchen did to her family—to all of us, really. She ruined your life. You were so distraught and miserable that you refused to help your brother, and you destroyed our lives when you would not help us flee the country."

"You live in a world of lies and confusion, Iris. Yes, Gretchen's disappearance caused me great grief. But Nicolai? There was no way to help him. Nicolai ruined his own life when he assaulted those young women, and what you may have forgotten is that you both took money from me. A robbery, as I recall, for which I never prosecuted you. Nicolai got what he deserved, and you made your own choices about your life, so now you live with the consequences that came with those choices."

"I had no choices after Nicolai went to prison. I had no life. I loved him, and he was gone. I waited for him, and he did not return. I had no other option, so I married a man for security, not for love. I never stopped loving Nicolai. Let us both find some answers and peace in all this. We now have the chance to do that after all these years."

She paused and looked away before continuing. "I asked you here because I would like you to finance the investigation into Gretchen's life. You have the means to hire a detective and pay his expenses to expose Gretchen. Get your revenge. Make her pay for what she did. You and I might even stand to gain monetarily if the story is what I think it might be. We are talking about a story that spans two continents and three decades and involves a girl with rare gifts. Possibly a book or a movie. Gretchen's life is high drama, according to one of the journalists."

Peter stood. "Iris, I have no need for money, especially money acquired in such a way. I am done with this subject and with you. I shall never speak of this again with you. Let it go. Live your life. Quit chasing shadows of what might have been. Find your peace elsewhere." He started to walk away.

She rose from her chair but did not follow. She raised her voice. "Perhaps I will. I will find Nicolai. I will find him on my own."

Peter froze. He turned and took a few steps closer to her. "Iris, I did not lie when I told you that I have not heard from Nicolai since his release from prison. I have not spoken to him." He paused, hung his head, and squeezed his eyes shut as though he might regret what he was about to say. "Iris, what would it take for you to let all of this go? How much?"

He wished he could reel his words back in. Instead, he walked briskly away before she could answer.

———•———

Tuesday evening in Moss Point

Sam and Angel sat comfortably in the library, Sam in his

lounge chair and Angel in her rocking chair. With the recording of Caroline's last recital playing in the background and a smoldering fire warming the room, Angel knitted the last round on another prayer shawl while Sam read his newest book on the Civil War, a gift from a former classmate and fellow retired judge in South Carolina. When the resonance from the last chord had faded into silence, Sam cleared his throat. "Our girl certainly makes beautiful music. You have been quieter than usual this evening, my Angel."

"Well, I couldn't hear Caroline's music if our jaws were flappin', and I certainly didn't want to disrupt some general's battle plans from a century and a half ago. You've been readin' those books for the last sixty years, Sam Meadows. The world's comin' unglued, and you're still fightin' battles that are already lost and won. Are you learnin' anything new?"

"Oh, there's always something I can learn. This one's a new biography of General James Longstreet. Interesting fellow, and he's buried just up the road in Gainesville. May want to ride over that way and visit his grave sometime." He laid the book on the table. "You do know, don't you, that history is shaped as much by the personalities of those in command as it is on the battlefields? A compassionate leader makes very different decisions than an angry, power-hungry man."

"Well, I think all those generals are a bit off center myself. Who wants to be sleepin' in a cold tent away from their families, eatin' cold beans and wonderin' when and where they're gonna get shot? You think they'd figure out a way to just get along. Or let women make decisions about war. Then there'd be no war. No woman wants to send her husband or her sons to war."

"Reasonable men or women might figure out how to get

along, but there again, not all men are reasonable. Women either, I might add. Principles and values worth defending call honorable men of integrity to the battlefield. At no point in history have we been able to get around that."

He watched as Angel wrapped the loose bits around the ball of yarn and placed it and her knitting needles in the basket beside her chair. "It's late, Sam, and that's too deep for me. I still think there ought to be a way to talk it out—just put it on the table and deal with it."

Sam took his walking cane propped against the ottoman and used it to scratch the top of his foot. "Are we still talking about mankind getting along and principles upheld, or are we talking about what's been on your mind since before supper?"

"You scare me sometimes, Sam. You read me better than you read your Civil War books. Am I not allowed to have a thought of my own?"

"Of course, you are, my sweet. I'll just keep my thoughts to myself, and you do the same. See, we talked it out, agreed, and all is well." He wiggled his toes inside his woolen socks, smiled on the inside, and started to count, knowing he wouldn't make it to five before Angel blurted it out.

"I talked to Caroline today. I'm thinkin' there's a gray cloud over Camelot, and they need to be talkin' it out and layin' it on the table themselves."

"And what would make you think that?"

"Somethin' in her voice wasn't quite right. No sparkle. And there was all this talk about missin' her students and longin' for her studio."

Sam was about to comment, but before he could, Angel continued. "And now she's decided she wants to learn more about Roderick' business. I don't know how that'll work out, but I know somethin's goin' on that's different."

"I think all is fine as frog hair. Why, Roderick called me the other day and asked what I thought about getting Ned and Fred to come and spend a few days to build a gazebo in Caroline's iris garden. He wants it done before Christmas." Sam paused. "Seems I remember he said he was making some changes in his business, but he's not too busy to think about how to make our girl happy. Caroline's just settling, I suppose."

"Settlin'? Settlin' what?"

"Think about it, Angel. They've been married close to ten months, and those months have been packed with all kinds of travel and projects. And now that winter's coming with a quieter life and schedule, they're settling down to life as most folks know it. Caroline has more time to think. And you know our girl doesn't have a lazy bone in her body. She's a hard worker and a planner, always thinking she's got to earn the air she breathes. I imagine she's trying to figure out what to do with herself. You know, settling into a normal routine."

"I hope you're right. You usually are, but that won't cause this *unsettled* feelin' I have to scamper away." Angel rose from her chair and walked toward the fireplace.

Sam joined her. "Don't you be worrying about our girl. God's been so good to take care of her, and He doesn't have a lazy bone either. He'll make things right."

He felt Angel's arms go around him and the tightness of her hug. "Caroline told me to give you a tight squeeze, and I told her I would. Am I doin' okay?"

Sam chuckled. "I'd say you are, my Angel. Now let's put aside the talk of wars and evil men and Caroline's settling, and let's go settle ourselves in for a good night's rest. I have a big day tomorrow. I have to pile up what I did today." Sam laughed.

Angel released him and stepped away. "Now that may

take some time."

He closed the glass doors to the fireplace and followed her. "What do you say we go by the kitchen and have one little sip of peach brandy? That'll make us dream of warm, sunny days where all is right with the world and everybody in it."

"Like I said, you scare me sometimes. I was thinkin' how warm that peach brandy is to my insides. Come on. You get the brandy, and I'll get the good glasses."

Chapter Three

Brooding

Thursday morning, September 17, at Rockwater

The hooting of the owl in the oak tree roused her. Without moving, Caroline opened her eyes and looked through the Palladian windows that were never shaded or covered with draperies. The eighteen-foot glass panes were her access to eastern skies that scrolled across the Rockwater horizon.

She recalled early March mornings when the morning star, Venus, had risen proudly, as if it were the only light in the dark sky, and had been framed in the window purely for her enjoyment. Many mornings in that last quiet hour before daybreak, she had watched it rise in the sky until the window could no longer contain it. Those were the early days of her marriage when she would lie awake next to Roderick, still trying to believe that she was his wife and how full her heart was and how much her life had changed.

There was no bright star on September mornings, only a sprinkling of faraway sparkles in a canopy of black. Seeing no hint of daybreak, she turned and reached for Roderick, only to find crumpled sheets and the cashmere blanket that had kept his parents warm.

Lilah had told her the story of the Adairs' trip to Rome when the house was being built and how Angeleah, insisting on the finest bed linens, returned with Frette sheets made of the finest Egyptian cotton and cashmere blankets for every bed in the house. In running the household after Angeleah's death, Lilah had carried on the tradition for as long as someone was living in the main house.

After his father died, Roderick had built his cottage under the large oak, steps away from the main house. He'd had no desire to live in the rambling, hollow French chateau whose halls echoed only memories. His cottage out back was where he slept and worked, and he only came to the main house to eat with Lilah or to see his administrative assistant who officed in the wing off the kitchen. But once married, he and Caroline made the chateau home. Before the wedding, Roderick had overseen a construction project in the office wing of the main house so that he and his new assistant Celia could office there. He no longer had need to escape the manor.

Caroline turned to see the clock. Four fifty. Sitting up in bed, she called his name softly, hoping he was still in the suite. No answer. She lay back down, curled up in a ball, and smoothed the sheet and blanket, wishing she could smooth her thoughts as easily. There was no time she could recall Roderick being so preoccupied.

He had worked late last evening and had agreed to come to bed with his stack of files only if she agreed to read quietly while he worked. When she asked about his work, he had dodged the question, explaining the time sensitivity of what he was doing, especially with their trip next week to Durham. Her solace was that he wasn't frequently jetting off to London or Hong Kong.

Springtime of the Song

The fussbudget she was, according to her mother, Caroline worried that he seemed so intense and focused. Even Celia had been putting in longer hours for the last few weeks, and it bothered her that Celia knew more about her husband's business than she did. Celia knew if what had captured Roderick's attention was a new merger, or the sale of one of his companies, or if finances were bad, or if there were internal problems with staff or some nasty legal battle. There had been many meetings with his legal team since July. And now senators were coming for a visit.

Although she had grown quite fond of Celia, especially with all the work she had done on logistics, travel, and paperwork for the Guatemalan Children's Choir visit, Caroline's pride had kept her from ever asking Celia about Roderick's business. And her pride would keep her from asking Roderick again.

She rolled to her back, stretched her arms beside her, and her fingers began playing Mendelssohn's "Spring Song" as though a cashmere blanket were an ivory keyboard. Mendelssohn would soothe her spirit. The poetic melody often came to her in the early morning as she looked out the Palladian windows to the rolling hills of Rockwater which were soon to be awash with the early dawn.

Unable to return to sleep, she rose, dressed quickly, and brushed her sable curls into a ponytail high on her head. The smell of coffee met her as she walked through the loggia on her way to the kitchen. She turned on the kitchen lights and before pouring herself a cup, she took the pot to Roderick's office. "Need a refill?" She approached his desk.

"You're up early, and yes, a refill is just what I need right after my morning kiss."

She leaned to kiss him and felt him caress her cheek. "You won the early-bird prize this morning."

"I tried not to disturb you. I couldn't sleep and knew

this mountain of paperwork could become an avalanche of details by noon if I don't plow through it. Celia's coming in this morning at eight. I promised her breakfast. We can all eat together."

She poured his coffee. "Celia's always welcome. I'm headed to the kitchen to make biscuits."

"Where's Lilah?"

She noticed the scowl on his face. "Lilah wanted to do the grocery shopping for the weekend before she comes in. Besides, I'm fully capable of making breakfast, and I told her I'd handle it this morning."

"If I had known Lilah was coming in later, I wouldn't have told Celia to come in early."

"You don't seem to be available for small talk lately, and I didn't think breakfast ranked in line with whatever is occupying your thoughts."

He responded as though he had not heard her. "Glad you and Lilah are working things out about the kitchen detail. It's not in her nature to allow you in the kitchen, you know." He turned to his computer.

"Well, it's not in my nature to be served all the time. So, this morning I'm serving biscuits with sausage gravy and grits and a bowl of strawberries if we still have some. It'll be ready at eight when Celia arrives."

He did not respond, nor did he turn from his computer when she left his office. She couldn't help but think how unlike him that was. She continued mulling over Roderick's behavior as she rolled out biscuits and stirred the gravy.

Breakfast was served in the morning room. Roderick was silent, scrolling through texts on his phone as he took infrequent bites of gravy-laden biscuits. The only conversation was small talk with Celia about the fall festival in Lexington and an update on the gifted boy who was a sixth-grade student of Celia's sister. On another day, Caroline might have been more interested and would have offered to assess the boy's musical abilities, but she was preoccupied with the unanswered questions about what dominated Roderick's thoughts and time lately.

He ate hurriedly. Celia offered to help Caroline clear the table, but Roderick not so subtly reminded her they had timely work to do.

Caroline was left to clear the table and clean the kitchen. Fifteen minutes later, she was wiping the counter when Lilah entered with grocery bags filling her hands and hanging from her shoulders. Caroline rushed to take some of them from her. "Good morning. You look swamped. Here, let me help you."

"Thank you. If I hadn't been anchored down with all these bags, I think the wind would have blown me into the next county. I can imagine my hair looks like that owl's nest in the oak tree."

"Oh, Lilah, you and that owl out there have a thing, don't you? I heard him this morning. Sounded like the chiff on the organ at the Methodist church, but I rarely get to see him."

"Don't tell me. I don't want to know. Hearing an owl hooting and having him live in a tree right out the back door? Well, it's just a bad sign. Think about Julius Caesar. A bad sign, I'm telling you. Nothing good to come of it, but I can't persuade Roderick to shoot him."

"Shoot him? Forget Caesar and think about how the Native Americans think of owls as being wise and helpful. Lilah, you're a fine Christian woman. Surely, you're not superstitious enough to want Roderick to kill that beautiful creature God made to delight us. And besides, I'm almost certain it's against the law."

"Well, it shouldn't be, and there's nothing delightful about a hoot owl. About as welcome as an overflowing chamber pot, as my poor grandmama would have said."

"I love having him here."

Caroline saw the quick turn of Lilah's head into almost a shiver. "Just a feathered messenger of bad news. We don't need any more bad news at Rockwater, not when things are happy and alive again. I want that bird to take up residence somewhere else. You know they're the only animals that can live with ghosts. If I could reach his nest, he'd have no home in that oak tree."

"Just think of him as a wise protector, and we're certain not to have any mice in the manor."

"Thank you, but I prefer a house cat. And close your ears so you don't hear him hoot three times. A sign of something bad, really bad. Gives me the shivers to think about it."

Caroline wrapped her arm around Lilah's shoulder. "Come on, I wasn't expecting you so early this morning. No more talk of owls. I saved you two biscuits, and I'll warm some sausage gravy and grits for you."

"Sounds good. I couldn't sleep, so I got up and had a cup of instant coffee and went grocery shopping. Your biscuits and gravy sound mighty good to this old biscuit maker."

Lilah started putting the groceries away while Caroline prepared her a plate.

"What is it with this sleeping business? I don't think Roderick slept much either. The moon isn't full for another week, and we had no after-dinner coffee last night, and still he was up and working before five o'clock this morning. When I woke and he wasn't there, I couldn't go back to sleep. In my old studio, when I couldn't sleep, I just got up and played the piano. That would always clear my head. But I didn't want to disturb Roderick." She brought Lilah's plate to the counter. "Here you go. You sit and eat. I'll finish putting the groceries away."

"I think I'll do just that. Don't remember when I had sausage gravy and grits and homemade biscuits that I didn't make myself. And by the way, get rid of your thoughts that your piano playing would have disturbed Roderick."

Caroline set down the can of roasted tomatoes. "Yes, it would. Everything that's not work related disturbs him these days. And he tells me nothing, not even when I ask." She bit her lip, thinking it would hold back her tears, but one escaped.

Lilah wiped her mouth and swallowed. "Dear girl, what's the matter?"

Caroline took a deep breath before she could speak. "I'm not sure, but something certainly is. Roderick and I have been close, so close, and yet I'm feeling this disconnection from him lately. It's like he's here but he's not. He's always working, taking calls, and shuffling papers. Then there's the steady stream of lawyers and deliveries the last few weeks, and he refuses to talk to me about any of it. And now senators are coming. I'm thinking that maybe the honeymoon is truly over."

"Well, Caroline, it's high time you had a conversation with someone besides yourself regarding these matters, and I'm mighty glad you're talking to me. You know I practically raised Roderick, and I know him well. I've seen him through his darkest times, and I'm watching him live through the happiest times of his life right now. He was just a mogul machine until he met you, with no time for anything except work. He adores you, and everything that man does, he does to make you happy." Lilah paused. "I can assure you that whatever he's up to, it will be good for you both. Just trust him and give him a little time."

"But why won't he tell me about whatever it is? I'm interested in whatever interests him."

"Roderick broods. He always has."

"What do you mean he broods?"

"It's like a mood only more productive. You must remember that Roderick's been a lone wolf in the business world for the last twelve years. I've watched him brood quietly for weeks at a time when he's working on something big. He sits tightly on all of it just like a pheasant sitting on her eggs until they hatch. And when the deal is hatched, so to speak, he comes back to us. That's just his way. He's never had someone to share his interests. And knowing him like I do, he's brooding and probably can't imagine you'd be the least bit interested in balance sheets and business plans and contracts. He just doesn't see you that way."

"How does he see me then?"

"Oh, you need to hear that from his voice, not mine." Lilah was about to take another bite, but she paused. "But hear this from my voice. I think you need something to do, Caroline." Then she took the last bite of the biscuit.

"Apparently Roderick and Sarah think the same thing."

"What makes you say that?"

"Roderick told me that he and Sarah had a conversation about me and what I should be doing these days. Seems that Sarah's worried I'll be bored now that the concert is over and our big travels are done for the year. And she decided to talk to Roderick about it without talking to me."

"Now, Caroline. They're not keeping secrets. Roderick told you about their conversation, didn't he?"

"Yes, he told me."

"They just want you to be happy, and they see you as this gifted pianist. So why don't you let Roderick go on about his moguling and his brooding, and you think about making music? Just think what you composed even while you were teaching back in Moss Point and doing your work at the church. Now you have all this time on your hands, and I wonder what you could do with so much freedom. Don't waste these quiet opportunities, sweet Caroline. They may not come again so soon."

"So, I'm to quit brooding—or maybe I'm just mooding. Either way, you think I should get busy?"

"Yes. Today. Orders from three people who love you. Joy will come when you're doing what you do best. Roderick has gone nowhere. You'll see. Now get to your piano, girl."

Caroline hugged Lilah. "Thank you. I think I needed this conversation. I'll get started on something with one condition—you stop worrying about the hoot owl and go comb your hair." Caroline chuckled as she left the kitchen and headed for the piano like a moth to a flame.

———·———

Lilah poured herself another cup of coffee and sat down with her calendar. She was enjoying Caroline's playing and making her list when the back doorbell rang. Lilah arrived at the door just before Celia. "Oh, I would have brought you the package."

"Thank you, but Mr. Adair was so anxious for this one, and I thought I'd save you a few steps."

"Then you answer the door and tell Harold to wait a minute. I have a bag of cookies for him. I'll go and get them."

Lilah bagged a dozen of the peanut-butter cookies Caroline had made yesterday and returned to the back entrance. She overheard Celia ask, "Harold, I see on your shirt your last name is Gray. Not many Grays around here. You wouldn't have a son named Piper who's in the sixth grade, would you?"

"Why, yes, ma'am, I do. How do you know my son?" Harold removed his cap and rubbed his forehead.

"I don't know him, but my sister, Leslie Cameron, is his teacher, and she talks about him all the time."

"Not sure I like the sound of that. Piper's a good boy, and I hope he's not giving Mrs. Cameron a hard time."

"My sister thinks he is a fine young man, and she thinks he's really a gifted singer."

"Yes, ma'am. That boy sings all the time. Don't know where it comes from. I can't carry a tune in a tin bucket, and neither can his mother. But Piper surely loves singing. Just joined the choir at school, and the director told us she thinks he could be something special if he had some singing lessons. But nobody around here I know of gives singing lessons."

Lilah had returned, and her antennae were waving like they always did when something resonated with her. *Caroline needs a student, and this boy needs a teacher.* She handed Harold the cookies. "Harold, do you go to church? Does the boy sing at church?"

"First things first, ma'am." He took the cookies. "Thank you. Mrs. Adair says you make some mighty fine cookies, and they'll be my mid-morning snack."

"I do make mighty fine cookies, but Mrs. Adair made these, and they're mighty fine too."

He held up the bag. "Looks like they'll be my dessert for lunch too. And to answer your question, Miss Lilah, yes, ma'am, we go to church, and Piper's been singing at church since he was about four years old. He makes all the ladies cry when he sings."

Lilah looked at Celia and winked so that Harold couldn't see. "Harold, I think I might have an idea about a teacher for your son. Give me a couple of days to work on it. Would you mind giving me your telephone number?"

Harold pulled a pen from his shirt pocket and tore off a small piece of the brown bag holding the cookies. "Sorry, ma'am. I don't have a card. But here's my number. I'd surely appreciate any leads you can give us on a teacher. We only have the one boy, and we work hard to give him everything he needs to become a fine man. And if that means singing lessons, then we'll find a way to pay for those."

Lilah took the scrap of paper from him. "I'll be in touch. You enjoy those cookies now, and you might even save one for your singing boy."

Harold thanked her again and left.

Lilah turned to Celia. "Girl, we got this. Caroline needs a student, and Piper needs a teacher. We're just connecting some dots this morning, and it's going to be a remarkable picture. Or maybe some beautiful music."

Celia didn't respond but looked up as though she was trying to remember something. "Didn't somebody say 'When the student is ready, the teacher appears'?"

"Yes, I do believe that was Buddha. But you can quote Lilah, because I'm about to say it like it is. When the teacher's ready, the student appears."

Lilah and Celia smiled at each other as if they shared a secret.

Chapter Four

---·---

Changing Shadows

Saturday morning at Rockwater

Caroline pulled on her new riding boots and stared into the full-length mirror, trying to recognize herself. For one who had worn tailored black or navy pants and white or ivory blouses almost every day for the last ten years, shopping for such specialized clothing for horseback riding seemed frivolous, but she had quickly learned that proper clothing was necessary for comfort and safety. And thoughts that this one riding outfit cost as much as she'd spent on clothes for an entire year reminded her that her life had truly changed.

She was decked out in khaki-colored riding pants with knee patches and a silicone seat to prevent chafing, boots with one-inch heels to keep her feet in the stirrups, a down vest and riding jacket, and leather gloves to avoid nasty blisters. Roderick had given strict caution about protecting her hands. She turned to look at the back of her form-fitting pants. As she hardly recognized herself in the mirror, she began to have second thoughts about riding horses and thought her idea of a bicycle was safer.

Roderick entered as she was surveying her backside in the mirror. "Wow. You don't look like the same woman who descended the stairs at Rockwater for the first time in icy pink, looking like you landed from someplace celestial. Today, you look like the mistress of the manor, a real Kentucky woman ready for a horseback-riding adventure."

"I suppose." She picked up the helmet from the dressing table, wondering how she'd get it over her ponytail. "But the helmet? Really, Roderick, I need a helmet?"

He approached and pulled her to him. "Yes. You do. You'll be riding Magnum this morning, and he's fifteen hands."

"Fifteen hands?"

"Fifteen hands means that at his shoulder, he's about five feet tall. That's where you'll be in the saddle. Being that far above the ground and the fact that you'll be moving make wearing a helmet absolutely necessary. It's not a fashionable accessory for horseback riding. You'll be glad for it in case you take a spill." He stammered. "But I'm there to make certain that doesn't happen. So don't worry, and just put that pretty little head of yours in the helmet and let's go." He helped her adjust the headgear and tightened the chin strap.

She looked up at him with questioning eyes. "I've only heard the word *magnum* used to describe guns—big guns, according to my brother. So, I'm guessing with a name like Magnum, I'll be riding a large and powerful horse."

"Not to worry. Magnum is average size, and he's a con-genial and patient sort. He's the horse Lydia rode while she was here. If he put up with Lydia's stubborn streak, he'll be a great ride for you. Besides, we'll take it easy and just ride out to the iris garden. We'll see how you feel after that, and if you'd like to ride farther, we will. But if not, it's not too far for us to walk back."

She took a deep breath and took his hand. "I'm ready. Let's do this. I suppose it's an initiation of sorts to life on a Kentucky horse farm."

Hand in hand, they walked down to the barn where Chip had their horses ready. Roderick and Chip were beside Caroline to guide her as she put her foot in the stirrup. Roderick instructed, "Here, take the reins and just hold them loosely in your left hand. Don't worry, Chip has already checked the saddle and has control of the horse. You're not going anywhere until your safely astride Magnum. Make sure your foot is securely in the stirrup." He checked her boot. "Now pull yourself up and come to a standing position."

As she pulled herself up, Caroline felt the muscles in her left thigh tense, more from nervousness than strain. "Okay. What do I do now? And hurry, please."

"Now lift your right leg, and Magnum would appreciate it if you didn't kick him in the rump as you swing that leg over him and then sit in your saddle."

In a matter of seconds, Caroline sat astride a horse for the first time in her life. God had skipped her when He was passing out adventuresome streaks. But if it took getting on a horse to spend time with Roderick this morning, then she was ready to ride.

"Now relax if you can. It's natural to try to hold on by tightening your legs, but try not to do that. Grasp the horn on the saddle and hold the reins loosely. Chip and I'll be here until you feel comfortable."

She listened to every word as Roderick gave instruction. She knew he had been instructed well as a boy and that he'd loved to ride with his mother. But when his mother died in a riding accident, he had stopped riding altogether until recently. Perhaps this was as much an initiation for him as it was for her.

She surprised herself as she grew more comfortable in the saddle. "I think I can breathe again. So, what's next?"

"Chip will lead you around the ring until you're comfortable. I'll get on my horse and ride beside you."

Caroline kept breathing deeply, trying to relax and remember the things Roderick told her. After a few times around the ring, she felt ready for the ride.

Roderick assured her, "No galloping or trotting, just a slow and steady walk to the iris garden. Let's go."

Chip opened the gate, and Caroline gazed at the horizon as they rode. She was grateful for level ground covered in lush grass that would buffer a fall if there was one.

"You know, I think the world looks so different when I'm astride a horse. It makes me feel powerful and free."

Roderick laughed. "I suppose it would. You're probably two to three feet taller on Magnum, and yes, that would give you a different perspective on the ground and tree limbs. And you do have the horse's power under you. Remind me never to let you behind the wheel of a race car." He gave her a once over. "Relax your legs, and don't hold the reins so tightly. And it's fine to hold the horn on the saddle if it makes you feel more secure. You're getting the hang of this. I'm not surprised."

They rode on and chatted about horses and the leaves that hinted at autumn. They stopped under the tree where the irises were planted. Roderick got down from his horse and moved to help her. "Next thing to learn is how to get off the horse."

"And why do I need to get off the horse? I'm just getting comfortable."

"Because I'd like us to sit here together for a few moments."

Just hearing his words gave her hope that he might tell

her what was going on in his work life—the thing he thought she didn't need to know.

He patted her calf. "Make sure this foot is solidly in the stirrup." He instructed and guided her until both her feet were on the ground. "Now stroke Magnum a bit and tell him how much you've enjoyed the ride."

"Really? I must do that?"

"Yes. You've heard of horse sense? Well, horses have plenty of sense. You've been giving Magnum nonverbal cues since we left the stable. He could sense your tension, the pressure of your knees and calves against his body, and his response was a gentle ride. I'd venture to say he'd understand some verbal cues too. He'll most certainly understand a gentle stroking and soft-spoken words."

Caroline followed Roderick's lead and stroked Magnum's neck. She walked round to face him, rubbed the spot between his eyes, and thanked him for allowing her to ride him.

Roderick then took the reins of both horses and tied them to a rough-hewn timber between two fence posts. "Chip came out yesterday and put in these fence posts so we'd have a place to tie the horses."

Realizing Roderick had taken care of every detail and planned this yesterday, she was almost embarrassed at her thoughts as of late. "You truly think of everything."

She felt his gloved hand take hers and lead her to the bench underneath the tree. "I'd say you're a natural, and I must say I'm enjoying riding again. Let's relax and enjoy the breeze for a little while." He handed her a bottle of water he had taken from his saddle bag.

She took a drink. "I'm not sure I'm a natural. My piano bench is more comfortable, but I surprised myself that I could even stay on the horse."

"I think I prefer you on your piano bench, but you're

right. Things don't look the same when you're astride a horse—a different perspective in so many ways. The world is bit different when we find ourselves astride or under other things as well. We just keep our eyes on the horizon."

Caroline sensed her hands growing sweaty and removed her gloves. Perhaps Roderick brought her out here to tell her something—the *something* that had claimed him for the past few weeks. "Are we still talking about horses, or have we moved on to something else?"

He looked at her and smiled. "You read me well, my dear. I would like to talk with you about something else. I wish I could keep it secret, but I can't keep it any longer and be fair to you."

Caroline's breath shortened, and she felt her face growing pale. "This sounds important."

"Not compared to what's going on in the world, but it's most important to me." He paused before starting again. "These last few months have just seemed to evaporate, and here it is already mid-September. The winter's approaching and that means Christmas and our first anniversary will be here in a few short weeks. What I want to tell you is that my gift to you will be a gazebo under the shade of this tree—a gazebo just like the one in the Meadows' Park in Moss Point, and Ned and Fred have agreed to come and build it. They'll be arriving after we return from Durham next week and will be with us for a couple of weeks."

Caroline had braced herself, and now she was so relieved that she laughed out loud. "A gazebo? What a fantastic idea and present. And you brought me out here to tell me Ned and Fred are coming for a working visit? You really had me worried that our lives were about to change in a big way. You've been so consumed lately, and you won't talk to me about what's going on."

She felt his arm go around her shoulders as they leaned

back against the bench. "Caroline, there is nothing for you to worry about. There are just several deals and projects going on right now, all hitting at the same time, and all time sensitive. Things will be different in a few weeks, and then I'll have some things to talk to you about. Right now, the business dealings are in preliminary stages. I want you to be free to spend your time however you wish, playing the piano, composing, shopping, reading—whatever it is that makes you happy."

"I trust you, Roderick, but I want you to know that I'm interested in the things that interest you. More than anyone, I'm aware that I know nothing about your business. It's like a foreign language when you begin talking about it. I just worry because you're so focused."

"Again, you're not to worry. Focusing is necessary to get the work done. When everything is settled, I promise I will explain." He paused. "There is one thing I do need your help with, though. Since the renovation and moving my office to the manor house, my cottage sits empty and could use a bit of renovating itself. I think it's time to turn it into a comfortable guest cottage in case your parents or Sam and Angel would like to come for extended visits. And now that Sarah and George have little Rosita, they might even be more comfortable in the guest house."

She couldn't hide the puzzled look on her face.

"Why that look? You don't like my idea?"

She removed her helmet and rubbed her brow. "It's not that I don't like it, but Roderick, the manor house is so large, with three guest suites already. And your cottage is very comfortable as it is. It seems such a waste of money, and honestly, I like having guests with us in the house."

"Even Lydia? There were times I wanted to send her to the barn."

"Yes, even Lydia. I know she's like a whirlwind, but she

always fills the room with such energy."

"But what about Sam and Angel or your parents? Wouldn't you like them to have their own place here? They may want to come for long visits, and they'd have their own cottage."

"They have a place here." She sensed his insistence. "Is this something you really want done, or are you trying to provide me with something to occupy my time?"

"Caught again. It's both. I don't like to think of you bored. But honestly, the cottage project was Lilah's idea. She reminded me that it's been several years since any work's been done out there. And she thought it would make an ideal guest cottage with some 'sprucing up' and 'getting rid of the bachelor pad look,' so she says. It does look like an office, and the colors are dark. I don't think Ned and Fred will mind, though. Although, they'd probably prefer the tack room."

"We'll make Ned and Fred comfortable, and I think I'd like to invite Sam and Angel to come with Ned and Fred. Are you sending the plane for them?"

"That's a great idea. Wish I had thought of it myself." He grinned. "Actually, I did think of it and gave them a call earlier this morning. They didn't hesitate."

She snuggled closer to him. "You think of everything." She paused. "Look, Lilah explained about your brooding. I understand now. You go on with your brooding because I am done with mine. I started a new composition on Thursday, and with our trip to Durham next week and the arrival of Ned and Fred when we get back, it may be a while before I get back to it. But if it makes you happy, I'll talk to Lilah about the cottage. We'll come up with something, and Angel has such good taste. She'll be helpful."

"I'll leave it to you three. Lilah knows which decorator to call. Christmas is coming, and I hope Rockwater will be filled with family for the holidays. I think it'll be convenient to have the extra room."

"I'll talk to Lilah, and we'll take care of it. Just give me a budget."

Now his face was puzzled. "Budget? Whatever it takes to make the cottage comfortable and lovely and up to Caroline standards."

His response was another reminder that her life had truly changed. Her standard of living had always required practicality, and she had lived on a budget, a meager one, with no thoughts of frivolous spending on a cottage that was already comfortable. Her worries somewhat diluted with this conversation and realizing that talk about business was not happening, she looked at her watch.

Before she could say anything, Roderick said, "You're right. We need to get back to the barn. I told Chip we'd be back before lunch. Besides, I'm craving one of your tuna-fish sandwiches with that coleslaw you make, and I think we have some packing to do for our trip tomorrow. Helmet on, please."

———◆———

After a light lunch, she followed Roderick to their suite to pack. Larger than the living room in her old studio, their closet was another reminder of the changes in her life. Roderick himself had designed the built-ins and the spacious island of drawers and cabinets that made packing so much easier. In her prior life, getting ready for a trip had been opening the suitcase on her bed and hoping everything would fit in her one bag. Now she had a whole set of world-class luggage and a marble-topped built-in where she could stack her clothes for organizing and her bags before packing them. Tomorrow, she'd be flying to Durham on a private jet.

It had taken the last several months for these changes to become less of a fairytale and more her new reality. Such luxury often brought on a sense of guilt when she had lived such a simple life and had seen so much poverty in Guatemala and even in Moss Point.

Roderick was done in ten minutes and placed his bags at the closet door. "I need to go out to the office and work for a while. Why don't you finish packing and take a long soak and turn on the jets for a water massage? Your body will thank you tonight. You did great today, but you can count on some sore muscles tomorrow. Muscles you didn't know you had."

"I think I'll take your advice, but I do need to call Gretchen first. We need to go over the schedule for Monday, and then I thought I'd touch base with Sarah to remind her of the time of our arrival tomorrow afternoon."

Roderick winked at her and said as he walked away, "I'll try to be done by dinner time."

She finished packing and went to the morning-room desk to get her calendar and call Sarah and Gretchen. The call to Sarah was a quick one to go over arrival time tomorrow. She knew the call to Gretchen would be longer.

Karina answered the phone. "Hello."

Caroline heard Bella playing Bartok in the background. "Hi, Karina, it's good to hear your voice, and I hear Bella. Sounds like they're introducing her to twentieth-century composers. But with her amazing abilities, I suppose it's all the same to her. I just wanted to go over a few things about Monday with Gretchen."

"Yes. Bella hears it and plays it—Bartok, Prokofiev, whatever they give to her. I'll get Mammá for you. She's out in the garden sitting in the sunshine. She seems not to be feeling so well the last couple of days. Maybe you can cheer her up. And I would be happy to email you the schedule."

"Thank you. Yes, just send me the schedule, then I can begin to gather my thoughts and make some notes. We will arrive tomorrow afternoon and spend the evening with Sarah and George, and I suppose I'll see you and Bella and Gretchen on Monday morning."

"Yes, I know Mammá is looking forward to your visit. And Peter will be here later in the week. It's a big week for Mammá. Wait a moment. I think I hear her coming in now."

"I'd love to speak with her if she's up to it." Caroline waited.

"Here's Mammá, and I will email the schedule right now."

Gretchen answered with a certain melancholy in her voice. "Hello, my friend. I will be more than glad to see you Monday."

"Yes, we'll be happy to see you as well. Karina says you're not feeling well."

"Oh, my. I must do better. I do not wish my daughter nor you to worry about me. I am well. I think the stress of the documentary and Peter's arrival have weighed my spirit down."

"Weighed down?" Caroline knew Gretchen far too well to accept this answer. "Those things should lighten your spirit, especially Peter's visit. Roderick and I are really looking forward to seeing him again. So, tell me, what's really dampening your spirit?"

"To trouble you is the last thing I want to do, but I have no one else to tell, and I must tell someone. I do not wish to pour my fears on Karina, especially right now."

Caroline held tightly to the phone and sat down as the pitch, rhythm, and volume of Gretchen's voice lowered. The words seemed to come like a recording on a slow speed. Caroline listened intently as Gretchen described the mysterious phone calls she had received over the past few days and her ideas of who it might be. "My life is so much brighter now, but things in my past still cast their haunting shadows."

"I certainly understand why this might trouble you, but so much time has passed. I can't imagine it's any of Ernesto's criminal friends. They're all in jail, and you'd think if someone was looking for you, they would have found you before now. Perhaps it's a reporter trying to get to you regarding the documentary. Try to stop worrying, and give your attention to Bella and Peter, and I'll call Sam. He's the one to properly check into this, and I know he'll be glad to help. But truly, Gretchen, I think it is nothing."

"But I heard the whispered voice say my name. Whoever is calling knows he has reached me."

Caroline had no fear-relieving answer for that fact. She said her goodbyes and laid down the phone, then continued to sit and silently process what Gretchen had told her. It was possible that Ernesto's partners were looking for her to press her for money, especially since Ernesto's death.

With all the media attention Bella had received, it could be Bella's biological father who had abandoned her and Karina and now wanted to cash in. Or Karina's old flame, Skeeter.

Or Nicolai. He could have found out about Gretchen's visit to Austria and about Karina and Bella.

Gretchen was right about the shadows. Even the bright light of freedom she lived in now could be dimmed by the shadows from her past.

The afternoon beams of gold came through the window and warmed Caroline's folded hands on the desk. Her eyes were fixed on the garden and the way the wind stirred the leaves and branches of the berry-laden shrubs. The crimson color and the berries of the flameleaf sumac were proof that given time, everything changed. She wondered if there was ever a true settling in this life or if life was a constant series of changes requiring acceptance and adapting.

Focused on Gretchen's report and wondering what could be done and if she should tell Roderick and when to call Sam, she hardly remembered walking into their suite and running her bath water. Gretchen's words of lament, describing how she had lived most of her life in the shadows, replayed in Caroline's mind. She tried to encourage herself with the same words she had spoken to Gretchen, reminding her that God had led them both through troubling and treacherous seasons of their lives before, and they must count on Him now.

Caroline stepped into the swirling waters of the bathtub and sank under the bubbles as if they would wash away all the reasons for her worries.

Chapter Five

———◆———

Dreaded Mystery

Monday afternoon, September 20, at Gretchen's house in Durham

For the director's interview of her, Caroline had chosen to sit on the piano bench with Bella beside her. Being at the piano was truly home for each of them. Caroline's interview was now over, and she felt comfortable that her comments and answers had educated the director and crew about Bella's rare gift and her capabilities.

The crew continued taping Bella at the piano as the crew director played tunes from his phone, asking Bella if she knew each one. Like a musical machine, Bella listened intently and then played one after the other to the amazement of everyone in the room, including Caroline. She knew that Bella would not have responded if the director had given Bella a title, but only when he played the music for her.

Caroline took a few moments to escape the intensity of the filming. She needed a break from the barrage of questions and the chaos of lighting and equipment that filled Gretchen's small living room. Escaping to the kitchen for a glass of water, she stood at the kitchen door and looked out at the back garden, marveling at how in less than two years Gretchen had recreated in Durham the Austrian cottage garden she'd loved as a girl—blooms of color, hedged privacy, with a willow tree in the rear corner.

Gretchen had money to buy something larger, but Caroline wondered if the aging willow tree was the real reason Gretchen had found this cottage so attractive. She remembered Gretchen's stories of the trysting place underneath the willows on the banks of the Danube where she and Peter had met often during their courtship and where, after thirty years, they'd renewed their relationship during Gretchen's visit to Austria in May. Caroline sipped her water and wondered what Gretchen dreamed as she sat in her garden chair underneath the willow tree now.

She looked at her watch. Three thirty-five. She had hoped to hear from Sam by now. She checked her phone for messages. While Roderick worked late on Saturday evening, she had called Sam to give him Gretchen's report of the shadowy calls. Sam had surprised her by not being alarmed, not even when she explained the caller knew Gretchen's name. Sam had said he had his reasons for not being worried but that he would give Caleb, Moss Point's sheriff, a call on Monday morning and get back to her.

She trusted Sam. It gladdened her that he and Angel had accepted Roderick's invitation to come to Rockwater with Ned and Fred and stay for a couple of weeks. There was a need in her to be with them.

Karina called to her. "Caroline, Mr. Stiles would like you to come back now. He'd like to record you and Mammá in conversation about the first time you met."

Caroline put her phone in her pocket. "Certainly." She took another sip of water, put the glass beside the sink, and returned to the living room.

Retelling how she had first come to meet Gretchen and Bella was like visiting an old friend she hadn't seen in a while. Their stories of Bella slipping out at night and hiding in the bushes near the studio window to hear Caroline play, and then Caroline's report of hearing Bella play for the first time, mesmerized Mr. Stiles and even brought a few needed smiles to Gretchen.

Karina and Bella sat quietly and listened as though the stories were about someone else. When the interview was over, the two of them said their goodbyes and excused themselves from the room. The crew's work was done for the day, and they packed up their gear and were gone by five o'clock.

Caroline sensed that ahh feeling and watched the muscles in Gretchen's face relax as she closed the door behind the crew and returned to her favorite chair next to the window.

Caroline and Gretchen had only begun to talk when Karina and Bella returned, dressed in jeans and T-shirts with purses in hand. Karina said, "Mammá, I know it is late, but I promised Bella ice cream when the shoot was over. It is closer to dinnertime than I thought, so if it suits you, she and I could get burgers and fries. You know how she loves them. And I could bring you two something."

"Yes, dear daughter. You both deserve to enjoy yourselves. I will visit with Caroline and straighten up a bit and get ready for another day tomorrow at the university."

"What would you like me to bring you?"

"Bring your beautiful smiles back through the front door. I still have soup from yesterday and the bread you made. That will be more than sufficient for me."

Without being prompted, Bella stepped to Caroline and kissed her cheek and then went to her Mammá and leaned to hug and kiss her. "I was good today. I get ice cream." She took Karina's hand. "I want my ice cream. I will be good tomorrow. Vanilla today. Chocolate tomorrow."

As the two left, Caroline smiled at the simplicity of Bella's language and still marveled that she had been playing the piano almost nonstop all day—everything from Beethoven to Bartók, without knowing the names of the pieces or anything about their musical history. "You know, Gretchen, I think sometimes I've become so familiar with Bella that I forget how truly rare she is. Seeing her through the eyes of the producer and the crew today was good for me."

Gretchen breathed a long sigh before she spoke. "Yes, my friend. I understand your words and their meaning. She is my Bella, my beautiful gift, but soon she will belong to the world, and I fear she will be my Bella no longer."

"You have no fears there. She will always be your Bella. You are her heart and her home, and she will always return to you."

"I pray she will." Gretchen laid her head back against the chair and closed her eyes as though she were resting on that promise. Then, like she had awakened from a dream, she sat up straight. "Did you hear from Sam today?"

"Not yet, but let me look again to see if I have a message." Caroline took her phone from her pocket. "No, nothing."

"What do you understand from his silence?" The furrow in Gretchen's brow deepened. "Do you think it might be that Sam does not wish to be the deliverer of worrisome news?"

"I really don't think we can make anything of it. Maybe he couldn't reach Caleb, or maybe he's waiting to hear from Caleb. But like I told you, Sam was not worried about Ernesto's old friends. They're all still in jail and will be for several more years."

"Yes, but they may have friends who learned of Ernesto's death and think that all his money came to me. And they could have given their friends instructions like those Ernesto gave to me. They still think of it as their money."

"Yes, money they made from drug trafficking with their trucking line. I imagine they think that the legal system took the money since it was obtained illegally. But not all of Ernesto's money came from criminal activities." Caroline paused. "I still think it's more likely a reporter trying to get the scoop on Bella's new documentary, her coming television appearances, and her concert schedule."

"Then why not identify himself or herself?"

Caroline had no quick answer for that question. "You couldn't tell if it was a man or woman?"

"I could not. It was a whisper that I think I was not meant to hear as the caller ended the conversation."

"I know it must be difficult not to worry, but please try to put this away and enjoy this week. This is what you've dreamed of for Bella since I've known you. And then with Peter coming later in the week? Why that's more than you ever dared to dream for yourself! Don't let your worries cloud this day or tomorrow." Caroline looked at her watch. "I hate to leave you without an answer, but I must get back to Sarah's. It will be dark soon, and remember, I'm walking."

"Oh, how thoughtless of me. I should have asked Karina to drop you off. Would you like me to walk with you through the garden?"

"I always enjoy your company, but perhaps after such a busy day, a few moments of quiet peace will be best for both of us. You sitting here in the serenity of your cottage, and me walking through the gardens for fifteen minutes before I become little Rosita's playmate. I'm hoping to Skype with

Sister Gabby and the Guatemala girls tonight. Rosita will enjoy that. And maybe a bit of rest before we have another day of this tomorrow."

Caroline rose from her chair, and Gretchen followed her to the door. She helped Caroline with her jacket. "The gardens will be lovely this time of day. Please call me if you hear anything from Sam."

Caroline kissed Gretchen's cheek and opened the front door. "Of course, I will." When she was out of sight of Gretchen's cottage, she pulled her phone from her purse.

———•———

Late Monday evening at Sarah's house in Durham

George, Sarah, and Roderick had been in conversation for the last two hours. Roderick looked at his watch. "I thought Caroline would be here by now. Maybe I should call and go pick her up. She insisted on walking over to Gretchen's this morning."

Sarah was polite. "I don't think that's a good idea, in case they're still recording, but I suppose your abrupt change in thought means you are done with this topic of conversation."

"For now. I've updated you on all the business transactions, and I'll send you the paperwork when it's ready for your signatures. The final documents won't be signed until the board meeting in another few weeks. Then the real work starts. And as far as the senators, I'll know more after their visit. But Sarah, you know where I stand on all these issues, at least with what I know now. You and I agree. Am I right?"

Sarah reached across the table to pat her brother's arm. "Yes. On all the business we have discussed, we're in agreement. I cannot tell you that I agree about your response to Senator Stone's initial ideas until I hear them fleshed out. Of course, I'll tell you what I think then, and I'll ask you a never-ending list of questions to help you think through things. But Rod, that must be your decision. Yours and Caroline's. Where we do have disagreement is that you haven't told Caroline any of this. She's in the dark, and all these changes will affect her life too."

"I will talk this over with her." He paused. "When the time is right."

"What you mean is that when all the decisions have been made, you'll just make an announcement. Or perhaps you'll just wait and let her read it in the news. The time to talk it over is now, while she can give input and feel that she's a part of this whole process." Sarah closed her eyes and shook her head. "Rod, Caroline's smart and sensitive. Don't you think she suspects something is going on? You're working night and day. You have all these lawyers coming and going. You're focused and engaged. And now a visit from a senator?"

Roderick lowered his head. "Yes. She's aware that something's different. Lilah told her I was in brooding mode. She keeps telling me that she wants to learn more about my business. There's no time to get all this done and educate her at the same time. I just keep deflecting and trying to keep her occupied with other things."

"I rest my case. I simply do not understand why you won't tell her now. It makes no sense to me."

"She trusts me. I have my reasons, and besides, I'd like to—"

A knock sounded at the front door.

Sarah rose from her chair. "Saved by the doorknocker, which I'd like to use to pound some sense into your stubbornness. And I won't have the chance, because it's probably your uninformed wife at the door. You know, the one who desperately wants to be involved in every aspect of her husband's life. But there again, perhaps you'd like it if she were keeping big life-changing decisions from you." As Sarah left the room, she turned. "I will not divulge your confidence, but we're not done with this conversation, my dear brother."

George broke his silence and spoke gently and quietly. "Rod, you know Sarah's right. And if you don't know it, then you should. You're blessed to have a wife like Caroline, and you're doubly blessed to have a sister like Sarah who will support you no matter what. He would be a wise man who chose not to disappoint either of them. That is all I have to say."

———•———

Caroline sat at the dressing table brushing her hair. She could see Roderick's reflection in the mirror as he chewed on a pencil while sitting in bed with his laptop. She had noticed this pencil-chewing eccentricity weeks ago. He had any number of expensive pens and mechanical pencils, but he preferred the old No. 2, school-bus-yellow pencil while he worked. Lately, she had found several chewed practically into pieces.

Caroline rose from the dressing table, walked across the room, turned out the light on the bedside table, and crawled in beside him. He took no notice.

"Roderick. Maybe it's time to put your work away? I've not seen you all day. I'd like to hear about your visit with Sarah and George and what you've been doing with yourself since early morning."

"Give me just two minutes to finish this email, and I'm

all yours."

Caroline lay back on her pillow and thought that it had been several weeks since he was all hers except for brief interludes.

He finally closed his computer, walked over to put it on the dresser, and returned to bed. He reached for the beside lamp switch. "Want the lights out?"

"Not yet."

He climbed in and adjusted the covers. "Full day? Tell me how things went."

"Yes. A full day followed by a full evening. I'm relieved to be done with my part of the filming. So tomorrow shouldn't be as intense, since I'll only be observing and consulting when needed." She felt Roderick curling her hair around his finger as he lay facing her. "I was hoping for a quieter evening, but it was enjoyable to Skype with Sister Gabby and see the girls. It was worth the time just to see the delight on Rosita's face."

"Oh yes. I think she doesn't feel the distance and separation so much when she can see and hear her friends, and it keeps her Spanish up. Sarah tries and does well, but nothing like children speaking to children."

"Children are that way, I suppose." What she wanted to say was that she was feeling distance and separation, and she was only inches away from him. "I disliked having to bow out so quickly, but I really needed to take Sam's call."

"Yeah, what was that all about?"

"Seems there's been no time to tell you, but Gretchen's had a few disturbing phone calls where the caller is on the line but refuses to identify himself or say anything. Only this one time she heard the caller whisper 'It is Gretchen' before hanging up. She has it in her mind that some of Ernesto's old friends have found her and will try to get money from her. Her stress reminds me of her old life of fear with

Ernesto. So I called Sam to get his advice."

"Seems unlikely it would be any of Ernesto's criminal comrades. It's been over two years, and they're all in prison. You'd think if they were coming after her, they would have done it before now."

"That's what I told her, and Sam confirmed it when I spoke with him tonight. Caleb did some checking, and they're all still in jail and will be for many more years. They were told all their assets were frozen by the government when they were convicted of drug trafficking, especially since it was across state lines. Sam doesn't think they would ever come after Gretchen."

"I agree. Then that leaves the unanswered question: who *is* making these calls?"

"Gretchen and I talked about that. My guess is that it's likely a reporter trying to get access to Bella, since she is about to become such a public person. Or it could be Bella's father. He fled Moss Point years ago when Karina told him she was pregnant, and they've not heard from him since. Or it could be that Skeeter guy that Karina left in South Carolina when she came to her senses and came home to her family. I gather he is not someone you'd want to invite to dinner."

"But why would either of them contact Gretchen? Why not contact Karina? It doesn't make sense."

"No, it doesn't. Maybe whoever it is thinks he could cash in somehow now that Bella is the subject of this documentary and her concert schedule has been published. The university has built a whole website around Bella with all kinds of information about her and her rare gift. Maybe they think she is making a fortune off these public appearances."

"Now that's possible, but it still does not sound likely to me. I ask again, if it were Bella's biological father or Karina's old flame looking for money or to be part of all this attention, why call Gretchen and not Karina?"

Caroline stretched and turned to face him. "Good point. But the person knew Gretchen's name. And I've wondered if a reporter would use her first name. That doesn't sound likely, either, the more I think about it. She couldn't tell from the raspy whisper if the caller was male or female, and she thinks she was not supposed to hear what she heard. She sensed the caller was just confirming that it was Gretchen to someone else while hanging up. Such a mystery. And I do not like mystery."

Roderick pulled her closer and pressed his lips to her forehead. "You're not to worry about this. Gretchen is safe, and she's surrounded by folks who will take care of these matters for her. Besides, all good mysteries are just waiting to be solved. Give it some time."

She enjoyed his closeness and traced his shoulder lightly with her fingers. "We can be grateful that she has you and Sam and George looking out for her, and what great timing that Peter is arriving late Friday. These calls have Gretchen a bit distracted, but I'm hoping Peter will be a more pleasant distraction."

"Speaking of schedules, I've had a bit of a change in mine. You know I told you initially I might not be able to stay the week here with you. Turns out matters have developed. I need to get back to Rockwater tomorrow. I have so much work and preparation to do, and then my visitors from Washington are coming in on Thursday morning. I'll fly back here on Friday. We can plan something special with Gretchen and Peter, and then we'll return home late Saturday or Sunday."

The gray cloud that had hovered above her head all day got heavier and darker. "If you could delay leaving until early afternoon, perhaps I could return to Rockwater with you."

"Caroline, you're needed here, and I'll be working and in meetings for the next three days. Why don't you stay and enjoy visiting with Sarah and be available to Gretchen and the crew? I won't be nearly such good company as they are."

She thought it sounded as though he wouldn't be company at all. "But the senator and whoever else is coming to Rockwater? Don't you want me there?"

"It would be a total waste of your time. Lilah can manage, and I'll enjoy telling them what my beautiful and talented wife is up to and why she's not there. That may be the most interesting part of our conversation. This is just an exploratory meeting. If anything develops, you'll be engaged later. But for tonight, we need to get some rest. Big day tomorrow for you, and I'll be flying out early. Come closer and kiss me."

Caroline kissed him. In only a few moments, she heard the familiar sounds of his breathing as he fell asleep and felt the muscles in his arms relax. She lay in the stillness, thinking of how much she hated mystery and the unknown and the feeling of being on the outside and not even being able to see in.

Chapter Six

---◆---

Sweet Home

Thursday, September 23, somewhere over the Atlantic

Peter had spent the night in Vienna to catch his morning flight to the States. With only a brief stop in Amsterdam and a quick change of planes in New York, in thirteen hours he would be stepping into Gretchen's world. Although it would be well past his bedtime, it would only be two o'clock in the afternoon in Durham.

The constant low-pitched hum of the plane and the slight vibration had almost lulled him to sleep. He closed his folder holding all the information his assistant had printed about savant syndrome and Adair Enterprises and put it away. He pulled the shade over the window, reached into his pants pocket to make certain the velvet pouch was still there, and stretched out in his first-class reclining seat.

The sale of his family's original market in the village of Melk had afforded him money to start a new business and to make investments over the last eighteen years. Moving from Melk to Linz had removed him from the shadows of his brother's crimes and Iris's meanness and vindictiveness. He had new friends, close business associates, and a lovely home, but he was still a single man in his late fifties with no one to spoil with his good fortune. Humility shaped from his earlier life made him uncomfortable with things like first-class plane tickets, but he justified this expense because he wanted to be rested upon his arrival in North Carolina.

Comfortable enough, he closed his eyes, but sleep would not come. He envisioned Gretchen and Bella and wondered if Karina would look like Nicolai—his brother, who had brutally attacked Gretchen, his bride to be, compelling her to abandon him and her family to avoid her shame. His brother, who changed so many lives with his evil deeds.

I will not think of Nicolai. I will only think of the blessing of Gretchen's return to me after three decades. I will think of her silver hair and her green eyes and her velvety skin. I will imagine my future with her. Nicolai robbed us of years of joy, but the memory of what he did will not stain one moment I have left with Gretchen.

Peter shifted his weight in the leather seat and adjusted his pillow, trying to soothe himself to sleep with thoughts Gretchen. He remembered their trysts under the willow trees on the banks of the Danube. In his twilight imagining, he walked the lane from Melk to the site near the grove of willows, where they'd planned to build a small cottage for themselves and the family they hoped to have. They had planned to grow old together there.

He remembered Gretchen's softness as he'd held her when they parted back in the spring. That embrace had given him hope he would not grow old alone. Subsequent conversations and this visit would cinch that.

A smile seeped across his face . . . until he thought of his last trip to Melk and his meeting with Iris—the won't-go-away, venomous, and manipulative Iris. He wondered if his offer of money had halted whatever she was planning, but sharp slivers of doubt pricked at his hope. He knew it wasn't money she wanted. She was still obsessed with Nicolai, and she would use whatever means she had, even Gretchen, to get to him. He could only hope that Iris would never find out that Gretchen had borne Nicolai's child.

———•———

Early Thursday morning in Durham

Gretchen smiled as she wiped the last crumbs of the scones from the breakfast table. Bella had come early to the kitchen, decked out in her new green dress and black slippers. Gretchen couldn't help but chortle at Bella's attempt at a ponytail adorned with a green ribbon. After breakfast, Karina had rescued the ponytail and sent Bella to play the piano while she dressed for work.

A Chopin prelude floated through the modest cottage. Bella had already displayed her excitement about Peter's arrival, and Gretchen could only hope she remembered Peter had told her Chopin was his favorite composer.

By the time Karina returned to the kitchen, Chopin's prelude had been replaced by a nocturne. "Mammá, Bella is enjoying herself. Might we have a cup of coffee together before I leave for work?"

Gretchen continued scouring the countertops. "But oh, my sweet daughter, I have so much work to do and so little time."

Karina took the dish towel from Gretchen's hands. "No, Mammá, you do not. We cleaned the house last night before bed. No more cleaning. Although you might check Bella's room, since it is our guest room for Peter."

"We hope that it might be. I know Bella insisted that Peter could have her room, but she does not do well with change sometimes."

"If Bella is unsettled after Peter arrives, he can have my room, and I'll move in with Bella." Karina led Gretchen to the table and poured two cups of coffee. "Here's your coffee, just like you like it with extra milk and two sugars." Karina sat down at the end of the table. "You might cut a few morning blossoms from the garden for the dining table and for the guest room, which ever one it might be, but there is nothing left to clean. Mammá, you will have time for yourself this morning, maybe even time for a long, warm soak before you must leave for the airport."

Gretchen held the coffee mug near her face and inhaled the pungent aroma, which brought thoughts of the coffee shops of her homeland. "I feel so guilty. You are doing all my work at the bakery today, and you arranged for Bella to spend the day with Sarah and Rosita. I will pick her up from Sarah's, and then we will pick you from the bakery on our way home from the airport."

"No, Mammá. You will not. I made other plans for today and this evening because you and Peter need time alone. When I close the bakery, I will walk to Sarah's and get Bella. We will walk through the gardens and catch one of the late-afternoon student recitals on campus. You know how Bella loves those." Karina stirred her coffee slowly. "And I have made reservations for you and Peter at the Counting House for a romantic dinner."

"The Counting House? But it's so . . ."

"It is so . . . one of the best places in the neighborhood. Do you remember Brandon, my friend from church? He works there in the evenings to help pay his tuition. He is reserving the best table and ordering an early three-course dinner just for you. Everything is taken care of as a gift to you and a welcoming gift for Peter from Bella and me. You must arrive by six o'clock. The only reason it is not a four-course meal is that I am making a special dessert to bring home from the bakery so that Bella and I might share it with you."

Gretchen was overcome. "You did all this for me?"

"Yes, Mammá, and to welcome Peter. After all those years of being apart, you two deserve something special. It is his first evening here with you, and I wanted it to be an evening to remember." Karina stumbled for words. "Ah . . . Should . . . I do not know how to address him. Should I call him Peter or Mr. Kornilov? I know Bella speaks of him as Peter, but I do not know if that is proper or if he is comfortable with that."

"My dearest daughter, you think of everything. And yes, he asked Bella to call him Peter, and I think he would like it if you addressed him as Peter too." Gretchen smiled on the inside as she thought of how Karina's return home had been a return to her truest self. After more than ten years away and living a different life, her genteel ways—the ways Gretchen had taught her as a child—had returned. She had allowed her short, smut-black dyed hair grow out to its original platinum, and her garish makeup was gone. Her love of music was flourishing, and she was responsible in helping Gretchen run the bakery. Most important, the relationship she was developing with Bella was more than Gretchen had ever prayed for. "Thank you for all you are doing today, and I ask you to do one more thing. You must sing for Peter tonight. He has been waiting to hear you."

"Yes, Mammá, I will sing, just for you and for Peter."

Gretchen detected the pensive look in Karina's eyes as she lowered her voice.

"Mammá, we do not speak of these things because I can never bring myself to ask, and I do not wish it to cast a cloud over your beautiful day, but I must know. Peter knows everything, and I mean everything? That I am his brother's biological child?"

Gretchen's smiling heart felt suddenly soggy with remorse, not for herself but for her daughter, who knew she had not been conceived in love. She had learned it from reading the letter Gretchen had penned. Gretchen had written the letter because she could not look her daughter in the face and tell her the painful truth. She had determined that reading it would give Karina time to process it before they ever had conversation about it.

She grieved for her daughter who had never known the love of a father as she herself had known—a love that had compelled her to return to her homeland after thirty years.

"Yes, Karina, Peter knows. Peter knows everything that happened and why I felt I had no choice but to leave. I learned I was not Nicolai's only victim, and Peter has accepted that truth as well."

The word *victim* left a horrid taste in her mouth as she said it. How Gretchen wished she could unsay the word. "Remember, I told you upon my return from Austria in the spring that Peter and Nicolai do not have a relationship. Nicolai went to prison and has contacted Peter only once before his release years ago."

"But . . . but how do you think Peter will see me? Will he be distant because he thinks of me as his brother's daughter?"

Gretchen felt the hesitancy in Karina's questions. "My dearest girl, you do not know my Peter, but you will come to see him as the loving and forgiving man he has always been. He will see you as a lovely and gifted young woman who is my daughter. Take your worries, and wipe them away. He is coming a very long way, yes, to see me, but also to meet you. And one day soon, I hope to take you back to Austria to meet my pappá and my sister and your cousins. Peter will take you to the great music halls of Austria. He has already said so."

Karina's gaze continued to question. "Peter has forgiven you for leaving and staying away so long?"

"Yes, I believe he has. We both have regrets, but we choose not to live in our past and allow it to rob us of one more day. And we choose the path of forgiveness so that our hearts may be at peace."

"But Mammá, do you never think of what might have been?"

Gretchen paused to give a thoughtful answer. "Honestly, I do. But I do not allow those thoughts to linger with me, for I do not wish to reinfect myself with the anger and sorrow I once felt as the frightened young woman I was back then. My heart changed when you were born, and then came Bella. With a heart filled with so much love, there is no room for anything else except the gratitude I have for all that God has done for me. For us."

"But think of all you missed, Mammá."

"But *you* should think of what I would have missed—the joy of being your mother, and the joys we have now as a family—if things had been different. The world needed Karina and Bella, and I had the gift of being your mother."

"Mammá, I will tell you now that I was afraid to come back home. I knew that Ernesto was no longer in your life, but I did not know if you could forgive me for running away and leaving Bella with you. With the ways I had lived, I did not know that I could adjust to settling back home again. But this last year has been the most joyful year of my life. With you and Bella and my music, I feel so complete and hopeful. I had lost all hope until I returned to you." Karina rose from her chair and walked to Gretchen. Her arms circled Gretchen's shoulders, and she buried her face in Gretchen's hair and allowed her tears to flow.

Gretchen's hands held tightly to her daughter's arms

wrapped around her. "I never, never lost hope that you would return. I prayed every day." Her voice constricted with emotion, she whispered, "I prayed, and God answered."

The moment was one they both needed. A buttoned-up flood of emotion now free. Words that had been begging to be said out loud.

Mother and daughter were still and silent for longer than a moment as a Chopin melody floated through the cottage.

———•———

Gretchen opened the cottage door. Amber light from late afternoon glinted through the windows, giving the room a warm, golden ambiance. "Oh, Peter, I have imagined inviting you through this door so many times, and now you are here." She closed the door behind him. "It is small and quaint and most comfortable."

She watched him as he put his bag down and perused the room.

"It reminds me of the cottage where you grew up."

"I suppose it would. I chose furniture and fabrics to recreate the house of my childhood. It was the place in which I was the most comfortable."

"I was always comfortable there, too, and I already feel at home in this room. I am so glad to stay here instead of a hotel. I will truly have the opportunity to see your life as you live it each day."

"That you feel comfortable makes my heart glad. Let us sit for a few moments." She led him to the chair where she would normally sit, and she took the seat at the end of the sofa. "You must be so tired from your flight delay. Again, I am so sorry there was no time to come straight home, but Karina had made such lovely arrangements for our dinner as a welcome gift to you."

"No. I would never have changed the plans Karina made for us. It was a lovely dinner and a most gracious way to start my visit—a couple of hours to see you first. I have missed you, and I must say that I have counted the days until I could see you again. And to see Bella and meet Karina."

"Oh, yes. For several weeks, Bella has been marking a calendar each morning, awaiting your arrival. She wanted her room to be the guest room where you would stay, but sometimes change is upsetting to her. We are prepared if that happens."

"I understand, and I would be happy on the sofa if it means I am under the same roof as you, my dear."

As she fumbled to reply, Gretchen could not help staring at the sunlight on Peter's white hair that had once been almost black. "Bella was so excited to see today's red circle on her calendar. She tidied up her room last night and got up and dressed herself this morning in her new dress and went straight for the piano and started playing Chopin. I am thinking she remembers that Chopin is your favorite." She watched the smile on Peter's face spread, that smile of contentment that she'd seen so often under the willow tree when he was happy.

"What pleasure to hear her to play again. She is so much like your grandmammá who played so beautifully, and now I will hear Karina's beautiful voice. But mostly, I want to look at you, Gretchen. We have spent hours on the phone over the last few months, but there is nothing quite like seeing your face." Across the arm of the chair, he extended his hand with his palm up.

Gretchen placed her fingers in his as she had all those

years ago, his hand that fit hers and always made her feel cherished and safe. "Yes, I am so grateful you are here in our little cottage."

The noise at the front door broke the spell of the moment. "Oh, my girls must be home." Gretchen and Peter stood at the same time, and she reached the door just as it was flung open.

Bella catapulted through the door and went straight for Peter. She wrapped her arms around his waist, squeezing him tightly. Gretchen took Karina's arm as they watched the embrace. Peter stroked Bella's hair as she repeated, "Peter is here. Peter is here. From Austria. From far away."

"Yes, I am here. And I am so happy to see you, Bella, and to hear you play the piano once again."

Their embrace ended as abruptly as it had started. Bella went straight to the piano. With her rendition of a Chopin etude in the background, Gretchen led Karina around Peter's bag, still at the front door. "Peter, I want you to know my precious Karina." She held her daughter close to her side, almost as if protecting her and presenting her at the same time. "And now, Karina, I want you to meet Peter."

The moment was awkward as Karina held out her hand as if to shake his. Instead, Peter took her fingers as though he were about to invite her to the dance floor, looked at her intently, and smiled. He then bowed like she was royalty and lightly kissed the back of her hand. It was a moment Gretchen could not have imagined.

"Karina, you are even more lovely than your dear mother has described. You are ever as lovely as she is."

Gretchen watched Karina's porcelain cheeks redden. "Thank you, sir. I am so very pleased to finally meet you. Mammá has told me that there is no one like you, and she always, always speaks truth. I am glad you are here." Karina turned to Gretchen. "Please tell me you haven't been in the kitchen or the dining room."

"We have not. We just arrived, put Peter's bag down, and were sitting here visiting while we waited for you."

"Then please sit for a few more minutes. Bella and I have something we must do." Karina went to the piano and whispered something in Bella's ear, and the melodious phrases of Chopin ceased instantly. Bella followed Karina step for step into the kitchen.

Moments later they returned. Bella went to the piano and sat, her hands clasped in her lap as though she must refrain from touching the keyboard. Karina stood in the curve of the piano and said, "Peter, Bella and I have prepared a song to welcome you to our home. And Mammá, this is for you, too, as you *are* home for Bella and me." She turned and glanced at Bella.

The introduction was sweet and simple, and then in the purest soprano voice, Karina began singing the English art song "Home Sweet Home."

The melody was familiar to Gretchen and immediately she was back in Austria, winging on the beautiful words and melody as Karina's voice caressed each phrase.

Mid pleasures and palaces though we may roam
Be it ever so humble, there's no place like home
A charm from the skies seems to hallow us there
Which seek thro' the world, is ne'er met elsewhere
Home! Home!
Sweet, sweet home!
There's no place like home
There's no place like home!

An exile from home splendor dazzles in vain
Oh give me my lowly thatched cottage again

The birds singing gaily that came at my call
And gave me the peace of mind dearer than all
Home, home, sweet, sweet home
There's no place like home, there's no place like home!

As Karina sang the last phrase, Gretchen looked around the room. A cottage in Austria had been her home. A cottage in North Carolina was now home. But the home of her heart was wherever Peter, Karina, and Bella were. Tonight, she was home.

Peter rose and embraced Karina and kissed her cheeks. "Your voice is a gift from heaven. That was truly exquisite, and I can only tell you that it moved me deeply in my spirit. Thank you. Thank you."

Karina smiled shyly. "I am so glad that it meant something to you, and welcome to our home. Now, stay right here, and I will return in only a moment." She reappeared in less than a minute. "Now for the real surprise."

Gretchen watched as Bella's excited clapping started. Bella stopped the clapping when she took Peter's hand and started toward the dining room. Gretchen followed with Karina at her side.

The room was magical: the table, covered in a delicate lace tablecloth, was set with the finest dessert plates and cups and saucers. The tea service, surrounded by bowls of fresh flowers and lit candles, sat at the end of the modest table.

Karina stepped into the room. "And now Bella and I will serve you a special dessert in honor of your visit—a Sacher torte I made just for you. I hope it will be the sweet ending of a much-anticipated day and a sweet beginning of many lovely days to come."

Gretchen moved to Peter's side and took his hand. She had no words.

Chapter Seven

———— ◆ ————

In the Willow's Shade

That weekend in Durham

*R*oderick's week had been full of meetings and phone calls. When he locked his office door before his return flight to Durham, he had closed the door on business for the weekend. Flying had enabled him to relax and unwind, and then he could breathe again when he was back with Caroline.

She picked him from the airport, and they had only the twenty-minute drive to Sarah's to be alone. Friday evening was spent with Sarah and George, catching up on their activities and a report of the documentary filming from Caroline, but he remained quiet about his own activities back at Rockwater, avoiding their inquiries by asking questions of his own. He needed a bit of private time with Sarah to tell her about his meeting with the senator, to get some sisterly advice about what to tell Caroline, and to hand over another stack of papers for Sarah's signature before returning to home on Sunday.

The loneliness he had felt at Rockwater without Caroline was unwelcomingly familiar, a feeling he had all but forgotten since their marriage. Before he met her, this kind of never-ending business and busyness had been his life—a continual itch that drove him to scratch with more work, more mergers, more deals. Lately, that itch had been more like the annoying prickliness from a scratchy wool sweater that would find its way to the rag bag. He longed for this to be finished, and for the life he hoped and planned for to continue.

After a light dinner and a bit of Caroline's and little Rosita's music making at her new piano, they retired for the evening. He rested soundly with Caroline in his arms and the anticipation of Saturday with Peter and Gretchen.

They slept in later than usual and shared a light breakfast with Sarah and George. Roderick entertained Rosita for a short while before it was time to meet Gretchen. As they stood at the door about to leave, Roderick asked Sarah, "Are you sure you won't go with us?"

"I am certain. Peter will be here for a couple of weeks, so you two spend some time with him today before your return to Rockwater tomorrow. Enjoy the gardens, and we'll meet you at the Nasher Museum Café at noon. Besides, we're planning dinner for them on Monday evening."

Roderick picked up Rosita and spun her around just to hear her giggle, put her down, and kissed Sarah on the cheek. "Okay, sis. I should have known you had a plan. We're off."

He felt Caroline's hand slip so naturally into his as they walked the few blocks to the gardens. No talk of work. Just marveling at the beauty of the morning. He spied Peter, Gretchen, and Bella at the entrance just as he expected they would be. He and Caroline picked up their pace. As they got nearer, he couldn't help noticing that Peter looked fresh, without a hint of jet lag. Nor could he miss that Peter held tightly to Gretchen's hand with his other arm around Bella's shoulder.

Roderick stood aside as Peter first kissed Caroline on both cheeks and hugged her tightly. He then took Peter's extended hand and shook it before he pulled him to a brotherly embrace. "Good morning, my friend, and welcome to America. You have brought us an amazingly beautiful day. And I do believe this air, or maybe something or someone else, must agree with you, for you look ten years younger than you did in May. How can that be? I've just gained a few more wrinkles."

"I suppose my joy at being here has lightened my spirit and my step. Shall we tour the gardens?"

Roderick wrongly assumed he and Peter would be following the ladies and that he would have some time to talk to Peter privately. Not so. Caroline took his arm, leading them through the five miles of garden paths as Peter held tightly to the hands of Bella and Gretchen and followed.

Caroline, having walked through the gardens three times this week and described them nightly to Roderick, conducted the tour. He loved how she could even make the description of the foliage and the ground covers sound musical. He always knew but was realizing more and more her love for the natural world. As of late, he wondered how she would react to the coming changes in their lives.

The crisp morning air and the fifty-five acres of autumnal colors did not disappoint. After nearly three hours of meandering through garden paths, they were joined by Sarah, George, and Rosita for lunch at the Nasher Museum Café as planned. A sumptuous luncheon was served at the best table George had reserved for them. Roderick was quiet, observing and listening to the conversation. He recognized Peter's look—the look of total enchantment with Gretchen—as the way he was always mesmerized by Caroline.

Finally, Sarah and George said their goodbyes and walked home, and Roderick and Caroline made the short walk to Gretchen's cottage to spend the afternoon. Bella entertained them with Chopin etudes until Karina returned home after closing the bakery. The minute she opened the door, Bella started. "Football. Football. Brandon. Football."

Roderick asked, "Football? Bella, I had no idea you liked football."

"I do not like football. I like Brandon." She briskly left the room.

With a bit of flush on her cheeks, Karina tilted her head and looked at the ceiling as though she was uncertain how to respond. "Yes, she likes Brandon, and I promised to take her to his intramural game this afternoon over at Williams Field."

Roderick chuckled. "You mean Brandon is a college student? Bella has a college boyfriend?"

Gretchen responded quickly. "Oh my, Roderick, she does not. She does *not* have a boyfriend. Brandon is Karina's friend from school and church, and Bella has grown quite fond of him."

"Well, I can relax now. I thought I might be going to a football game this afternoon to chaperone and check this Brandon out."

Karina spoke. "I can assure you that neither of us needs a chaperone. Brandon is our chaperone. Like me, he's a few years older than most college students. He served in the military and got a late start for his education. Actually, I first met him at church, as we both sing in the choir." She was about to leave the room but turned to say, "He is majoring in sports medicine, but he does not play football. He's just there to coach and help out where needed. But Bella loves all the excitement. And frankly, she loves all the attention even more. So, Brandon is her chaperone and really looks out for her."

"I already think I like this Brandon. Maybe Caroline and I could meet him on our next visit."

"I would like that, and I am certain Brandon would. I must go and change clothes." She turned to her mammá. "We will probably go for pizza after the game, and maybe a movie. So you enjoy your afternoon and evening. We will be having fun, and I will have Bella home by her evening bedtime."

After they left the room, Gretchen proudly responded, "Karina is so wonderful with Bella." She stood. "It is such a beautiful day, and I am drawn to spend more time outside this afternoon. The winter will keep us indoors for months, and the summer heat has kept us in with its mosquitoes, but today is perfect—warm sunshine and a cool breeze. I know we spent the morning in the gardens, but it was dark when Peter arrived last night, and he has yet to see our cottage garden out back. Would you mind if we continued our conversation there?"

Caroline stood and was the first to speak. "I'd love that. I was sitting here imagining that if Roderick and I were home, we might even be riding horses on such a beautiful afternoon. The leaves were beginning to turn before I left a week ago."

Roderick joined her. "Peter, I think I've made a Kentucky horsewoman out of this Georgia Peach."

Peter surprised them. "I know all about Georgia peaches and the ones from your neighboring state of South Carolina. I hear they are almost as delicious as our Wachau Valley apricots, though not as sweet."

Gretchen responded as she led them through the kitchen door onto the small porch. "Peter, there is nothing much better than a warm Georgia peach picked from the tree. Fruit is always better if left to ripen on the tree." She led them to the back corner of the garden, where four Adirondack chairs were arranged around a small homemade firepit of stacked stones.

Roderick watched Peter's face as he spied the large willow tree filling and shading the back corner of the garden and wondered what he must be thinking. It didn't take long to find out.

Peter put his arm around Gretchen and stood in admiration of the billowing branches. "Speaking of trees, you did not tell me you have a willow tree in your garden. I could not have imagined that willow trees so beautiful grew anywhere but along the Danube."

Smiling, Gretchen looked up at him. "Yes, a willow tree. The very reason I purchased this property. George and Sarah took me to see so many houses, some larger and farther away from the campus. But this garden with its willow tree and the quaintness of the cottage rose to the top of the list as cream rises to the top of milk."

Roderick winked at Caroline. After hearing Gretchen's stories about the willow trees along the Danube and having seen them, they had often speculated that Gretchen chose this cottage because of the tree. Now they knew.

Gretchen pointed to the chairs. "Let us sit in its shade. It is so lovely with the late-afternoon sun shining through. You can see the leaves are just beginning to turn a paler green to yellow, and its leaves will provide shade until the first snow."

After the conversation had come almost full circle with catching up on the Guatemalan Children's Choir concert, Bella's fall school schedule, and Peter's business, but nothing of Roderick's activities, Gretchen and Caroline went inside to make tea and bring out the box of pastries Karina had brought home from the bakery.

In their privacy, Peter excitedly spoke as though his

words were now unbridled and waiting for the gate to open. "Roderick, I am planning to ask Gretchen to marry me."

Roderick laughed heartily, not as though he had just heard a joke, but as though from sheer joy. "I am not surprised, my friend, and I couldn't be happier for either of you."

"I know it may seem a bit soon since we have spent so little time together. But she is and has been the love of my life, and I know in my deepest places that God has answered my prayers. I feel we have no time to waste."

"It's not too soon, my friend. I would have married Caroline the day I met her. When you know, you know." He paused. "Have you already talked with Gretchen about this?"

"I have not. We have declared our love for each other as we have talked and emailed over the last few months, and I am aware we would have many things to work out. It is in my heart to make whatever change is necessary to make her my wife and spend all my days with her." Peter cleared his throat. "I have the ring in my pocket, and I will ask her tonight. I do not wish to wait until late in my visit. Asking her this soon will give us time to seek wisdom from her friends and to make the best plans. That is why I tell you now, and will you please tell Caroline?"

"Of course. She will be thrilled to hear this news. And I understand there's no need to wait. Make the most of the time while you're here. But are you saying you would move to America?"

"Yes, if that is Gretchen's desire. Her life and home are here with Bella and Karina, but secretly I am hoping that she would like to spend some time in Austria each year to visit her family. That way I can keep my business going for a few more years until I can make certain transitions. And I am looking for a small American company to purchase.

Owning a business might make things easier for me to live and work here and become a citizen."

"I do understand transitions, and it sounds like you have given this much thought."

"I have. Gretchen is never absent from my thoughts. I am so happy to have observed that Karina is taking more responsibility for Bella now. That may ease Gretchen's fears of leaving Bella for brief trips. She is providing them with everything they need to be independent."

"I agree. Caroline and I have gladly perceived the same. Karina's come such a long way since returning to Gretchen. Knowing Bella's happy and well cared for would make it easier for Gretchen to leave for extended periods of time." Roderick paused. "So, tell me, when are you planning to ask her?"

"This evening. I have no need to wait, and the ring has been in my pocket since I left Austria. I felt I must speak with Karina about this, and we did have opportunity for a brief conversation early this morning. She is the only one who knows of my plans, and I have her blessing to make this proposal. She spoke maturely and honestly about her fears that I would not be able to accept her as Nicolai's daughter, but I assured her that I would love her as a father would love his eldest daughter, and I would love Bella as well."

Roderick nodded. "Oh, now I get it. That's why the football game." He watched the puzzled look on Peter's face transform to a smile when he understood.

"Oh yes. Karina arranged the time for our privacy. I showed her the ring and told her I would like to make my proposal early in my trip for the reasons I told you."

Roderick moved to the edge of his chair. "Well, my friend. You're wise in so many ways, and I can feel your happy anticipation. I will help you out. We'll drink our tea and skedaddle." Again, he saw the puzzled look on Peter's face. "Forgive me. Your English is so good, I forget that it's not your first language. *Skedaddle* just means we're getting out of here. I can tell you're ready to pop the question."

Roderick reached out in midair to catch the golden leaf floating in front of him. He turned it over in his hand, remembering a night in Atlanta when he and Caroline had been surrounded by autumn leaves and he was bursting to tell her how much he loved her but afraid that his proclamation would frighten her. "And then I want to make this offer. I will send our plane for you and Gretchen next week to visit us at Rockwater. I'm certain Gretchen and Caroline will have plans to make."

"Your plane? But could we not drive?"

"You could, but it would take between seven and eight hours, and a flight would take just over an hour."

"But riding eight hours alone with my Gretchen would bring me only pleasure."

Roderick smiled. "I have no doubt it would be pleasurable just to be together away from everyone and everything else, but my offer stands. So, you pop the question this evening, and we'll pop the cork of bubbly next week at Rockwater to celebrate, no matter how you get there."

"Yes, my friend. To celebrate love and life."

Roderick heard the chatter behind him as Gretchen and Caroline returned with tea and pastries. He looked at his watch. "It's three thirty. We'll be out of your hair at four. Then it's all up to you, my friend." Roderick nodded at Peter as the ladies approached.

———•———

Peter was quiet during the next half hour, allowing Gretchen and Caroline to carry the conversation. Eventually, he saw Roderick look at his watch and smiled.

Roderick placed his empty teacup back on the tray, took one more petite lemon tart from the crystal platter, and turned to Caroline. "We must go before I empty this platter and embarrass myself. These are the finest pastries I've eaten since we were in Austria."

Gretchen smiled. "Thank you, dear Roderick. That will make Karina so happy. I wish she were here to hear your words for herself. I will tell her, though. But must you go so soon?"

"Yes. We need to get back to Sarah's. I need to spend some time with her, and I know Rosita is dying for Caroline to get back to play the piano. And we must get ready to fly out in the morning." Roderick stood from his chair and went to Caroline. "So, my love, let's leave these two alone to enjoy this late-afternoon sunshine before the cool air forces them inside, or else I hope Peter's good at building a fire in that pit."

Peter responded. "A fire. That sounds perfectly lovely. I believe I saw the wood stacked next to the garden shed. Gretchen, maybe you could see them out while I get the wood so we can enjoy this beautiful afternoon underneath this willow a little longer. I will need some matches. Would you bring them?"

Gretchen chuckled. "Yes, and if you have trouble with starting the fire, I have grown quite skilled at it."

They said their goodbyes, and Roderick quietly reminded Peter of his offer before saying to both of them, "I'm sure we will see you again before you depart, Peter."

The wood was stacked perfectly when Gretchen returned with the matches, and in only moments, flames were flickering. Peter pulled their chairs closer to the fire and to each other.

Gretchen drew her shawl more tightly around her

shoulders. "Sitting next to you with the smell, the feel, and the sound of this fire is a perfect ending to a perfect day."

Her silhouette against the light through the willow was the thing of which his dreams were made. He wanted to pull the pouch from his pocket and get on his bended knee at this very moment. "And what makes you think this perfect day has ended? We still have hours to enjoy together."

"I suppose we do, and that makes for a glad heart. These months apart have dragged on, and I am certain our days together for these two weeks will take wings. Then it will be time for you to return to Austria, and our parting will be more painful than ever before. Every hour—no, every moment—is precious."

He felt her sudden sorrow at thinking of saying goodbye again and could bear not one more moment of sadness for her. He would give everything so that no shadow would ever be cast upon her. He wanted every day to be filled with hope and anticipation as they planned their lives together. As certain of her love for him as he was for God's love and blessing on both of them, he could wait no longer.

"My precious one, I think I have a solution that will keep us from parting ever again." He stood, and as he did, he reached for the velvet pouch in his pocket. He turned to kneel before her chair. The look of wonder on her face fueled his words. "My dearest Gretchen, I knelt before you years ago to ask you to marry me. I know that our parents had somewhat arranged our marriage, but I was so in love with you that I wanted to profess my devotion to you for myself. I kneel before you again today, under the shade of another willow tree in a land far from our homeland, to ask you to marry me and to spend the rest of your life with me."

Deep joy filled his heart as he saw tears trailing her cheeks. He pulled the ring from the pouch—a rose-gold band with a diamond and two rubies, the same ring he had given her almost thirty-three years ago. "Gretchen, will you accept me as your husband and allow me to love you and to take care of you until God calls one of us home?"

She choked on her words. "Yes, my love. Yes, with the same excitement in my heart as when I was a young girl, and the same commitment to love you as your devoted wife until, as you say, God calls one of us home."

He slipped the ring onto her finger, and their embrace was one of longing and fulfillment bound together with a lasting love. Tears, snubs, soft laughter, deep sighs—varied sounds of joy filled the air under the willow tree.

"You have made me one happy man, my love." He rose from the ground and sat beside her, never letting go of her right hand.

Gretchen held her left hand out in the last rays of sunlight. "Peter, it is the same ring, your grandmammá's ring?"

"Yes, it is. She told me something I have always remembered when she knew that I would ask you to marry all those years ago. Grandmammá said, 'The two rubies on each side represent you and your darling Gretchen, and the diamond in the middle represents—'"

Before he could finish the sentence, Gretchen continued with him, "'God, the One who binds you together forever.'"

"You remembered too."

"Always. And your grandmammá was right. Together forever."

"You left the ring, and your pappá returned it to me months after you disappeared. He was so certain that you were dead. I could never accept that. My heart told me you were alive."

"Oh, how it pained me to leave, and I could not bear to take the ring with me, so I placed it in my jewelry box. I knew it had great value to your family, and I knew when it was found it would be returned to you."

He kissed her hand that he held. "And finally, the ring is where it should be—on your finger."

"I will never, ever remove it again."

"Gretchen, you must have so many questions about our marriage, our wedding, where we will live, and how we will spend our time. I know that your home is here with Bella and Karina, and I could never take you from them. I am prepared to move to America. My work in Austria is secure with trusted men to continue the business, and I hope you would consider returning to Austria from time to time to visit your family, and I could take care of business there as well."

"I have wrestled with these thoughts these last few months, always wondering how we could be together, but no answer came. But now, you are saying you would make your home with us? What about your home in Linz and your friends?"

"I will keep the house, but my home is where you are. We will stay in my house when we are in Austria. My close friends and business associates will be so happy for me. I have no ties that would keep me from living here."

"I can hardly believe this, Peter. You, my Bella, and Karina, all here with me. My heart is so full." She paused and peered at him. "I have spent many sleepless nights over the last few weeks, dreaming of being your wife but unable to understand how that could be as we live such different lives on two continents. I could only talk to God about my hopes and my concerns."

"There is much you do not know, Gretchen. With my import business, I have all the proper credentials to do business in America, and I am thinking of purchasing a small company that might make things easier. Roderick is advising me."

He saw the question in her eyes. "And if you marry me, you will become a citizen?"

"Not automatically, but my attorneys tell me that I should find it easy to get a green card, and in time I will become a citizen. I will have dual citizenship here and in Austria."

"That is good." She stopped, and her face filled with surprise. "We must tell the girls right away."

Peter smiled sheepishly. "Karina knows."

"Karina knows? How can that be?"

"Because she and I had an early-morning conversation while you were in the shower, and I asked for her blessing. She is happy for us, and she gladly made all the arrangements to take Bella to the game to give us some time this afternoon and evening. I told her I could wait no longer. I wanted to make the most of my visit."

Almost as a sigh, Gretchen whispered, "She knows, and she is happy." Gretchen's whole body relaxed in peace as she leaned her head against the back of the chair.

"And forgive me, but Roderick knows, and I asked him to tell Caroline. I was bursting and told him while you were making tea. He has invited us to Rockwater for a few days while I am here so that you and Caroline can make plans."

Gretchen sat up straight in the chair. "Plans?"

"Wedding plans. Caroline is your best friend. We were certain you would want her to help you."

"Of course, wedding plans." She cocked her head and smiled. "Am I the last to know?"

Peter chuckled. "I suppose you are."

She stood excitedly. "When may we marry, Peter? Our marriage is more important than a wedding."

He rose to stand before her. "I would marry you today, my love, if we had the proper papers and a priest."

"Do you think we could be married before you must return to Austria?"

"If that is what you would like, nothing would make me happier."

Chapter Eight

———— ◆ ————

Bright Yellow Days

Late Saturday afternoon in Durham

Roderick and Caroline strolled the sidewalks taking them through a historic neighborhood back to Sarah's house. He pretended to listen and occasionally responded as Caroline gave commentary about the gates, fences, and front porches of the houses they passed, but he had no interest in wooden gates versus iron gates. He was rehearsing his talk with Sarah, and he was waiting for just the right moment to tell Caroline about Peter's proposal.

They were nearing Sarah's when he spoke. "My dear, you seem to be so interested in the architecture and curb appeal of all these houses, but I think I have something that might interest you even more." He kept a steady pace at her side.

"Well, then, I suppose I'd like to hear what that is."

"Yes, I think you'll rather enjoy it." He looked at his watch. "Let's see. We left Gretchen's about fifteen minutes ago."

"Sounds right."

"I think by now Gretchen has said yes." He watched Caroline stop in her tracks and clasp her hands, a nervous habit.

"No. No way. Are you saying what I think you're saying?" Her hands flew into the air, and he thought her legs might follow.

Coyishly, he answered, "If you think I'm telling you that Peter is proposing to Gretchen as you're talking about gates and fences, then you'd be right."

Caroline's arms flew around his neck. He embraced her and twirled her around before stopping so she could put her feet on the ground. "I don't recall your being this excited when I proposed to you."

She looked up at him. "Because I was in disbelief that you would want to marry me, and I had no idea how to respond. But Gretchen and Peter! They have belonged together all these years. I hope she will say yes." She sputtered. "Of course she will say yes. Surely she wouldn't refuse." She took his hand again.

"Do you think there is a possibility she won't accept his proposal?"

"Possibly." She paused. "Peter lives across the Atlantic, and even as much as she loves him and her homeland, I don't see Gretchen uprooting the girls and moving now that she is settled."

They started to walk and talk again. Roderick asked, "But what if Peter was willing to move to North Carolina? And now that Karina is taking a more responsible role with Bella, Gretchen might feel more freedom to return to Austria to visit her family occasionally."

"If that were the case, then I think she would say yes. A thousand times yes."

"Then she's saying yes. Peter said he's willing to make whatever changes in his life that would make Gretchen agree to become his wife."

"Wait a minute." She stopped in her tracks again. "How do you know all this?"

"When you and Gretchen were making tea this afternoon, Peter was giving me the scoop. You were hardly out of earshot when the announcement came out of his mouth like a cannonball. He could hardly wait to tell me, and he could bear to wait no longer to ask Gretchen. He had already talked to Karina early this morning to get her blessing, and he had the ring in his pocket."

"I'd say he's not wasting any time."

They were nearing the corner where Sarah lived. "Peter thought, and I agree, that it would be best to propose early in his trip so that they could spend these two weeks making their plans."

"Yes. They will have lots of plans, and I'll help. Gretchen was always there for me."

"One other thing. I know that Ned and Fred and Sam and Angel will be arriving Tuesday to spend a couple of weeks with us while the gazebo is being built, but I also told Peter that we would love for them to come and visit us at Rockwater for a few days. I hope that's all right with you."

She dropped his hand and clasped hers together in excitement again. "It's better than all right. I know Gretchen would love showing Peter off to Sam and Angel. And Angel is so good with plans, especially weddings. Why, she's hosted more bridal and baby showers than the rest of the women in Moss Point combined. Let's walk faster. I can't wait to call her."

"You mean call Angel?"

"No! I want to call Gretchen."

"Don't you think you should let them savor these moments together, just the two of them, for a little while? She will call you."

He saw the reluctant acceptance on her face.

"You're right. But I must tell somebody. May we tell Sarah and George?"

"I see no reason we shouldn't." He unlatched the wooden gate at the entrance to Sarah's house.

"And what about Sam and Angel? I'd like to tell them."

He encouraged her, as he knew this would give him a few minutes alone with Sarah. "Yes, go right ahead. I'm certain when the two of you are finished talking, the wedding will be planned. And besides, I have some papers for Sarah to sign. That'll only take a few minutes, then we can have a lovely evening together. Albert will be picking us up early for our flight home in the morning."

He paused before opening the door. A sudden and unexplainable flash of memories of all those silent years at Rockwater, those years when he'd had no family, no celebrations, and no hope that he ever would. Now, Rockwater was alive again. He sighed with deep satisfaction. "Now maybe you'll get busy and get my office out back refurbished for a guest cottage. Our family's growing." He kissed her cheek gently. "We don't seem to have many quiet moments around Rockwater, do we?"

—•—

They had all taken comfortable seats in the sunroom when Caroline broke the proposal news to Sarah and George in the presence of little Rosita. Her innocent questions precipitated a comedic explanation of love, marriage, proposals, weddings, and starting a new family. Rosita quickly and adamantly proclaimed she was never getting married, and she was never leaving home. She liked the family she had and saw no reason to have another one.

Roderick was certain that Rosita's declaration delighted Sarah and George.

"Caroline, maybe you should go and give Sam and Angel a call, and Sarah can sign these papers before dinner." He patted the briefcase next to his leg and turned to Sarah. "That suit you, sis?"

"Yes. We're picking up for dinner tonight. We found this wonderful little Guatemalan restaurant not far from here, El Chapin Grill, and Rosita is so fond of their corn cakes with all the trimmings topped off with their banana milkshake. It has become our Saturday-night treat. Hope that suits the two of you."

Roderick patted Rosita's head. "Can't say as I've ever had a banana milkshake, but then again, I've never had a milkshake I didn't like."

George got out of his chair, "Come on, Rosie, let's go look at the menu and call in our order. It'll be the best Guatemalan meal Uncle Roderick and Aunt Caroline have had since their last trip to Xela."

Rosita moved from Roderick's side and took her father's hand. "And we don't have to get in an airplane to get it."

When the chuckles settled, Roderick reached for his briefcase and opened it. He saw the immediate change of expression on his sister's face.

Sarah asked, "Do we need to move to the desk or a table?"

"Not necessary. Just two places to sign, and all the paperwork is complete and will be filed next week."

She moved to sit next to him on the sofa. "Give me the pen and the papers, and tell me about the meeting with your entourage from DC. I've been dying to hear, and I suppose you've still said nothing about this to Caroline."

He shuffled through the documents until he found the right page. "Sign here and on the next page." He pointed to the signature line and watched as her name appeared in the beautiful script she had perfected as a child.

When she finished, she handed him the papers and his pen. "Finally. It's done. That must be a relief. I guess with this final document, you can check off many things and start a new list. But what concerns me most is what will be on that new list? What did you tell the senator?"

He looked at her as he instinctively put the papers in his briefcase and shut it. "Sarah, what do you suppose I told them?"

"I hope it was absolutely nothing."

"Our parents raised shrewd kids and taught us to listen. That's what I did. I listened to what they were proposing, and I can assure you I said little, and not one facial muscle movement belied what I might have been thinking."

"Good. Now, tell me what you're thinking because your face tells me you're thinking something."

"I'm thinking that I've been successful for the last fifteen years because I practiced what I was taught and followed my gut instinct. Seems like we both inherited Mother's discernment about people and Dad's instinct for business." He put the briefcase on the floor and settled back on the sofa. "I told them I would give some thought to what they were asking of me, and I would let them know in a few days."

"Have you decided what you'll tell them?"

"No, but it's only been a couple of days, and I need a few more sleeps on it and a walk down to Blue Hole to be quiet for a while. Staring into that blue spring is like looking into a crystal ball." He paused and looked directly at Sarah. "I can't yet say that it doesn't interest me, but neither can I say it's something that excites me. I've learned through the years that I need to be excited about something to give myself to it."

"Of much more importance to me is when you will engage Caroline in the process."

"I know. I know, Sarah. I will speak with Caroline." He tried to hide his agitation.

"Better sooner than later, little brother."

"It seems Rockwater will have a full house with Sam and Angel and Ned and Fred arriving Tuesday, and then I've invited Peter and Gretchen to join us all. So as soon as the manor is quiet again, I will speak with her."

Sarah sat up straighter and got the stern face Roderick remembered all too well, the muscles in her face speaking loudly. "Twice now in the last thirty seconds I've heard you use the word *speak* with her. There is a difference in *talking* and *speaking*, Roderick. I'm *speaking* to you now: my advice is that you converse with her, talk to her—and talk to her soon. That's it. I'm done." She got up from the sofa. "No, I'm not done. You listen to her too. Ask her the questions that you want answered and listen to her. Now, I am done. I need to check on George and Rosita."

———◆———

Glad to be alone, Caroline plumped up the pillows on the bed in the guest suite, grabbed her phone, and lay down across the bed. As instinctively as her fingers played a Mendelssohn's *Song Without Words*, they pressed the numbers for Sam and Angel. She knew the familiar sounds her phone made when calling them. It was almost a melody.

Sam answered. "Hello." No one could say hello like Sam, sounding like he was still wearing his judge's robe.

"Hello to you—"

Before she could say another word, Sam stopped her. "Wait, let me get Angel. She'll want to hear everything you have to say."

She could hear him calling Angel and waited impatiently, about to explode with her good news. Then she heard Angel. "No, Sam, not that button, or you'll cut her off. The speaker button is on the right."

"All right. Got it." Sam's voice boomed. "Caroline, can you hear me?"

"All the way to Durham, I can hear you." She secretly smiled and shook her head. She imagined Sam was sitting in his library reading and had called to Angel in the kitchen. And as usual, Angel was better with the latest technology.

"And Angel too? You can hear her?"

"I think I could if you'd let her say something." She heard them both laughing.

"My goodness, it's so good to hear your voice, Caroline. Did you say you're still in Durham?"

"Yes, ma'am. We fly back to Rockwater tomorrow morning early. I've finished my work with the documentary crew, and we've spent the day with Gretchen and Peter. So good to see him again."

Sam asked, "Oh, how is dear Gretchen? Is she still worried about those annoying phone calls?"

Caroline could finally say it. "As a matter of fact, I think the only thing that might even come close to worrying her right now would be all the plans she must make to become Mrs. Peter Kornilov."

"Come again?" Sam asked.

Angel interrupted. "Oh, Sam, stop it. Peter has asked Gretchen to marry him. Why, that is the best news since Roderick walked down to your studio to put pink diamonds and pearls on your ring finger, Caroline. What a love story for those two! See, like I always told you, Sam, true love is for all time."

"Yes, it is. Peter asked her this evening, and he's even

moving to America."

"And of course she said yes." Caroline could practically hear Angel grinning.

Then Caroline recalled that she didn't know for certain. "The truth is Peter told Roderick he was asking her this evening. So I'm assuming he has already proposed, and she said yes. I mean, how could she refuse?"

Angel's voice squeaked. "You know she said yes. How could she refuse the man she's loved since she was a girl?"

Sam added, "Especially since he came halfway around the world to ask her. Why, I would have stayed down on my knee until Gabriel blew his trumpet or Angel said yes, whichever came first. I wasn't about to let her slip through my fingers. And I'll just bet my old fishing hat that Peter feels the same way."

Caroline pictured the look on Angel's face. She could only hope that she and Roderick and Peter and Gretchen would know love like Sam's and Angel's—long and satisfying. "Gretchen loves him, and now that he's willing to move here, there are no obstacles to their being together. She must be the happiest she's ever been."

"Well said, sweet girl! And next to you, if anyone ever deserves some happiness, it would be Gretchen. My, what gray days she's had. It's high time she had some bright-yellow ones."

Sam blurted out, "With all she's been through with that scoundrel of a husband in Ernesto Silva."

Angel stopped him. "Sam, don't go speakin' ill of the dead. Mr. Silva made his restitution, and don't go draggin' all that up on the happiest night of Gretchen's life."

"Well, she's not here to hear it, and you know it's true."

Caroline felt she was eavesdropping on their conversation.

"Sam Meadows, you were a judge. You know that just

because somethin's true doesn't mean it necessarily needs to be said. 'Nough about that."

Sam retorted. "You're right. Enough about that. I'm just grateful she's about to enter a new season in her life." He paused. "Come to think of it, Peter's bringing a new season to that whole family."

Caroline heard Angel breathe. "Now, the minute you find out for sure, you let us know, you hear?"

"Of course, I will. And Roderick has invited them to come to Rockwater next week. In fact, you may see them before I see them depending on the flight plan. Albert may pick all six of you up on the same trip. Either way, I'll see you two on Tuesday. I'm really looking forward to your visit and having you around for two whole weeks."

Angel responded. "It'll be a delightful time. Don't know what Hattie's goin' to do, though. She's been groanin' and moanin' for the last few days. Says that our bein' gone for two whole weeks is just too long. She's bringin' two of her youngest grandchildren over to stay in the house while we're gone. They'll enjoy the park and bein' in town. I'll make certain there's plenty of ice cream in the freezer before we leave."

"Hattie will be fine with her grandchildren around. The change will do her good too. I just had to tell you about Gretchen, and I'll call you the minute I hear from her. She knows our flight time is at early-thirty in the morning, so I'm thinking she won't call until tomorrow. Roderick's talking business with Sarah, and I need to get my things packed before dinner. You all have sweet dreams tonight just remembering dreams do come true."

"Will do, sweet girl. We can't wait to see you, and tell Lilah I'm expectin' some of her cinnamon-raisin scones with my Tuesday afternoon tea."

"That will make Lilah happy and me too. Love you."

She lay there holding the phone for a few minutes as though that would make Gretchen call. She then thought about all the activity the next week could bring to Rockwater and called Lilah to inform her they were having two more guests next week.

Caroline sprang from the bed and grabbed her luggage. She was too anxious not to be doing something. She gathered her clothes, folded them neatly as was her custom, and placed them in perfect order inside the bag, even the ones that would go straight to the laundry basket when she got home. Another bag for shoes and accessories. And yet another bag for toiletries. Roderick's bag was across the room leaning against the closet door. One bag, and he would throw what little he brought in it without thought. Lilah had always been there to take care of him.

But Lilah wasn't here, so Caroline took his two shirts from their hangers in the closet and folded them and placed them in his bag, even though she knew Lilah would send them to the dry cleaners. She foraged the room for T-shirts, socks, and his jacket, and put them in as carefully as if they were her offering to him.

As she packed his things, she remembered he had said these were the last of the documents that Sarah must sign. Would he explain everything to her now? Maybe, just maybe, she was nearer to learning what had claimed his time and most of his attention the last several weeks. She would not ask again, knowing if he did not tell her before their guests arrived on Tuesday there would be no serious conversation for the next two weeks. And absolutely no chance of serious conversation if Gretchen and Peter took him up on his invitation.

She was folding the last pair of socks when her cellphone rang. It was Gretchen. Her sophomoric squeals were probably heard all over the house. Caroline, normally reserved and contained, could not hold back her emotions.

She was saying goodbye when Roderick walked into the room. "I would assume Gretchen said yes. We heard you all the way to the sunroom."

She jumped up, flung her arms around him. "Gretchen said yes to Peter. And they said yes to your invitation to Rockwater. They will arrive on Thursday."

"I hoped they would."

"She didn't hesitate. She said the ones that mattered to her would all be there."

"Well, except for Bella and Karina."

"No. They're coming too. They're all making the road trip."

"Oh, I told you last week we would need the guest cottage. No time for that project now, but at least you and Lilah will have a couple of days to get Sam and Angel settled and Ned and Fred started on the gazebo before the rest of them arrive."

She looked at him coyishly. "And time to make plans for a wedding. Another magical wedding at Rockwater."

"They want to get married at Rockwater?"

Not often did she get to see a look of surprise on Roderick's face. "Yes, on Saturday."

Chapter Nine

———— ◆ ————

Decisions

Sunday morning in Melk, Austria

Sunday morning. Iris's day off, but she could not bear her dusty, hollow, lifeless cottage. She had nothing to do, no one to even share Sunday brunch, and nowhere to go except to her office. She donned her sweater and walked the eight blocks to the hotel.

Once there, she grabbed the morning paper from the lobby counter, snapped at the hotel desk clerk about his wrinkled tie, and hissed all the way down the hall to her office. She slammed the heavy wooden door hard and tossed her bag and the morning paper onto her desk before she crossed the room to the window, which looked out on the terrace garden restaurant.

There was one empty table, with the rest of the seats filled with tourists visiting the area for the autumn grape harvest and other families on their last holiday before Christmas. Fall festivals were always good for hotel business, but those happy faces only drove Iris deeper into the mire of envy she lived in lately. She begrudged whatever the hotel guests had that made them smile so much.

The young couple sitting under the vine-covered cupola caught her eye. She wondered if they even noticed the fading purple wisteria blossoms that were dropping daily. They probably gave no thought that the cupola would be bare in just a few weeks and would stay barren until spring. She wondered if they were newlyweds. Were they on holiday? Then came the soul-crushing questions: What would her life have been like if only Nicolai had never gone to prison? Would they have sat together on a Sunday morning enjoying the sunshine and each other's smiles?

Seeing no future for herself—no satisfying future—Iris lived in the dark, dead-end alleys of what might have been. Memories of winsome Nicolai, the most handsome young man in town. Every girl in Melk had fancied him, but she had caught his eye. They had partied and spent almost every night together for weeks. Inseparable they were—until he started going out in the evenings without her to meet his friends at a local bar. She convinced herself if she was patient, he would return to her and ask her to marry him. He did return, but only when he was a suspect in a police investigation and needed her help.

She heard the sordid stories and chose not to believe them. Nicolai vowed to her he had never done the things those women accused him of doing. He begged her to help him, to vouch for him, and when he was out on bail, he asked her for money. She had none, certainly not enough to hire legal counsel or to flee. Instead, she helped him concoct a plan to get money from Peter. When Peter refused to help, they had stolen from him to finance their escape from Austria. But Peter and the police had set a trap, and Nicolai was apprehended.

She hated Peter for destroying her life with Nicolai.

Iris had been inconsolable for months after Nicolai was

convicted and sentenced. She wrote to him regularly for the first few years he was in prison, promising to wait for him. She visited him as often as she could. She maintained Nicolai's innocence to anyone who would listen to her. The few friends she had soon crossed the street when they saw her coming.

Even marrying Mr. Brandhof had been part of a grand scheme to get his money. She would use his small fortune to get a new trial for Nicolai. She would marry Mr. Brandhof, take care of him for a year or two, divorce him, and get everything she could. Then she and Nicolai would be financially set when he was released from prison and could start their lives together. That had been the plan.

But no retrial was permitted, and Iris had ended up wedged between her obsession with Nicolai and her miserable marriage to a sickly, elderly man. When Nicolai had served his sentence and was released, he did not return to Melk, nor did he even contact her. When someone else told her about his prison discharge, she'd been devastated all over again. She convinced herself that he could not return because he would not be accepted in the community. His parents were dead. Peter had sold the family business and moved to Linz. And she was married.

Iris's excuses for Nicolai continued until they didn't. Her questions, anger, and bitterness had smoldered for the last few years since her husband's death. If only she had known he'd willed almost everything to his two grown children who despised her. She had assumed since she was the one who had given care to him, the bulk of his estate would be hers. She lamented that she was left with only a small cottage and must work to live.

For some reason not even Iris understood, Gretchen's return to Melk last spring had ignited her, bringing back so many memories, most of them unpleasant. And then there had been seeing Peter again. She knew little about Gretchen or Peter, but her curiosity had consumed her. What had she to lose by digging? She had nothing, so there was nothing to lose.

She had learned from Peter that he had spoken to his brother only once since his release. She had no notion of where to start, but she would not rest until she found Nicolai.

Peter's final words had ricocheted through her thoughts and deprived her of sleep for over a week. *"Iris, what would it take for you to let all of this go? How much?"* There was something to be gained here, and perhaps there might even be a bonus.

She looked at her watch. Almost ten o'clock. Peter would be on his way to church soon. She dialed his number, not really expecting to hear his voice but hoping she would.

When he did not answer, she left a brief message. "Peter. It is Iris. You asked me what it would take for me to let this go. I am ready to tell you. Call me." She put her phone in her pocket.

Still gazing at the young couple and standing so near that her breath fogged the window, she whispered, "Peter will call. And if he does not, I will continue to call. I will use your brother's money to find you, Nicolai. You will return to me, or I will make your life as miserable as mine."

———•———

4:00 a.m. Sunday morning in Durham

Not from jet lag or fatigue, Peter slept soundly and peacefully like he had not in weeks. It had been a late evening with Gretchen and the girls, making plans and talking about the future. So much laughter, and even a few tears of joy. They made plans to leave for Rockwater on Thursday. Karina would make arrangements to close the bakery for a few days. Gretchen would be making wedding plans with Caroline. There would be shopping for wedding attire, and Peter would be making plans for the life he had all but lost.

His grateful heart knew that only God could have led him to this new season of his life. It was like spring again, a latent spring with new life and hope. No more thoughts of growing old with only a business to keep him company. He now had Gretchen to love and care for, and she loved him as well. He would love Karina and Bella as his own daughters, and he had hope that in time they would grow to love him too.

With such pleasant thoughts and the scent of lavender on his pillow, he had drifted tranquilly to sleep well past midnight, imagining that in exactly one week Gretchen would be his wife, and Bella and Karina would be his family. He was all too pleased that the coming week would be one of joy and anticipation.

The ringing phone startled him. Remembering he was not at home in Linz, he turned over and reached for the lamp switch and his phone. The clock read three fifty-five. Who would call him at four o'clock in the morning? Only someone who did not know he was traveling. Or it could be business related. But it was Sunday and midmorning in Austria.

He studied the number on the screen. It looked vaguely familiar. He declined the call and lay with the phone in his hand until the voice mail message popped up. He listened. The sound of Iris's voice was smothering.

Peter's principled father had taught him as a young man to behave each day so that he would not live in the shadow of regret. It had been good advice—advice he had tried to live by whether in business or his personal life. In last week's meeting with Iris, he'd known immediately he would regret asking her that last question before he left her standing in the hotel dining room. But he had asked it, and she had heard it. He had walked away briskly without giving her time to respond.

Over the last few days, he had considered his response if she ever contacted him again. He had begun to look at Iris as a tragic character, another life left in the wake of his brother's tidal wave of transgressions. He had forgiven Nicolai for the pain he had caused, but forgiving him did not mean he had forgotten, or even that he should forget. He had purposefully steered clear of his brother after that one painful visit years ago. It was enough to know that Nicolai now lived in Germany. Neither brother desired a relationship with the other; and like Nicolai, he planned to have nothing else to do with Iris.

Giving her money would be never-ending, and he would be no party to any of her destructive schemes. She might be a tragic figure, but he knew full well she was a self-serving woman. He had maintained his distance for several years, and it had worked. And now he would be married and nearly five thousand miles away from her clutches. He was done. No return phone calls. No answered emails or letters. No money. No more talk of Nicolai or Gretchen's past. No more Iris. Only Gretchen.

The winter of his life might be approaching, but it felt like spring, and he would allow nothing and no one to cast shadows from the past. He basked in the light of a new season of life.

—————•—————

Springtime of the Song

Sunday morning at the airport in Durham

The morning breeze blew wisps of Caroline's curls across her cheek as she stood on the tarmac. She brushed them away from her face and looked at her watch. Almost seven o'clock. Familiar with their habits, she knew Angel would be in the kitchen and Sam would be sitting at the breakfast table turning the pages of the Sunday edition of the *Atlanta Journal-Constitution.* She called to Roderick, "I'll board in just a moment. I promised to call Sam and Angel as soon as I heard from Gretchen, and it was too late last night."

Roderick responded, "Don't take too long. Albert has filed his flight plan, and we need to get going."

In seconds she heard Angel's squeaky morning voice. "It's Sunday, so I know it's a good mornin'."

"Yes, it is. A beautiful morning indeed. It's Caroline."

"Tell me somethin' I didn't already know."

"Gretchen said yes."

Angel laughed loudly. "I already knew that too. Now tell me somethin' I really don't know."

"We have a wedding to plan. Peter and Gretchen are getting married at Rockwater on Saturday. She said all the people she cared about most would be there, and they wanted to marry in the presence of all of us who are like family to her."

"Well, I didn't see that one comin'. Bless Pat, whoever she is, we're gonna have a weddin'. Did you hear that, Sam? Gretchen and Peter are getting married at Rockwater Saturday!"

Caroline started up the steps to the plane. "I must go now, but I'll call you later this afternoon. Just wanted you to know she accepted Peter's proposal. Be thinking. You always have such creative ideas, but remember, nothing elaborate. Gretchen wants to keep it simple."

"Not a thing wrong with simple. We'll make it simply elegant, just like Gretchen."

"I like the sound of that. Talk later. I love you both."

Caroline dropped her phone into her bag and climbed the remaining steps. Roderick helped her through the door and closed it. "You know the drill. Seat belt and get comfortable, little wife. I'll join you after takeoff."

"Yes, Captain." Another wave of disbelief came over her. She had just boarded their plane—not *a* plane, but *their* plane—headed to Rockwater, her home now. When would all the trappings of this new season of her life become more real? Or perhaps it was beginning to.

As much as she had enjoyed her week with George and Sarah and then with Peter and Gretchen, she missed Rockwater. She missed the serenity, the beauty, Lilah, curling up in a chair in the library, her morning walks with Roderick, and her treasured piano.

Being at home would be good. Two days before guests arrived, but a flurry of activity every day. She couldn't wait to see Lilah's face when she gave her the news of another Rockwater wedding.

———•———

Sunday morning in Durham

Sunrise could not come early enough for Gretchen. Today was Sunday, and for the first time since she was a girl, she would sit in church next to the man she loved. She would smile with pride at hearing Karina's bell-like voice above all the rest in the choir, and Bella would be sitting beside her.

They would begin this week with worship and thanksgiving. This would be the first Sunday in the new season of her life, and this time next Sunday she would be Mrs. Peter

Kornilov.

She rose early, showered, and dressed for the day before heading to the kitchen. She chose her white Sunday apron trimmed in Battenburg lace and put it over her green skirt and ivory-colored blouse. As she reached for the cannister of coffee, she gazed at the glistening gemstones in the ring on her finger, and a smile spread across her face.

The sound of footsteps caused her to turn. Peter.

Gretchen went to him and embraced him tightly. "Good morning, my love, and pardon my apron." She inhaled the lavender that lingered on his hair from his pillow. "I see you're up and dressed for church."

He kissed her cheek, held her hands, and took one step back. "I am. I hope you like this suit. Or perhaps you would prefer I buy a new one for our wedding."

"It is dashing, and I see no reason to buy a new one. But that decision is yours, my love. I am glad you rose early. I was simply too excited to sleep. I was thinking of so many things. All through the night, I would wake, turn on the light, and add something to my list."

"You make lists?"

"Yes, Caroline taught me to make them. I find list making so helpful." She stepped to the counter where the coffee cannister sat and immediately turned back to him. "My goodness, I do not know if you prefer coffee or tea in the morning. I have so much to learn of you, my love."

Peter took a seat at the breakfast table—not the seat at the head of the table where he assumed Gretchen would sit, but one on the side. "I prefer whatever you are having."

She reached for two mugs. "Karina must have her morning coffee made in this percolator, and she has taught me to drink it with her. And I have taught her to drink tea with me in the afternoon. So, will you have a cup of coffee with us?"

"Yes, and I will have a cup of tea with you this afternoon. May I help you?"

"Oh no. Just sit and talk with me. We have a few traditions, and Sunday-morning breakfast is one of those. Bella must have her *kaiserschmarrn* with maple syrup and bacon on Sunday mornings. Is that agreeable with you?"

"*Kaiserschmarrn*? You did bring some of Austria with you."

"Oh yes. Tomorrow, you will see the bakery and the other delights I have brought from our homeland, and Karina makes them so well."

"Then there will be nothing I shall miss by living here with you and the girls and Karina's Austrian pastries."

"We will work to make you happy and your life complete." She added water and measured the coffee carefully before putting it into the percolator basket and plugging it in. Coffee on, she reached for the flour and a mixing bowl.

"My life is already complete. I know we have so many plans to make, and I could not be happier that we will be married at Rockwater on Saturday. But I was thinking . . . Fairly soon, I must return to Linz to take care of some business."

Gretchen stopped what she was doing and spun to face him.

Peter continued. "I am hoping that in mid-October we could return to Austria together and have our honeymoon in the Alps before the winter sets in. I have a small chalet just outside of Innsbruck. I would love to take you there, and we could visit your pappá and Elfi."

"Return to Austria? In all my thoughts these last twelve hours, I had none that you must return to Austria. Of course you must, and I shall look forward to returning with you." She felt a sudden flush. "How long will we be gone?"

"No longer than two weeks." He waited a moment for

her to respond. "I know you must be thinking of Bella, and we can take her with us if that would please you. I know you have never been away from her."

She wiped the flour from her hands and sat down at the table with him. "Peter, your kindness has only grown through the years. I am grateful you would think such things, but I am learning that Karina's relationship with Bella is deepening, and she is most responsible with her. I must speak with Karina, but I think she will gladly take care of Bella while I am away. It would be best not to upset her school schedule."

Peter took her hands. "I want you to know that I will never come between you and your girls. I will always support you and give care to them myself."

"What comfort that gives me. Neither of the girls ever had a father who loved them the way pappá loved me. You will be God's gift to them as well as to me." She stood from her chair and leaned to wrap her arms around him. "I truly love you, Peter."

"And I you, my precious Gretchen."

She moved away. "Now that we have made our honeymoon plans, I must get on with the scrambled pancakes. That is what Bella calls *kaiserschmarrn*."

"Having this settled pleases me. It means my waking hours in planning last night were successful."

She sifted the flour and measured the sugar. "Speaking of waking, I thought I heard your phone sometime during the night."

"Yes. Nothing to concern you. Not everyone in Austria knows that I am in America with you. I did not take the call. I wanted nothing to disturb my sweet thoughts of the new season in our lives."

"And nothing shall."

Karina and Bella joined them exactly at eight o'clock,

dressed in their Sunday best. The scene at the breakfast table filled Gretchen's soul. They talked and laughed and ate their breakfast of scrambled pancakes with Vermont maple syrup and salt-cured bacon. And with the last bite, Bella was off to the piano. In only moments, Chopin filled the cottage. Gretchen and Karina began tidying the kitchen while Peter sat at the table and enjoyed his second cup of coffee.

Gretchen watched as he sat back in his chair with ease, closed his eyes, breathed deeply, and smiled. She did not know if he was enjoying the aroma of the coffee or the sweet scent of newfound happiness. He spoke without opening his eyes, "I think I shall grow to love living in this cottage filled with so much love and Chopin and strong coffee."

Gretchen looked at Karina, and they both giggled softly and continued their cleaning.

At exactly nine fifteen, the music stopped, and Bella announced. "Time to go to church."

Gretchen removed her apron. "Bella is right. It is time to leave for church. It is a most beautiful morning for our walk." She and Peter joined Bella at the front door. While they waited for Karina, Gretchen took the silk scarf Peter had given her from the shelf and draped it loosely around her shoulders and neck. "Do you recognize this scarf?"

"Do you think I would not recognize the scarf that I searched for—the perfect one to bring out the green in your eyes? I chose wisely."

She felt his arm slip around her shoulders. "Shall we go?"

They were out the door and halfway down the walkway when a phone rang. Peter retrieved his phone from his pocket, looked at the number. "Nothing important. I am turning my phone off. We are headed to church."

Chapter Ten

---◆---

Revelations

Sunday afternoon, September 26, at Rockwater

Albert, bags in hand, followed Roderick and Caroline up the back steps. Roderick searched his pocket for the key. "Thanks for a safe flight, and I'll see you on Tuesday morning, bright and early. Let's attempt a flight plan that will have us home by lunch, then you can park the plane for at least a couple of weeks. I'm staying put. We'll have guests, and I need to let the dust settle."

"Yes, sir. I'll be ready to fly whenever you are." Albert headed toward the truck.

Roderick waved goodbye to him and inserted the key into the back door. The last time he had returned home, it had been without Caroline and to a silent manor house. Today was different, and he liked it.

They walked into the kitchen, and she put the bag of Chinese takeout on the counter and went immediately to open the curtains covering the bay windows overlooking the garden.

"Roderick, look at the flaming sumac. Oh, how it's

changed in the short time I was gone. The color is spectacular." She sighed. "I'm beginning to think autumn is my
favorite season at Rockwater. That is until we have a white
Christmas, and then I'll likely change my mind again."

He stood holding the bags and gazed out the window
over Caroline's shoulder. "I say that too until I see the acres
of spring daffodils and blooms on the fruit trees. And come
next April, you'll have large beds of irises around the gazebo.
What do you say? You put our lunch on plates, and I'll get
these bags to our suite. We can nap and unpack after
lunch."

"Yes to getting our lunch ready and unpacking, but I'm
not certain I can nap. I'm so happy to be home, I think I'll
just wander these halls until I find a place to sit and start my
list making."

"Whatever is your pleasure, but you must not deny me a
walk down to Blue Hole this afternoon. The sun's shining,
it's still warm, and we should take advantage of such a quiet
autumn afternoon. There won't be many of those in the
next couple of weeks. Besides, there's nothing like sitting on
the boulder above Blue Hole to clear our heads and get
ready for a busy week."

What he refrained from telling her was that he could not
answer his sister's call Monday morning if he did not talk
with Caroline about what he'd been doing. He knew if this
conversation did not take place today, it would likely be
another two weeks before they had a few hours to themselves. The time was right, and he was ready and
determined.

"Certainly. Sounds like a perfect afternoon, and I can't
wait to see the color on those hills around the stream." She
turned to him. "Go on. I'll have our plates ready before you
get back. I don't like cold Chinese food, and right now, it's
still hot. We'll eat in the morning room. So glad you

thought of picking up something and coming home. I don't think I could bear walking into another restaurant today."

Before he left the kitchen, she opened the refrigerator for a couple of bottles of coconut water and found a note from Lilah. "Would you look? Lilah's note says she came yesterday. She left us her homemade chicken salad and that spicy coleslaw you love. Sounds like we'll have a real picnic at Blue Hole."

They had eaten the last spring roll when Caroline's phone rang. He sat silently and listened for a few moments as she chattered away with Gretchen about music and candles and who was doing what. He was antsy, so he picked up both their plates and headed to the kitchen. He cleaned their plates, put the leftover food away, and returned to the morning room, where he motioned that he was headed to his office. He could at least lighten his briefcase and stack the files on Celia's desk. He was finally done with these files. The last paperwork had been signed, and it would all be sealed and filed tomorrow. Their lives were about to change.

He closed his office door. Caroline was still at the table talking to Gretchen and taking notes when he passed the morning room. He kept walking, went to their suite, and dumped the contents of his one backpack on the floor. He put his bag away and tossed everything—the clothes that Caroline had neatly folded and put in his bag the evening before—into the oversized laundry basket.

Next, he picked up her bag, placed it on the marble countertop, and unzipped it. He smiled as he opened it. Her bag was packed as though she had held a ruler to the two stacks of perfectly folded clothes. Then there was her shoe bag with four pairs of shoes inside nylon shoe bags. The blouses, skirts, and pants in her hanging bag were the same way—buttoned properly, blouses together, then the skirts, then the pants. He wondered how she could tell what needed to be laundered, but this was Caroline. His Caroline. Orderly. Staid. Her life had been predictable until the cyclone of change blew in with Bella and then he blustered in with the backdraft.

He had marveled at how well she'd adapted to the changes in such a short time—stepping up to guide Gretchen through the turmoil in her life and her move to Durham, starting the Guatemalan Children's Choir and almost losing her life while doing it. Then there were more changes when she married him. She gave up her career, moved from a small studio to a vast estate, and said goodbye to her students, friends, and the people with whom she had been doing life. Yet she had done it all with such calm.

Still, although her music remained the constant in her life, he had lately sensed a new uneasiness about her. He wondered if she had grown weary of all the changes and was missing her old life, or if she was bored, but he didn't want to hear from Sarah or from Lilah that his secrecy was partly the cause.

And now there was about to be another change, a life-altering one that she couldn't have seen coming. His life would be the most affected, but he hoped she could adapt. As he had done for the last fifteen years, he did things his way, made his decisions, and then moved forward with unchecked certainty. He could only hope now that his secrecy had not been a mistake.

He unpacked her bags and did his best to stack her clothes as neatly on the countertop as Caroline had placed them in her bag, removing her shoes from their bags and lining up them up beside her stacks of clothes. He returned the luggage to its place on the top shelf, glad that he would not be needing it any time soon. That done, he placed Caroline's toiletry bag on her vanity and walked back to the morning room.

Caroline was still on the phone with Gretchen, so he grabbed the paper he had picked up in the airport in Durham and sat down to read. He was almost done with the business pages when he heard Caroline finally say goodbye.

"Sounds like you two covered all the details."

With her notepad in hand, she turned from her chair at the table to face him. "At least the big ones, but there are still so many small decisions they must make. Good news is they both want a simple ceremony in the loggia on Saturday morning at eleven o'clock. Bella will play, Karina will sing two songs, and for the first time in my life, I will be the matron of honor. I have always provided the music for weddings, too many times to count, and now I get to stand beside the bride. Oh, and Sarah and George and Rosita are coming. And you, my husband, will be the best man. I'm letting you know in advance. Gretchen said Peter will be calling you later today, so act surprised when he asks you."

Roderick folded the paper and dropped it to the floor. "Me? Best man for Peter? I can handle it. Did that for two of my fraternity brothers, and this will be a pleasure. Besides I think I'll enjoy standing there looking at you, reliving our own wedding day."

"You will, will you?" She winked at him. "Your only duty—and it's a big one—will be to secure our pastor to perform the ceremony."

"I can certainly make an attempt, but I do hope they have a plan B if he's not available. This is short notice, even for a small-town pastor."

"Yes, they have another plan. I suggested Sam. He's a judge."

Roderick waffled. "Hmm, I'm not sure that will work. Sam's retired and from another state. I should check with our attorney. We do want them legally and properly married, especially since Peter's not an American citizen."

"Maybe you could call the minister this afternoon, and if he's available, we'll have no need to fret about Sam." She looked down her list. "The other big things: Peter will be hosting a dinner on Friday evening for all of us at the Castle, and the two of them will return there for their wedding night. Bella and Karina will stay with us, and they'll leave on Sunday to return to Durham."

"Short honeymoon."

"They need to get back so that Karina and Bella can stay on their school and work schedules. And don't worry about the short honeymoon. Gretchen and Peter plan to leave for Austria in mid-October to honeymoon at the base of the Alps in a small chalet in Innsbruck. Peter owns it. And Gretchen's leaving Bella with Karina."

Roderick rose from his chair. "That's a big step for her. For all of them, really."

"Truly it is, but she's at peace about it, and so is Karina." Caroline put her notepad on the table. "And the last thing is that I insisted we have the pleasure of hosting a wedding brunch on Saturday. We all must eat, so we might as well make a party of it."

He approached Caroline and took her in his arms. "Nobody loves giving a party like Lilah does. I can only hope my parents are aware that you have brought Rockwater back to life and so many happy occasions are shared here with the people we love."

She looked up at him, their noses almost touching. "That was a sweet thing to say, and perhaps God lets them in on the happy things that are going on in the lives of their children."

He kissed her deeply and then held her to his chest. "What would you say about trying to take just a short rest? After that, I'll put the things together for a picnic while you put your things away, and we'll head down to Blue Hole for an early supper."

"I'll follow you anywhere."

Her words surprised him, and he hoped that was true. "You mean all the way over to the daybed in the bay window. View's nice, and the warm sun coming in will put us to sleep."

———◆———

Roderick had the picnic basket strapped to his back, and Caroline had the quilt tucked under her arm. They walked the path to Blue Hole, marveling at the forested rolling hills spangled with reds, golds, and yellows. Caroline commented, "Oh, I do hope the colors will last another couple of weeks so that our guests can enjoy them. I suppose the horse-drawn sleigh we use at Christmas only works on snow."

Roderick squeezed her hand. "You'd be right about that, but I'll get Chip to clean up the carriage. Our guests can enjoy a carriage ride to see the leaves. They haven't even begun to reach their peak. We'll have color for another month unless we have an unexpected early freeze. September's almost over, and September freezes are rare."

They walked on until they reached the boulder that guarded the blue waters of the spring below. Roderick removed the picnic backpack from his shoulder.

Caroline unrolled the quilt she had been carrying and unfurled it in the afternoon breeze. Roderick helped her spread it over the sun-warmed boulder. They sat and feasted on Lilah's chicken salad, coleslaw, a sliced apple with soft Gouda, and a sleeve of butter crackers. They chuckled about eating from paper plates and drinking a glass of cabernet from Waterford crystal. Picnic talk centered around wedding plans, where to put their guests, and whether to stain the new gazebo or paint it white.

When they finished eating and the small talked waned, Roderick reached for the picnic basket.

Caroline quipped, "No. Don't tell me it's time to go. This was the perfect supper for such an afternoon. Lilah takes such good care of us and always keeps the fridge stocked. Here, if we must go, let me help you put things away."

He was scrambling to the bottom of the basket. "Not so fast, my lady. We have dessert."

"Dessert? I didn't see any dessert in the fridge. What is it?"

"A surprise." He looked her straight in the eye while still fumbling in the basket. "What did I promise you on the night I proposed to you?"

She tittered. "Oh, let me see. I do recall a couple of little things, like promising to love me always and that you would do your best to keep me smiling all the days of my life."

"I did promise those little things, but there was something else." He pulled two Baby Ruths from the basket. "Remember our engagement dinner in your studio, and you lifted the dome over the dessert tray to two of these. You had told me they were your favorites. And I promised that I would always have Baby Ruths for you. Lilah keeps those for us too—some in a secret place for me and a few in the freezer for special times like this afternoon."

"A special time?" Taking the one he offered her, she felt a familiar tightening in her stomach. She forced a smile and looked away as she removed the wrapper. "Well, these must have been in the freezer, and I'm not certain they're thawed."

"Just lay them on the rock in the warm sunshine.

Shouldn't take long." He paused. "You know, Caroline, Blue Hole was always my special place when I was a child and even when I became a man. It was the place where I came to clear my head and think things through. Then when you came to Rockwater for the first time for the parlor concert and we walked to Blue Hole, for me it became our special place, not just mine. And I remember thinking and hoping for a lifetime of walking to Blue Hole with you after our first afternoon here."

"Really? You never told me that."

"I should have told you. It's true. We've had some serious conversations here in the past. This is where you told me about losing David in a Guatemala flood, and I told you about the afternoon of my mother's accident and why I no longer rode horses. Right here on this rock, we've talked about some of the most significant events that really changed our lives, and I remembered how you prayed out loud right here one morning."

Her stomach grew tighter. Was he about to tell her what he had been keeping from her for the last several weeks? Did she really want to know? Her stubborn pride had kept her from asking him again. Her gaze was penetrating and her voice shaky. "Are we about to have another conversation about a significant event?"

"Yes. That's why I brought you here. There is something I've been keeping from you until I was ready to tell you. That time has come. There are about to be some very significant changes in our lives. Mostly mine." His head dropped as he said those last words.

Caroline felt the blood drain from her head and the edge of dizziness take her. All she could think of was losing him. "Roderick, are you ill? Are you dying?"

What?" He looked up and chuckled. "No. Whatever would make you think that?" When she gasped for air in relief and became quiet, his grin faded. "Speak to me, Caroline. What would make you think I was sick?"

She squeezed her eyes shut to hold back tears of relief and exhaled calmly. "It's just that you've been so secretive, and you said you were getting things in order. And I know you would dread telling me something like that."

He reached for her and pulled her closer to him. "Oh, Caroline, I'm so sorry. It never crossed my mind that you would jump to such conclusions."

She buried her face in his shoulder and sniffed. "Honestly, I didn't think of those things until you started talking about the serious conversations we've had right here. And then my mind flipped through all the files of the past few weeks when you were so distant and you refused to talk to me."

He took her chin and held her face up to his and kissed her. "My precious, I truly am sorry that I have caused you one minute of stress. What I am about to tell you is a most wonderful change." He paused. "I'll give you the bottom line, and then I'll unpack it for you. I, with Sarah's agreement and blessing, have sold Adair Enterprises." He stammered. "Well, most of it."

"You sold your business?" She was totally perplexed. "Will we be moving?"

"No, Rockwater is our home and always will be on this side of heaven as far as I'm concerned. It's just that Adair Enterprises has been my life until I met you. And I have learned there are more important things to do in life than just business. When I joined my father in the company and it became my responsibility when he died, my goal was to be successful—to honor all that he had built and be even more successful. And I have been. The net worth of the company has doubled in the last thirteen years. But I'm weary of it, and I have other interests."

Caroline was finally able to breathe normally again. Roderick was safe, and he seemed peaceful. She pulled away from him to focus on his face, to read every expression. "Other interests? Like what?"

"You're aware we've always had our family foundation, the charitable arm of the business. And Sarah's done a great job of managing that while I was increasing the fortune. But she has other interests now too. You don't know it, but about half of the businesses we owned were in smaller communities along the East Coast. I have observed some things in these small communities over the last several years, and I have some ideas about what I can do to help them. I have a different idea about wealth now, thanks to you."

She felt his hand brush back the tendrils of hair from her face. "Thanks to me? How can that be?"

"I watched you manage the Guatemalan Children's Choir and what joy it brought you. I observed how you organized things and made them work synergistically. All of that with what I had already observed just spurred my thinking."

She sat up straighter and became more engaged. "Is this why the senators came to visit you?"

"Not exactly." He sighed. "I will go ahead and tell you. They came because they would like me to run for Congress in two years, but they need an answer right away."

"Are you going to run?"

"I'd never make a decision like that without talking to you, but I really think I could do more to help communities by sticking with my plan. But honestly, it's not totally out of the question."

"So how will this change our lives?"

"Perhaps I overstated that. It will change what I do with my time every day, and I will be more of the master of my activities. I will get to pick and choose, and I won't be constantly on guard and going over quarterly reports and spending my time in lawyers' offices." He looked at her intently. "And I have ideas about how you can help. Your people skills are wonderful, and you're so discerning." He stopped. "I don't want to get into all the details right now, but I just wanted you to know what I've been doing and that it is done. All done. The final paperwork will be filed tomorrow, and the funds should be available within a couple of weeks."

"So, am I to understand you no longer have a paying job? Will I need to go to work? I don't mind."

He laughed out loud. "No, my blue-eyed beauty. I have retained the two companies started by my grandfather, and they will provide a very fine living for us and Sarah and George for our lifetimes. And if they don't, we have a sizable trust." He shook his head in disbelief. "And I *will* have a job. My job will be developing some new ideas and using our money to do good, and I expect you to help me. I can assure you we will never be destitute."

"I wasn't worried about being destitute. You know that I'm happy with a very simple life."

"Yes, I know, and that's one of the reasons I love you so much. Our lives will be more to our liking, but we will be making our mark and leaving a legacy."

Head down, she whispered, "Our mark and our legacy." She looked up at him. "Roderick, how I love you, and I am so proud that you have made these decisions. I will do whatever you ask of me. You know that." She paused. "Now is not the time, because what you've told me are reasons for us to celebrate, but we must have a conversation about how we relate to each other in the future. I've been miserable with all this secrecy. Oh, Lilah told me about your being a lone wolf and about your brooding and making decisions on your own, but we must come to a clearer understanding for our future."

"I do understand, Caroline. And I promise I will do better, for I never want to disappoint you. I just wanted to surprise you and make you proud of me. I wanted it all to be done, so that we could start a new season of our lives right away."

"Well, I'd say you accomplished your purpose and a few other things you didn't intend. But for now, let me say again, I am proud, so very proud of you, and I look forward to hearing every detail. Thank you for bringing me here to tell me. I want Blue Hole to be our place not only of serious conversations but of celebrations too." She inhaled the moment deeply and went naturally to him for his embrace.

"Yes, it is a celebration, my precious one. And on another subject before we head back to the manor—forgive me for keeping it secret, but we do have our minister for Gretchen's wedding."

She gave him a raised eyebrow. "One thing you must know about me is that I do not like surprises. But this one makes me happy."

Chapter Eleven

---◆---

Secrets Revealed

Monday morning, September 27, at Rockwater

Caroline sang sweetly in muted tones the words to "Some Enchanted Evening" as she moved about the kitchen in the early morning. Sunday evening had been truly enchanting, and her returned sense of closeness to Roderick had brought sweet, worriless sleep. The burden of his secret no longer weighed either of them down. And for the next two weeks, she would enjoy her guests and the wedding before she and Roderick embarked on new work. The details of that work could wait now that he was no longer brooding.

Roderick waltzed light footed through the kitchen and kissed Caroline on the neck as she scrambled the eggs. For the first time ever, he tried to join her in song. Spatula in hand, she turned to look at him with surprise. "You know I love you, but you really shouldn't sing."

Roderick grabbed his chest. "Oh, that was painful. I've always known I wasn't a singer, but I just felt like trying this morning."

"I'm glad you want to sing, but maybe you could just pour us both a cup of coffee. I think it's ready."

"I was so otherwise engaged last evening that forgot to tell you I phoned Celia yesterday, and she's coming in early this morning. With my flying out tomorrow morning and then a house filled with guests for two weeks, I am taking this time off. My plan is to get everything done today, and I'm giving Celia the next two weeks off unless you think she could be helpful with the wedding plans."

"Oh, no need for Celia. Lilah and Angel and I will be able to handle things. This wedding will be simple. Give Celia the time off. She deserves a break. She's been working long hours for the last few months."

He put her mug down on the countertop. "Your coffee's ready when you are." He sipped his and reached for a piece of the crispy bacon on the platter next to the stove. "Celia has been tireless and uncomplaining, but I can assure you she's been compensated very well for all her hard work. Her biggest job was keeping Liz Bevins at bay. Remember her?"

"You mean your former assistant Liz, the one green with envy whose deliberate negligence nearly got me killed in Guatemala? Well, I'd say she has turned to solid brass if she'd be willing to call you after what she did and after you fired her."

"Yes, that Liz. She got wind through the business grapevine that I was selling off some major companies. She knows the worth of those companies, and I'm certain she was trying to feather her own nest by acquiring them for the group she's working for." He took another piece of bacon. "But I might have sold them at half the price to someone else to keep them out of her grubby hands. Fortunately, the deals I made were lucrative. No more companies. No more deals. Nothing to interest Liz. Celia handled her like a pro, and I don't think she'll be calling again."

"Then by all means, give Celia two weeks off. Lock the office door, and let's enjoy our guests and being here together with family for a few days. Oh, and if Celia would like to have breakfast with us, she's welcome. I have plenty, except we may be a bit short on bacon." She grinned at him. "Lilah's on her way. I called her earlier and told her I was cooking."

"Did you tell her there'd be a wedding here next Saturday?"

"Not yet. I wanted to tell her in person."

Roderick headed to his office, and Caroline finished preparing breakfast and had it all on the table in the morning room when Lilah and Celia arrived. Scrambled eggs with cheese, crispy bacon, hot biscuits with fig preserves, and slices of mandarin oranges, blueberries, and fresh pineapple.

Lilah took her seat, and Celia joined them only for a quick cup of coffee. Before heading back to the office, she asked Lilah, "Did you tell Caroline about Piper Gray yet?"

"Not yet. This is the first time I've seen her in several days."

"Who is Piper Gray?" Caroline inquired. "Sounds like a movie star."

"Well, I was going to wait to talk to you about this. Piper is the son of Harold, the delivery man. Celia's sister is his teacher, and apparently, he's a very gifted singer in need of a gifted teacher. I thought maybe you would find that interesting."

"Possibly. But later, not for the next couple of weeks at least."

As Celia left the room, Roderick said, "I'll be there shortly. I'm determined to deadbolt the office door by early afternoon." He finished his third biscuit with his second cup of coffee. "Honestly, I don't know how Celia turned down

the biscuits with these figs. That's pure goodness on a plate."
He wiped his mouth, put his napkin on the table and stood.
"I know you two have much to talk about, and I have some
work to finish." He turned to Lilah. "May I be excused,
ma'am?"

Caroline giggled when Lilah rolled her eyes and retorted, "You're asking the wrong one, Roderick. I thought you
understood that when you married Caroline."

Caroline raised an eyebrow. "Oh, I think he has a better
understanding of that now. At least, I hope he does."

When Roderick was safely out of the room, Lilah looked
at Caroline. "What's going on? My antennae are wiggling
again at high speed."

"Two big things. Roderick finally told me what he's
been keeping from me all these weeks. I still don't fully
understand exactly why he thought he should keep me in
the dark, except that he said he wanted to surprise me when
it was done."

"That's Roderick, the lone wolf. So, tell me—what's he
been up to?"

"He has sold most of Adair Enterprises and put all the
money in the family foundation and plans to spend the rest
of his life using the money for good to improve smaller
communities. He explained that he's observed so many of
these communities with the same issues, and he thinks he
has some creative ideas that would solve at least some of the
problems. He wants to create a model that can be replicated
in communities around the country. I don't know much yet,
but I will learn."

Lilah took Caroline's hand. "That's our Roderick. He's
brilliant, creative, resourceful, and that boy has always been
able to make things happen. But I think what moved him to
do this was no more observing these communities than it
was walking backward through the cabbage patch. It was

you, Caroline. Like I told you, he loves you so much, and he wants you to be proud of him in ways that you understand. He wants you two to work together. You've shown him with the Guatemalan Children's Choir how much good a bit of money can do."

"He says we will leave our mark and our legacy." Caroline paused. "There is a fly in the ointment, though. You were here when the senator and his colleagues came last week. They want Roderick to get into politics, run for Congress in two years. He's considering it, but he promised to include me in his decision-making."

Lilah put her coffee mug down. "You needn't give that another thought. I told you—Roderick's a lone wolf. Lone wolves don't handle bureaucracy well. Besides, he'll want to raise his children right here."

Caroline raised both eyebrows. "Well, that's a leap ahead. But you're right. Rockwater is the place for our family, whenever that day comes."

Lilah took one more biscuit from the basket. "You want half?"

Caroline shook her head. "Thank you, but no."

"Good. I wanted the whole biscuit for myself. Now pass me those preserves again. I need to call Hattie and get her recipe. With the fig trees Fletcher planted, we'll be making our own preserves next year." She smeared the sugared figs over her buttered biscuit and looked askance at Caroline. "You said two things, didn't you? What's the second?"

Caroline couldn't help but chortle. "We're having a wedding here on Saturday."

Lilah nearly choked on a mouthful of biscuit before she replied, "A wedding? Another wedding here at Rockwater?" She stopped, chewed, and swallowed the biscuit. "I knew it. Gretchen and her gentleman, the one from Austria."

"Yes. Peter proposed Saturday night, and they decided

there's no need to wait longer than the thirty years they've already waited. They were coming to visit us next week anyway, and with Sam and Angel here, they decided to bring Bella and Karina and get married right here at Rockwater. Sarah and George are coming too. The wedding will be simple. Just family. We will host a wedding brunch on Saturday morning, and we'll get flowers—simple flowers, Gretchen kept saying—and that'll be it for us."

"Oh, my goodness, girl. Having this house full of folks who love each other is the absolute best thing to make us all happy. And nothing I like better than throwing a party. I already had the menu planned for the week with Sam and Angel and Ned and Fred. I'll just go over that with you, and we'll make whatever changes we need to make and add some more soup to the pot."

"Look, Lilah, you don't have to do this all yourself. We will have a houseful for a few days, so if you want to call in the caterer, you might reach out to her today and line her up for a few days the end of this week. And I can help a bit, but with Sam and Angel here, and the rest arriving on Thursday and Friday, I'll be busy hosting. So, call for whatever help you need. That would ease my mind that you're not overworked." Caroline stood from the table and started stacking dishes. "Oh, and don't count on Celia. Roderick's locking the office at noon and giving her the next two weeks off."

Lilah helped clear the table. "Good for Roderick. We can handle this, but we must have a lovely party on Friday night."

Caroline balanced the plates and juice glasses on her way to the kitchen. "Peter's hosting the party on Friday night. I promised to help him make the arrangements for a dinner party at the Kentucky Castle for all of us. He insists. Then he and Gretchen will spend their wedding night there, and everyone will return home on Sunday. Just a wedding brunch will do."

Lilah started filling the dishwasher. "Then we will have a wedding brunch to remember."

Caroline smiled with satisfaction. "I have no doubt. Do you think we could go to the florist today? I have some special requests. I want to use willow branches and fall leaves and berries. They're earthy and in season, and I think Gretchen will be so pleased. Maybe we could even get the florist to gather some of the material from Rockwater." She stopped what she was doing and turned to Lilah to ask, "Do you recall a willow tree on the property?"

"I don't know, but Fletcher would. I'll give him a call and ask him to come up today and talk to you. He can scout the property, and he'll be helpful to the florist in gathering the other branches and berries."

When the kitchen was in order, Caroline dried her hands. "Sounds good. I'm headed to the piano just because I feel like playing for a few minutes this morning. Then we'll head to town to see the florist." She was almost out the door but stopped. "Oh, Lilah, guess what woke me around five o'clock this morning."

Lilah nodded. "If it was that wicked owl, I don't want to know about it. I don't want him screeching his bad luck around this place."

"Oh, but it wasn't just the owl. I think now there are two of them. One is a bass and the other an alto. They were hooting to each other. It was wonderful."

"Like I said, I don't want to know about it, especially if there are two now. Just twice as bad."

"They sounded like a pair of barn owls. You know they mate for life, don't you? When we heard them, Roderick said barn owls are rare around these parts. But we had a pair in Ferngrove, and I do know what they sound like. They were there for years and kept the mice out of my dad's barn and workshop."

"For years, you say? They may eat rats, but the sounds they make still give me the shivers. You go on now, and fill this house with some music—happy music—and don't talk to me anymore about owls."

Caroline hid her giggle and headed straight to the piano.

———•———

Monday morning in Durham

Karina left early for the bakery. Sarah had volunteered to take Bella to the university for her instruction and a still photo session with the university's photographer. Sarah had told Gretchen what Bella would need for the session, and Gretchen had made certain to put in a couple of extra outfits in Bella's backpack in case the photographer needed her to change.

Gretchen was glad to have the morning with Peter to finalize some plans. They took a morning walk around the neighborhood, chatting about the activities of the next couple of days before leaving for Rockwater. When they returned, they continued their conversation at the breakfast table with a midmorning cup of tea.

"I was so pleased to hear the minister is available on Saturday, and Caroline has agreed to make the arrangements for dinner at the Castle on Friday evening." Gretchen smiled. "She will email the menu today, and you may make selections of the food and wine."

"I would prefer if she made all those decisions. She knows more about the preferences of our guests than I do. American cuisine is still new to me. Tell her my only desire is that it will be a most memorable dinner in every way."

Peter caressed Gretchen's hand.

"It will be. The people I love will be there, except for Pappá and Elfi. I will call them today with the good news. I am anxious for you to know Sam and Angel, and then you must meet Ned and Fred. They are at Rockwater building a gazebo in Caroline's iris garden, and I have invited them to the wedding and to dinner on Friday night. They have been good to Bella and me."

"Ned and Fred. I think you have spoken of them before. The twins?"

"Yes, they are eccentric bachelor twins, but such fine men." Gretchen never dreamed she'd be sitting at her table with Peter and talking about such pleasant things. "Oh, to see the Castle again. It is magical and will remind you of the castles on the hillsides of the Wachau Valley. Bella is so excited—" The phone rang. "Excuse me. I should answer. Bella or Karina might need me." She stepped across the kitchen to answer the phone at the small desk. "Hello." No answer. "Hello." Still no answer. "Who might this be?" Nothing. She put the phone down and returned to the table.

"Was no one there?" Peter asked.

She hoped the worry in her thoughts was not apparent on her face. "I suppose it was the wrong number." She could not return to conversation about the Castle with the fear and dread rising in her throat. She must tell him. She would not begin their married life with secrets.

"Peter, I do not wish to bring up anything that would lessen our happiness, but there is something I must tell you. In these past few months of writing and in our phone conversations, I have tried to tell you everything about my life these past thirty years. I told you about Ernesto and how he was an unkind and brutal man who kept his dark secrets. You know that he went to prison for the illegal things he did. What I did not tell you is that he had partners who committed crimes with him. He warned me that someday they would come after their money."

She saw the deep furrows in Peter's brow as he listened, and she hated to worry him. "I have been receiving these strange calls for the last few weeks, and I worried that it might be someone connected to Ernesto. Sam has assured me that it is not possible for these criminals to be calling me, and I believe him. They are still in prison and will be for many more years. Sam said they were told the money they gained by criminal activity had been taken by the government. I trust Sam, and I no longer fear that it could be Ernesto's partners." She cleared her throat. "Caroline thinks it is related to all the publicity Bella has been getting recently, and that it could be reporters who might wish to speak with me or to find out if we are at home. That does not make so much sense to me. If it is a reporter, why not identify himself and ask a question? I am still bothered by these calls, and I find myself not even wanting to answer the phone."

Peter moved from his relaxed position, slid forward on his chair, and put his arms on the table. "Does this person ever speak?"

"No. There is much static on the line each time." She stopped. "But last week at the end of one of these calls, I heard someone say in almost a whisper, 'It is Gretchen.'"

Peter's voice became more serious as he folded his arms. "Was this person male or female?"

"I do not know. It was a whisper, and then with the static, I could not tell. But the caller knew my name."

She watched as Peter bowed his head, almost as if he were praying. Then followed what seemed a long silence. When he lifted his head, the muscles in face were tense, and he looked straight into Gretchen's eyes. "You have been so open to tell me everything, Gretchen. Now there is something I must tell you."

She felt more heaviness and the dread of what he might say. She had no clue as to what it might be, but nothing in his voice or face implied pleasantries.

"You heard my phone ring in the middle of the night on Saturday, and you saw when I refused to answer my phone Sunday morning as we were leaving for church. I think that our calls might be coming from the same person."

"But who is such a person?"

"Iris Brandhof."

The wringing feeling in the pit of her stomach tightened. She remembered her sister Elfi's caution about Iris. Jana, Elfi's doctor friend, had cautioned her too. But they had been vague with their comments, simply saying Iris could not be trusted. "Why would Iris do such a thing?"

"Because Iris is a bitter, vindictive woman, and she is incapable of accepting responsibility for her misery. And she certainly is incapable of putting any blame on Nicolai. It seems that she needs someone to blame, and she has chosen me. And in a way, she is blaming you. In her perverted mind, she has concocted this story that your disappearance made me so distraught that I turned against my own brother. She has concluded that I could not bear to see Nicolai happy with her when I was in such misery. She thinks that is why I refused to give them money and turned him in to the police officials before he could escape."

Gretchen was slightly relieved but even more puzzled. "But Peter, that is irrational."

"Yes, my love, it is. But we cannot expect rational thinking from such a disturbed individual—one who is determined to force others to join her in her misery."

Gretchen pushed away her cup of tea. "But I do not understand why she is calling me, and really why she is calling you."

"Your visit in the spring disturbed her and sent her into the past again. She started calling me about a month ago with threats and insinuations. I have not told you, but I went to Melk to meet with her several days ago, just before I traveled here. She is convinced there is more to your story, and she has done enough research on her own to learn more about Bella. She thinks there is money to be gained."

"Money. But how?"

"She has talked to a couple of reporters, including one who covered the story of your disappearance all those years ago. You may recall that Bella made big news when you were in Melk. Her picture was in the paper with that lovely article. It seems that Iris has contacted this one reporter to tell him Bella is quite a celebrity in the States. He is interested in a follow-up story. She thinks the reporters will pay her for access to you, but she is seriously misguided on that. A professional reporter has no need of Iris to get his story."

Gretchen was curious about so many things. "Does Iris need money? I thought she married an older gentleman with money."

Peter nodded. "Yes. Marrying Mr. Brandhof was part of her plan with Nicolai. She assumed that her husband would die, leaving his money to her. Wisely, he left most of his estate to his grown children, and much of his money was used for his care in his later years. She was left with a small cottage and a good job and no one. No husband. No children, and apparently few friends."

"God never intended for one to live that way. How sad for Iris."

"It is only a woman with a good heart who could have pity on such a person. And you are correct, God does not intend for us to be alone, especially alone with so much bitterness. She has been disappointed many times over. When Nicolai was released from prison, he cut all ties with her and never returned to Melk. She is an angry, bitter woman with nothing to lose. She is determined to find Nicolai, and she wants money to pay a professional to get that done."

Gretchen reached for Peter's hand. "God brought us back together after all these years, and we will not allow Iris to cause us any worry or sadness."

"Those are my thoughts too." He stammered. "But I said something to Iris when we parted, and I wish I had not said it."

"What did you say to cause such regret?"

"I asked her how much it would take for her to drop all of this, and then I walked away before she answered."

She squeezed his hand. "You mean you offered her money?"

"Yes, I suppose I did, but I should never have done that. I have decided I will have no further contact with her. She is thousands of miles away and not very resourceful. She will eventually tire of this and move on with her life."

"I have hope that she will move on, but I have learned that meanness rarely rests."

"With me in America and Nicolai out of the picture—and she has no idea where he is—she has no one to strike with her meanness."

Gretchen forced a smile. "Yes. No one within striking distance." She hoped it was true.

Chapter Twelve

---◆---

Settled for a Season

Tuesday afternoon in Rockwater

It was as though Caroline's gloom of the last few weeks had been whisked away by the fresh autumn breezes and the anticipated arrival of Sam and Angel and the Pendergrass twins. After telling Lilah Monday morning about Gretchen's coming wedding, the afternoon had been spent preparing the house and seeing the florist about wedding flowers. Tuesday morning, Albert picked up Roderick at the crack of dawn as planned for their flight to Moss Point, and Lilah arrived early with bags of last-minute fruits and vegetables from the market and two bundles of fresh flowers.

When Caroline and Lilah finished arranging the blossoms, there would be smiling sunflowers and coral-colored lilies in a copper kettle on the morning-room breakfast table and more lilies with fresh ferns and eucalyptus in crystal vases for all the guest rooms. Lilah assured her the flowers would last the rest of the week.

Bed linens had been freshened Monday afternoon after

seeing the florist. Caroline had fixed trays of bottled water, baskets of packaged snacks, fresh tea sachets, and everything needed to make a cup of tea in all three guest suites. She had spent time in their library carefully choosing reading material she thought Sam and Angel would enjoy and left stacks on their bedside tables. She relished the fact that Roderick's father shared Sam's interest in everything Civil War, and she had chosen accordingly.

As she prepared the guest suites, she thought about what she might do with Roderick's cottage out back to make it the most comfortable guest house in Kentucky, but in her frugal and practical way, she still preferred using the guest suites in the manor house. But Roderick was right. With a growing family, the guest cottage would be useful.

Lastly, with vases of flowers delivered to the guest rooms, she fluffed pillows and checked for anything out of place. Sam and Angel would stay downstairs while Peter, Gretchen, and the girls would stay in the suites upstairs. Sarah and her crew would be in Roderick's cottage across the courtyard, and Ned and Fred would take up residence in the barn's tack room. For their last visit, it had been outfitted with everything they needed and more, including a big-screen television.

Caroline looked at her watch. Roderick would be back by noon, and almost everything was already checked on her morning list. Fletcher would be here to pick her up in fifteen minutes for a ride around the property.

As Caroline went singing from room to room, she remembered her first visit to Rockwater and how Roderick had shown her all the suites and allowed her to choose where she wanted to stay. She had selected the corner upstairs suite, the one farthest from the rest of the activity in the house. It had been on the balcony of that suite, where she could look down on the gardens and Roderick's cottage, that she first felt those twinges of attraction that had long lain dormant in her. Those feelings had frightened her at the time.

But she couldn't help smiling as she opened the door to that suite this morning. She put the flowers on the table next to the window and stepped out onto the balcony and looked at the stairs leading to the courtyard. They were still covered in moss just as they had been the day she had walked down to Blue Hole and was caught in a rainstorm. Roderick had come to rescue her and brought her to the gate where she could go upstairs to her suite without the others seeing her drenched and shivering. She remembered how he had cautioned her about the moss-covered steps and how he didn't want his guest pianist to have an accident that would mean cancelling the parlor concert. Two and a half years ago she had been a guest in the suite with only thoughts of playing her childhood piano again, never even fantasizing Rockwater would become her home. Now she was lady of the manor, still almost a dream to her.

While Roderick and Albert were in the air somewhere between Moss Point and Lexington, she and Fletcher scoured the nearby forests for the most pristine foliage and a willow tree. He made note of the best places to bring the florist to gather the most vibrant leaves, seed pods, and berries, and then he put a song in her heart when he took her straightway upstream from the covered bridge to a weeping willow that shaded the shallow rapids in the creek bed.

She imagined Ned and Fred would be thrilled to build the rustic arch she had described to Fletcher and asked him to sketch yesterday afternoon. Their overall fasteners would be popping with pride on Gretchen's wedding day. Roderick agreed that the arch would be a worthy project after Fletcher said it could be used in one of the many gardens after the wedding. The ten-foot arch would be shaped exactly as the two-story loggia windows and would be framed by the view of the hills through the windows. The florist would dress it in fall leaves and berries and soften it with branches from the willow tree. Gretchen would marry Peter underneath a cascade of willow branches. It would be one of Caroline's surprises for her dear friend.

Fletcher dropped her off at the kitchen door in time to help Lilah finish lunch preparation.

After lunch and a rest, the guys would be off to the hardware store and the lumberyard for materials for the arch, and Caroline could look forward to an afternoon with Angel, probably their only private time until after the wedding. She had realized over the last few weeks how much she missed Angel. Sam and Angel had provided a soft place for her to land at Twin Oaks during her grief when she lost David, and Angel had been her anchor in the drifting she did for the next six years. Caroline loved her mother but could not bear to burden or worry her with her never-ending sadness. Angel was always there to listen and guide, making the harshness of life a little gentler around the edges.

Caroline thought of Angel while harmonizing on "Swing Low, Sweet Chariot" with Lilah as Lilah tended the big sizzling pot on the stove. From the looks of the serving bowls on the counter, Caroline assumed Lilah was not planning to be outdone by Hattie. Caroline had often mentioned Hattie's cooking, and Roderick had raved about it. In between watching what was in the big pot, Lilah filled the remaining bowls with deliciousness that would rival Hattie's table any day of the week.

Caroline was elbow deep in dishwater, trying to keep up with the pots and pans Lilah had emptied, when she heard Sam's booming voice preceding him through the front door. God had truly gifted him with the voice every judge craved—strong, resonant, resolute, and clear—the perfect voice for pronouncing judgment. She dried her hands and almost sprinted to the front door.

She opened the door wide and embraced Angel on the porch. "I don't know when I've been happier to see you." She released Angel and buried her face in Sam's broad chest. "And you too, Sam. I have missed you both so much." She and Angel had slowly trained Ned and Fred to hug, but she was still cautious, knowing they were not natural huggers, at least not Fred. She stood between the twins and hugged them to her side. She turned to the open door. "I'm so glad you're all here. Please do come in. Lunch is almost ready."

Sam's voice filled the marble-floored loggia. "Well, that's good because my stomach is gnawing on my backbone. It's been a while since breakfast."

A plenteous lunch followed with laughter and conversation around the table. After a slice of Lilah's butternut cake, Roderick delivered Ned and Fred to the barn, and Sam and Angel escaped to their suite for a rest. Caroline helped Lilah with clearing the table and then last-minute decisions on final meal plans.

———•———

Fully rested after an hour, Angel held tightly to Sam's arm as they walked from the suite through the loggia to the morning room. She refused to use her walker when Sam was around. They had been keeping each other upright for years. He steadied her on one side, and his cane steadied them on the other. They stopped in the kitchen when they saw Caroline and Lilah sitting at the counter going over a list.

Lilah closed her notebook. "Well, friends, did you have a pleasant nap?"

In a sonorous voice, as if Lilah might not understand him otherwise, Sam said, "I can assure you I did, dreaming of that fried chicken, cream potatoes, and green beans. I don't know what you did to the green beans, Lilah, but I do believe they were the best I have ever eaten. Angel will tell you my usual verdict on green beans is that they should be fed to the horses. But you must tell Angel your secret so we can tell Hattie."

Angel watched Lilah beaming. "Why, Judge, I'd be happy to give Hattie my recipe. It does have one secret ingredient, but I'll gladly reveal it since you enjoyed them so much."

"I do hope there's at least a serving of those beans and one chicken leg left for my supper," Sam replied.

"I wouldn't dream of serving you that for supper. You go on now with Roderick to town, and you let me take care of supper." Lilah stood. "And Caroline, you and Angel go get yourselves comfortable in the morning room, and I'll bring you a cup of tea in just a few minutes. You all could use a good visit. I'll let Roderick know the judge is up and ready to go to the lumberyard and hardware store."

Angel turned to Sam. "You're sure you'd rather go with the boys than stay with us?"

"Just as certain as I am that I'll have another slice of Lilah's butternut cake before bedtime, maybe with a glass of cold milk."

Caroline slipped from the stool where she was sitting and took Angel's arm. "Yes, we could use a visit. I need to fill you in on all the details. And Lilah, tea sounds lovely."

Caroline led Angel to the chair by the window with the best view of the sumac, and Caroline took the chair opposite her. They both propped their feet on the ottoman between them. While they waited for their tea, Caroline went on about the arrival of the other guests and the plans for the remainder of the week, especially wedding decoration plans.

Angel listened patiently and inquired when appropriate, but the minute their tea had been served and Lilah was out of the room, she looked at Caroline. "Now, Miss Blue Eyes, I think I've heard quite enough about weddin' plans and about who's stayin' where and who's doin' what. I find myself much more interested in what's goin' on with you these days. You've been a bit out of tune the last few weeks, like my old upright piano. So, what's been goin' on? You seem like you might have had a good tunin' or else you're puttin' on a good show."

"Oh, Angel, you still read me like a book. And to use your term, I suppose I've had a good tuning."

Angel smiled believingly. "I like the sound of that, but what I'd like to know is what got you so out of tune. Sam tried to convince me you were settlin' in and acceptin' the reality of your new life. He thought you might be missin' some parts of your old life. Is that true?" She watched every muscle in Caroline's face.

"You haven't forgotten how to ask a penetrating question, have you? And to give you my best answer, I do think there's some truth in what Sam was thinking. Lately, I've had more time to reflect. You know, I lived in a cocoon for more than six years with very little change. I had settled into a certain comfortable monotony, and honestly, I was afraid to even think about the future. But then Bella entered my life at about the same time Roderick did, and for the last two years, change has been what was constant." Caroline put her teacup on the table beside her.

"Well, sweet girl, you figured it out. Life, that is. There are a few more constants in life, but change is certainly one of them." She watched as Caroline curled her legs up under her like an adolescent and wrapped her arms around her knees. Her body language might have said she was shutting down, but Angel had seen this before. She knew Caroline was listening and preparing to spill her story. "I'd say for six years, you had spackled the cracks in your heart and shellacked your feelin's real good, and it just takes a while for the shellack to crack and peel away. So, how are you dealin' with all that crackin' and peelin'?"

"That's certainly what it feels like. Sometimes, Angel, I feel like Cinderella. I mean, who gets to fall in love with and marry Prince Charming in real life? Our courting and the first few months after we were married were magical and like a fairytale. I could hardly catch my breath between learning how to be Roderick's wife and all the travel, and then the children's choir debut back in the summer. It was all so much, and when those events were over, life settled down. Things grew calmer and quieter, but I had prepared myself and grown to expect the activity."

"You mean calm and quiet like it used to be for you?"

"Maybe a bit. But as things quietened down, so did Roderick. And I mean that literally. He dove back into work like I'd never seen him, and he seemed rarely to come up for air. When I would ask him about his work, he just said he'd talk to me when the time was right."

Angel leaned her head against the back of the chair. "And that frightened you. You wondered if that was a new reality you'd be settlin' into as well. Am I right?"

"As usual, yes, right on, like the perfect pitch of a tuning fork. I talked to Lilah, and she explained that Roderick was doing what she called *brooding*, completely focused on work. She told me to be patient and that he would eventually return."

"By the smile you've been wearin' since we arrived, I'm guessin' he did."

"Yes, but not until Sunday afternoon. We took a picnic down to Blue Hole where he announced that he has sold most of Adair Enterprises and put the money into the family foundation. He did it so that we could work together to use the family fortune to do good."

Angel perked up in her chair. "He just up and sold everything?"

"Almost. He kept two companies that have been in his family for three generations, but he sold everything else. He has some creative ideas about helping smaller communities with some problems they all have in common."

"Help how?"

"I haven't a clue yet. He just gave me the big picture, and he promised to explain his ideas when we have more time to talk, and when they're fleshed out more. He said we would be leaving our mark and legacy and making life better for others." Caroline sighed. "And if that wasn't enough, while I was away in Durham last week, a senator and his entourage came here to talk to Roderick about running for Congress in two years."

"Oh, my. Not politics! Small-town politics are nasty enough, but Washington politics? Well, that's another whole kind of nasty." Realizing her unbridled disdain had escaped, Angel tried to cover. "But oh, how we need honorable men with integrity in high positions. I'm certain Roderick could do some good. Is he interested?"

"I'm not sure, but he says I'll be part of that decision since it would require living in Washington. Lilah thinks he'd never do it. She says he's a lone wolf used to getting things done his way and quickly, and lone wolves don't take to established bureaucracy. I tend to think she's right." Caroline put her feet on the floor and leaned forward. "I'll admit I'm intrigued about working with Roderick. He says I have people skills and discernment that will be helpful. He must see something in me I don't see."

Somewhat relieved, Angel settled back comfortably in

her chair again. "Well, my sweet girl, I think what he has done is a tribute to you. He has determined he doesn't want to be jet settin' off to faraway places, cuttin' deals, and leavin' you behind. He prefers to be with you. I think you've given him a whole new set of values. Not that he wasn't an honorable man with integrity before, but I think his passions have taken a new direction."

"He says we are financially set for life with no worries, and that frees us to concentrate on how best to use this money to do good in the world." Caroline shook her head. "Just when I thought things were settling down and was thinking of taking on a few music students and getting back to my composing. And here comes another tsunami."

"Oh, sweet girl. Another thing about life is this: there's really no such thing as settlin' down. That's what you talk about and keep hopin' for, but there's no real settlin' till you get to heaven. Oh, now there are some important things you must settle—the big stuff like your faith and how you're goin' to relate to the ones you love, and your purpose for bein' on this planet to begin with. Then the rest of life—the circumstances—well, they only settle for a season, and then the seasons change. Who you *are* on the inside won't change with the seasons, but what you *do* during that season is always up for change."

"You seriously don't think I'm any different with all the changes in my life?"

"I most certainly do not. You're still the same serious-minded, cautious, carin', and gifted Caroline you've always been." Angel giggled. "Girl, I can't tell you how many seasons Sam and I've been through. When you've turned over as many calendar pages as I have in over eight decades, believe me, you see lots of seasons. And I don't mean the ones just determined by the equinox. And trust me, they're not all as lovely and hopeful as spring. But you already know that. Some of them are like the dead of winter, but you're hopin' spring will come again, like it did for you and Roderick and now for Gretchen and Peter." She paused. "Seasons come and go, but we're still the same down deep on the inside, just more like ourselves with the changin' seasons."

Angel gazed out the window. "I remember somethin' Sam's mother told me after we got married and moved into Twin Oaks. She was on up there in age at the time, and she was the sweetest woman I think I ever knew. She said that the older we get, the more like our truest selves we become. I took that to heart, and I've worked at bein' sweet and sassy since then. And look at me now! How am I doin'?" Angel laughed so hard her belly jiggled.

Caroline joined her laughter. "I guess I'd better start thinking about how I want to be when a few more seasons have passed in my life. Thanks for your winter wisdom. I think I get it—we settle for a season, and the seasons change, but we don't allow them to change us on the inside."

"You got it, girl, that is unless you need changin' for the better on the inside. Then you ask the good Lord to take care of that part, but you don't let the circumstances of a season make you afraid or bitter. You just hold on and trust till the new season comes, just like it did for you and now for Gretchen. And what an excitin' new season she's about to have, and you, too, Caroline."

———•———

Same afternoon at the hardware store

Ned and Fred, in starched jeans and matching, rust-colored plaid shirts, walked down the aisle of the hardware store shoulder to shoulder and in step. Ned leaned over and whispered in Fred's ear. "Fred, I ain't never knowed a man who don't have no tools. He wants us to buy ever'thing— hammers and nails and saws, ever'thing we need, 'cause he ain't got nothin'. Can you believe it? I ain't never in my life had to buy so much stuff. I don't think I know how."

Roderick and Sam walked behind them, Sam pushing a large cart that was still empty.

Ned turned around to Roderick behind him. "Now, Mr. Roderick, I wanna be sure I got this right. We're buildin' this here arch for Miss Gretchen's weddin'?" He pointed to the sketch on the paper in his hand. "And we s'posed to build it afore we start on the gazebo? And we s'posed to git ever'thing we need today, and we won't have to look at the price or haggle with the store help? And that means all the tools we need too?"

Roderick nodded in agreement. "That's right, Ned. The arch is for the wedding, but Fletcher plans to use it later in one of the gardens. He's already ordered the lumber for it, and it will be at the front desk. The sketch looks fairly simple to me. How long will it take to build?"

Ned scratched his head, looked at his twin, and read his lips. Fred had not spoken since they arrived. "Fred says 'bout two days. Says all them pieces got to be cut jes' right or it'll look like the Carson brothers built it, and we ain't havin' none o' that."

"We're counting on you two to do it right, Ned. I trust you."

"Thanky, sir. But I got one more question. Do you have some place to put all this stuff when we git it put together? I ain't seen no sign of a workshop at Rockwater."

"Yes, I do. I'll take you to it when we get home, if we ever do. Chip has cleared out a storage room that will be a perfect workplace for the arch. And then we can transport what we need for you to work on site for the gazebo."

"That's good."

Sam had been silent. "Ned, I've been pushing this basket around this hardware store for the last thirty minutes, and there's nothing in it yet. If you and Fred don't start filling it up, I'm crawling into the basket, and Roderick'll be pushing me around."

"Yes, sir, Mr. Sam. We'll git on it."

Within an hour, Ned and Fred had filled three large carts with boxes containing work benches, a circular saw, a jig saw, a table saw, a miter saw, drills, nails, bolts, glue, screws, stain, a power sander, two hammers, and a set of screwdrivers. "This is better'n Christmas, Mr. Roderick. Ever'thing brand-spankin' new."

"I'm glad you're having such a good time. But guys, we're working against the clock here, and the wedding is Saturday. I see all these things in boxes. Won't these tools have to be put together? I'm thinking we should ask the manager if he has someone we could hire to come out and help you gentlemen put these things together and get them in working order."

Ned shook his head. "No, sir. Don't you worry 'bout none of that. Me and Fred'll have more fun doin' that than we had with tinker toys when we wuz boys. We ain't never had no vacation like this one, and this is the best vacation we could ask for. We got good beds and a big-screen television in the nail room, and good eatin', and plenty to do."

Roderick laughed. "Ned, I hate to correct you, but it's the tack room—you know, where we store and clean the gear and equipment we use with the horses. But it's a fairly nice apartment too. Lived there myself until my cottage was built. I'm so glad you're comfortable there."

Ned laughed at himself and even Fred let out a quiet

chuckle. "We thought the best part was gittin' to see Miss Caroline, but better'n all that is we git to see Miss Gretchen and her feller finally git married after waitin' thirty years." He elbowed his twin. "There's hope for us, Fred."

Chapter Thirteen

---◆---

Surprises

Wednesday afternoon, September 29, in Melk, Austria

Iris paced. The hotel was filled to capacity with guests enjoying the autumn season and the festivals. Yet she was working, her desk piled with accounting details to be recorded and a deposit to be made. But she could not focus to record receipts and accounts payable.

She had called Peter several times over the last three days, but there was no answer nor an opportunity to leave a message. It was possible he was traveling, but she presumed he was deliberately ignoring her. He knew nothing of her resolve and that she would not be ignored. She had called Gretchen twice with no answer. Gretchen could not be avoiding her since there was no way for Gretchen to know. She guessed Gretchen might be traveling for Bella's public appearances. She would not give up. She would keep calling because she was ready to talk to Gretchen now.

The phone on her desk rang. Assuming it was business related, she stopped her pacing, walked to the desk, and answered. "Iris Brandhof. How may I help you?"

The gruff voice on the line was not business related nor the voice she wanted to hear. She knew why he was calling. "Ms. Brandhof, this is Herbert Wurm. I am ready to start your work, but I will need a certain sum for my retainer. As I explained, I will require money in advance for my expenses, which I have learned could involve a certain amount for travel. I have checked, and the money you assured me would be wired to my account is not there. Is there a problem? Are you prepared to pay?"

He knows something if he knows he must travel.

"Mr. Wurm, I am happy that you are ready to begin the search for Nicolai Kornilov. It pleases me, but I need more time to acquire the funds. Your charges are steep for a woman of limited means. I can assure you that I will pay you. Nicolai has a rich relative who wishes to find him as much as I do. I will have the money soon."

"I believe that is the same answer you gave me last week. I will tell you that I do have a lead, but I will do nothing further until I am paid."

Iris felt short of breath. Her pulse rang in her ears as she sank to her chair. "Have you located Nicolai? Do you know where he is?"

"That is all for you to know until there is money received from you in my account. You have my number, and you know what must be done. Good day, Ms. Brandhof."

An abrupt click. Exasperated, she raised her arms in the air, still clutching the phone. She wanted to scream. She hung up the phone, put her head in her hands on her desk, and closed her eyes. She had assumed Herbert Wurm would be seedy because his name came from an unsavory source. But her source had assured her Mr. Wurm could and would get the job done.

Queasiness made her weak. The memory of him in the chair opposite her desk during their first meeting filled her closed eyes. He had the appearance of one who had never seen sunlight. He was dark haired, middle aged, and of medium build supporting a slightly bulging belly, with sallow, oily skin, and deep pockmarks on his face. His pale hands were colorless and without blemish, but what she remembered most was the strange, rancid odor about him.

He knows. That repulsive man knows where Nicolai is. Peter, you must give me the money, or you will pay, truly pay.

Iris raised her head and reached for her cell phone. She dialed Peter's number again. One ring. Nothing. No answer.

Could he be blocking my number?

She wanted to throw something. Then she saw the cash box sitting amid the mounting paperwork on her desk. Determination replaced her queasiness. She opened the box. Because of the current high occupancy at the hotel, more money than usual lay there. She began to count the bills and coins. It was more than double the amount Herbert Wurm required, and there would be more cash in the box by the end of the day. And it would be another week before she'd be required to give an end-of-the-month report.

Peter, once again, you have put me in this position. You have money that would take care of this matter. You will not answer my calls. But you will come through before I am done. And until you do, I have what I need.

She put a stack of bills in an envelope and the rest back into the cash box. She did not take the full amount Wurm was asking, but enough to make him know she was serious and that more would be coming.

One last attempt. She knew the name of Peter's company in Linz. She would call him at work. Surely, he would answer there, or they would help her contact him. She dialed the number. When a polite and professional voice answered, Iris requested to speak with Mr. Peter Kornilov.

"I am sorry. Mr. Kornilov is out of the office for the

next three weeks. May I direct your call to someone else who might help you?"

Iris panicked. She should have given this more thought before she called. "No. I need to speak with Mr. Kornilov now. It is personal, very personal, and I must speak with him."

"I am sorry. Again, he is not here. You may leave your name and number, and if he calls in, I will gladly give him your message."

Iris fumbled. "My name is Iris Brandhof. He has my number. Just give him the message that I have information about his brother, and it would serve him well to return my call."

"Yes, Ms. Brandhof. If he calls the office, I will tell him what you said."

"When might he call you?"

"I have no way of knowing, ma'am."

"Where is he? Is he ill, or is he traveling?"

"Ma'am, I am not allowed to give out such information. All I can say is that if he checks in, I will make certain he receives your message."

"It would be wise of you to do just that."

Iris slammed the phone on her desk, picked up her bag that now held the envelope, and locked the door to her office. As she passed the front desk, she barked at the clerk. "I must go to the bank to make a deposit. I will return shortly to finish my work." She nearly knocked down a guest as she charged through the glass-front door.

———•———

Wednesday morning in Durham

Peter had the morning to himself. Bella was at the university. Karina was at the bakery, preparing the employees for her absence, and Gretchen was doing some last-minute shopping and picking up their wedding apparel. He had rented a comfortable van for their road trip to Rockwater, and he and Gretchen would pick it up later this afternoon.

Moments after Gretchen left, his phone rang. One ring. He looked at the blocked number. Iris again. Then, in less than a minute or so, Gretchen's phone rang. He dared not answer it, thinking it might be Iris. He wanted his theory about Gretchen's strange phone calls to be wrong, but he feared he was right. He knew that Iris could easily get a listed phone number.

He decided to escape to the quiet peace of the garden, choosing the garden chair that gave him a view of the cottage. The breeze was gentle, just enough to stir the wispy willow branches above him. Contentment washed over him as he looked through garden to the rear of the small house. The cottage was quaint, and it had become more and more apparent that Gretchen had attempted to recreate the home of her past in Austria. Her love for her homeland and memories of her youth made him happy. And sitting under the shade of this willow tree made him even happier. It was a reminder that she'd had thoughts of him, of them, long before she journeyed to Austria to find her parents and Elfi.

Early on after their reunion, he had wished that Gretchen had returned to Austria to search for him, but he understood. Gretchen explained her assumption that he had moved on and had a family and that she had no desire to disrupt his life. She confessed that she could not have borne the pain of losing him twice. Looking back on how it all happened, he was grateful. He knew that it was not luck or coincidence or happenstance. It was meant to be. It was an act of God that had brought them together for the church's anniversary celebration, and he would honor God's gift to them by not allowing anything to mar their happiness.

Peter scanned the roofline of the cottage against the morning sky. He could certainly afford to buy her a much larger home. Not an estate like Rockwater as she described it, but something a bit grander than this cottage—larger rooms, a great room for the girls and their music, a private suite for him and Gretchen, and beautiful gardens. That conversation would come later, if ever. For now, her cottage was comfortable and convenient. He was quite content to live here and to be able to take Gretchen back to their homeland on occasion.

He shuffled through the file folder. This was something else God had orchestrated. Roderick was advising him on small companies or businesses he could buy that would make his citizenship easier to obtain. He thumbed through the pages of business profiles. Nothing in the Durham area. Some possibilities in Tennessee and Virginia that were three to four hours away. He saw nothing that really interested him.

He kept coming back to the idea of asking Gretchen to allow him to buy the bakery and expand it to include a specialty grocery store that would have food products from Europe. He knew the import-export food business, and this seemed natural to him. If this bakery business was something Karina could grow into, it would be hers. If not, they would find good employees to run it. Durham was populated with college students looking for jobs. This business would give them something to do together, something they loved and knew, and yet the freedom to enjoy their lives.

It just made sense. His mind was made up, but he would get Roderick's counsel and then find just the right time to speak with Gretchen.

He leaned his head against the back of the chair and

closed his eyes and felt the cool breeze on his face. Floating through his mind like the gentle zephyr wafting through the garden were images of Gretchen at Innsbruck, of Gretchen in his home in Linz, of Gretchen back in Český Krumlov with her family, but mostly images of Gretchen right here with him. He imagined joy-filled days.

The ringing of the phone in his pocket snatched him back from his daydreams. Iris again. The call would have been a most unpleasant jolt if he had not seen Gretchen walking through the back door and into the garden. She balanced two teacups and a paper bag. He stood from his seat and approached her, kissed her on the cheek, and took the bag from her. "Would this be something sweet from my dearest?"

She took the seat next to him. "It would be if Karina is your dearest. I stopped by the bakery after my errands, and she wanted you to try her almond crescent cookies. I can say they are quite good. She has a most skilled hand with the butter and flavors."

"Dear girl. She is as thoughtful as her mother."

Gretchen smiled shyly. "And a better baker, I might add."

"Did you get everything done? And do you have a wedding dress?"

"Yes, my love, I did. I picked up my dress and the dresses for the girls, and I have your new suit. The tailor did fine work in hemming the pants. I could have done that so easily if only time had permitted."

She opened the bag and passed it to him.

He reached in for a cookie and examined it. "Time. Such a gift we take for granted until it is running out. And it is time we get married, and no time for hemming pants. We should talk about our leaving tomorrow. Since you and I will pick up the van this afternoon, could we leave early in the morning? I have calculated a seven-hour trip, and slightly longer if we stop for lunch. I would like to arrive at Rockwater by mid-afternoon." He took a bite of the cookie.

"Of course, let us plan to leave at seven, and we should be there by three o'clock. The girls are early risers, and I shall be so excited I may not sleep tonight. Karina is planning to bring boxes of baked goods home this evening—some for the trip and some for Caroline and Roderick, so there will be something quick and easy for breakfast. We could even pack the van this evening. What an adventure! A road trip with the four of us."

"How I hope it is the first of many to come, especially if there is a bag of these cookies for the road. These are the best. Better than from the coffeehouses at home."

"Oh, Karina will be so happy. Please tell her." Gretchen paused. "Peter, with the many twists and turns of our lives, dare I believe that we will truly be married in three days? It is all so dreamlike to me, especially when I tried on my dress in the dress shop. Dare I trust this beautiful dream?"

He reached across the arm of the chair and took her hand. "Yes, my love. God planted that dream deep within our hearts so long ago, and now He is making it come true. Everything is now happening just as it should."

"It truly is, is it not? Even the timing. My dearest friends from Moss Point are already at Rockwater. And Sarah and George will join us. In the absence of my family from home, God gave me such a beautiful family here, and now you will join it. What a glorious time in our lives, Peter!"

"Yes, a most glorious time, and we will live each day that way: gloriously. We know the desolate feelings of being alone, and we will be grateful for every day—no, every hour—we have together." He squeezed her hand. "Would you answer this question for me, my love? Think of the most perfect place anywhere and the most perfect moment you dream of. What is that place and moment for you?"

Gretchen sighed and answered quickly. "That place is right here in the shade of this willow with you."

"It would not be in Austria or some other beautiful and peaceful place from your memory or your imagination?"

"My perfect place and moment are wherever we are together. I have learned to be content, Peter. I have so few desires, only that we be together, but I desire that so very much."

"Then we shall plan our lives so that we spend every moment together."

His phone rang for the third time this morning. One ring. He looked at the number. Iris again. "Let us finish our tea and these cookies, and then we shall pack and move toward our glorious future."

———•———

Late Wednesday afternoon at Rockwater

Lilah was in the kitchen with the caterer. Sam and Angel were perched in the library reading, Sam devouring the collection of Civil War books Roderick's father had collected. Roderick persuaded Caroline to take advantage of a few minutes to walk to the barn to check on Ned and Fred. He knew she was anxious about the arch, since it was the only decorative piece for the wedding. Ned and Fred were perfectionists, and she had no reason to worry about the arch being anything less than a one-of-a-kind piece of wooden art, but he had been up to something.

Roderick called Chip from the phone in the morning room. "Hey, Chip, can you step over into the shop area and let Ned and Fred know we'll be there in about ten minutes." He wanted to give them a heads-up he and Caroline were coming so they'd be ready for their mischievous surprise for her.

As they walked, Roderick engaged Caroline in conversation. "Explain something to me, Miss Blue Eyes. How is it that you can imagine an entire musical composition with every single instrument's part, every note, every nuance, and every harmony, and yet you cannot imagine what a simple arch should look like?"

"I wish I could explain it, and even more, I wish I could visualize things. That's why I've been hesitant to start your cottage project. I'm not good at decorating and imagining what things could look like. I'm just amazed that Fletcher could take my meager ideas and hand motions and sketch something so perfectly. His ideas of having the lines of the arch reflect the lines and angles of the loggia windows was so artistic. Now, if only Ned and Fred can take the sketch and make it real."

"Oh, I think you can check that off your worry list. We'll see what they've done, and hopefully they'll be finished tomorrow." Roderick was laughing on the inside, imagining the scene getting ready to unfold. "Look at that." He pointed in the distance. "We really should bring Sam and Angel on a carriage ride to see the color on these hills."

"That's a great idea. Tell me about those trees. I recognize a few."

"Fletcher might give you a better answer, but I think the near purple ones are dogwoods and sumacs, and the reddish ones are sourwoods and sweetgums." He pointed to the east. "Those orange ones over there are sugar maples, and the goldish-yellow ones are hickories.

"Seems those spring and summer showers we had are paying off. The confetti of color on those hills is worth a few thunderstorms and lightning bolts. I think a carriage ride late tomorrow afternoon for everyone would be quite a treat.

Maybe even a picnic if it's not too cool. But right this minute, I am much more concerned about the arch."

"We're almost there. You have no worries. Just enjoy the walk, Miss Blue Eyes. Don't let your worries cause you to miss this color. In a few weeks those leaves will carpet the forest floor and the limbs will be bare."

"I know. I know. Ned and Fred will do a great job, but they are slower than molasses, and they must finish tomorrow so the florist can work her magic. I wouldn't be so concerned if there were other decorations. Maybe some candelabras or other floral arrangements. But Gretchen really wanted nothing but the beautiful loggia windows. She said that view was all she desired, but the arch was my idea, sort of a floral frame for the long view."

As they approached the barn entrance, Chip met them. Roderick eyed Fletcher slipping into the makeshift workshop and bought a couple more minutes by giving Chip instructions about having the carriage ready for rides on Thursday afternoon.

Ned and Fred came out of the workshop to meet them. "Miss Caroline, you came just in time. Your arch is finished, and me and Fred think it jes might be the purtiest thing we ever did build. We think we could make some more o' these when we git home and we could sell 'em at the county fair. Come on, we jes cain't wait to show you."

Roderick tried to contain himself and ushered Caroline into the shop. He watched her blue eyes grow larger and her mouth open with a gasp.

Before she could respond, Ned asked, "What do you think? Me and Fred think Miss Gretchen is gonna look mighty purty standing under this with her feller. We even wired some flowers on it so the florist won't need to do that."

Roderick could hardly keep from laughing as he stared

at the white PVC pipe strung together with bailing wire, looking more like a jungle gym covered in purple and pink plastic flowers with white ribbon streaming from every angle.

Ned spoke up again. "We think it's even purtier than that drawin' Fletcher gave us." He paused. "Why, Miss Caroline, I think we done gone and made you speechless."

Roderick watched Caroline's chest rise and fall with her deep breaths. "Yes, Caroline, what do you think?"

Caroline stammered. "Well, you are right, Ned. I am speechless. I . . . I don't know quite what to say."

Ned laughed loudly, and even Fred covered his mouth and chuckled. "And we done gone and pulled yo' leg, too, Miss Caroline. But don't you go bein' mad as an ol' wet settin' hen with us, now. This was all Mr. Roderick's doin's. He wanted us to play a joke on you."

Caroline laughed out loud in relief. She turned and grabbed Roderick's ear. "Your ear didn't get pinched enough when you were a boy, or you'd know better."

Roderick took her in his arms and swung her around until she grew dizzy. "Well, the boys needed to have a little fun with all you ladies going on about the wedding plans."

"Please put me down, Roderick. This is making me nauseous."

He immediately released her, and she steadied herself and took a deep breath.

Fletcher appeared in the doorway. "Come look, Mrs. Adair. Ned and Fred have truly created a masterpiece."

Caroline cautiously entered the back room. Roderick walked beside her, watching her eyes again as she gazed on the real arch, a superb piece of craftsmanship made according to Fletcher's sketch with the addition of some scroll work suggested by Fred. Fletcher had draped a few limbs of colorful leaves just for the effect.

"It is perfect, truly perfect, in every way. It is so perfect I might even forgive you for such a cruel joke." She walked farther into the room and around the free-standing arch. "This is better than I even imagined. I cannot wait for Gretchen to see it." She turned to Fletcher. "Ned and Fred have done a magnificent job, and now it's up to you to make certain the florist honors their work with her best work."

"Yes, ma'am. You can count on it."

Roderick took her arm. "These men haven't even slept since they got here. They worked all night after we picked up the supplies yesterday afternoon and all morning to make certain they finished. We need to go and give them time to take a shower. Lilah's preparing an early dinner so Ned and Fred can get to bed early. They have a big day tomorrow."

Ned moved toward the arch. "Yes, sir. That sounds mighty good to me. And nothin' could make us happier than knowin' we built somethin' that put a smile on Miss Caroline's face."

"Then you should be happy, really happy, because I'm smiling inside and out." She hugged them both, causing them to blush.

"Come on, Roderick. I need to get to the kitchen and make sure Lilah's preparing all of Ned's and Fred's favorites."

They walked out of the barn and headed to the house. She turned to him with her right eyebrow raised. "I've decided to give this arch to Gretchen for a wedding present, and now I'll need another one for our garden. And don't even think you're getting by with this cruel joke. Remember, I had two brothers. I know about payback, and you will recognize payback, handsome. No question." She grinned.

Chapter Fourteen

———————— ♦ ————————

Gardyloo

Thursday, September 30, at Rockwater

aroline woke early but stayed quiet as Roderick slept.
She waited for daybreak to appear through the window
that framed the sunrise this season of the year. She imagined
Gretchen was moving around her cottage, preparing
breakfast, and getting last-minute things done for the road
trip. She relished knowing that Sam and Angel slept soundly
just down the hall. Since Ned and Fred were customary
early risers, she assumed they were already in the workshop
to start work before breakfast at seven thirty. She had made
them promise they would work only until noon and take the
afternoon off for Gretchen's arrival.

The quiet, soothing melodies in her mind's ear began to
frolic as the deep corals fringed in gold stretched upward on
the horizon, giving the bedroom a cordial glow. She
remembered her days of waking up alone in the studio and
walking barefoot into the great room where she would watch
the sun peep through the limbs of the magnolia tree that
shaded the patio. Those glints of morning sun had their own

beauty but could not compare to daybreak skies over Kentucky's rolling hills. Her heart was happy, and the halls of Rockwater would be filled with people she loved today. Even the sun smiled this morning.

The golden baritone voice that still sent pleasant shivers through her interrupted her private music. "Enjoying the morning skies, Miss Blue Eyes?" She felt the familiar weight of his arm around her waist as he slid closer to her.

"Shh. Yes, and I'm listening to a lovely symphony too. It will be over soon." She pulled his arm closer and took his hand and held it between her breasts. They lay quietly together for a short while and watched the vibrant colors fade as more light filled the sky. Finally, she rolled over to face him. "Well, I've had a splendid start to this day."

"I caught the sunrise, which was spectacular, but I wish I could have heard your symphony."

"Perhaps one day you will. It's percolating, and I think it will be quite lovely when it is finished."

Roderick rose slightly and propped himself on his elbow. "Are you composing again?"

She responded coyly, "Maybe. There is always a little ditty gamboling around in my head."

"'Gamboling'? Never heard of gamboling before. I hope it's not painful."

"Oh, gamboling is quite pleasant. It's a new word I learned from Ned—means running or skipping playfully. He's still into learning new and unusual words every day. Angel said Ned thinks an extensive vocabulary of unfamiliar words will make him sound more intelligent. She's still keeping a notebook of Ned's New Words."

Roderick chuckled. "I guess we shouldn't tell him his words are comical and send us all to the dictionary, should we? I wish Ned could see himself as the intelligent man he is. Too bad he didn't have the opportunity of an education.

And yet look at the young men and women who have been educated by those two," he added, speaking of the students the twins' money subsidized.

"Amazing. And to think, those young people haven't a clue as to whom to thank. I think it's scandalous to keep it such a secret, but that's the way Ned and Fred want it."

"It's their right, my dear, just as how we move forward with our new venture will be our right. I'm planning to have some serious conversation with Sam about our plans. I'll wait until the wedding's over and the house is a bit quieter, maybe early next week. He's wise and has good judgment, and we both trust him."

"That's a fine idea. I'd really like to be a part of that conversation." She smiled. "What would you say about getting ready for the day and helping Lilah with some breakfast? She'll be here in a half an hour."

"I'd say 'yes' to both right after my morning kiss."

They rose, dressed for the day, and made their way to the kitchen to find Lilah already at work, and Sam and Angel in the morning room, drinking coffee. Ned and Fred joined them right on time.

Breakfast and the morning disappeared quickly. As Caroline and Lilah were putting lunch on the table outside, Ned and Fred came ambling through the courtyard, all cleaned up for the guests' afternoon arrival. It was the first time Caroline had seen them in casual pants and sports shirts with buttoned-down collars. She assumed Angel had something to do with that.

When their lunch was winding down, Sam leaned back in his chair. "You know, we've been sitting out here in this beautiful courtyard enjoying Lilah's most delicious lunch. Now Angel and Ned and Fred, over there, had a view of the gardens and these hills that go on for miles, but my view is of those windows. They remind me so much of the windows we put in Angel's studio at Twin Oaks—the windows where Caroline's piano sat for seven years. And I couldn't help but notice through those loggia windows sits the piano that brought you two together. Here it is Thursday, and I don't recall having heard one sound from it yet. I was thinking about a short nap followed by some piano playing. Anybody around here know where we might find someone who'd play for us?" He looked and Caroline and winked.

"I think I might know someone." She looked at her watch. Twelve fifty. "Let's meet back around the piano at two o'clock." She turned to Sam. "Does that give you enough time for a nap?"

"Most certainly."

At two o'clock, as if a bell had been sounded, they gathered in the loggia around the piano, and Caroline took her seat on the piano bench. Even Lilah joined them all.

Roderick took his favorite chair, enabling him to see Caroline's hands and her silhouette against the Kentucky sky. "So, Miss Blue Eyes, what about a preview of the symphony you were listening to this morning."

She eyed him with a raised eyebrow. "It's not really a symphony, and it's not ready." She looked away and then back with a smile. "But I will let you hear the theme of the first movement." She gazed at the western sky, doubting there was anyone who could not make music or paint canvases while looking through those magnificent windows. The melody flowed through her and out her fingers— lyrical, lush, and romantic. She stopped abruptly as one phrase came to a cadence. "That's all for now."

Her listeners clapped, and Fred let out an ear-piercing whistle that startled them all. Sam's sonorous voice filled the hall. "Well, if I may assume that you're taking requests, I'd really like to hear your "Rockwater Suite." Haven't heard that one in a while, and sitting right here in the halls of

Rockwater and looking out on these hills is the perfect place to hear it again."

"Well, Judge, I think I can oblige you." Caroline cupped her hands, laid them gently in her lap, closed her eyes, and breathed deeply. With eyes still closed, her fingers moved knowingly to the keyboard, and she started to play.

The third movement was interrupted by the bell at the front door. Caroline snapped to reality, returning from the place that was hers and hers alone when she played the piano. A smile broke across her face. Gretchen had arrived.

Roderick answered the door. "Finally, you're here. We're so happy to see you, and please do come in. We've had to endure Caroline's piano playing while we waited for your arrival." He chuckled. "Honestly what a gift it is for her to play for us. I can't think of a better way to spend an afternoon."

Caroline joined him as he ushered their guests through the door and into the foyer. She found herself embraced heartily by Bella, and then the girl went quickly to Roderick.

Caroline intentionally hugged Karina before she went to Gretchen. "Oh Karina, I've been waiting to hear your lilting voice fill this hall. I am so glad you have finally made it to Rockwater." She noticed that Roderick had taken Peter's arm and led him into the loggia to meet the others, and Gretchen stood quietly as though she was taking it all in. "And Gretchen, my friend, I can hardly believe it. You're here, and in two days, you'll be a married woman, right here in the same spot where Roderick and I were married."

She saw an immediate look of alarm on Gretchen's face. "Oh, how insensitive of me. This is your place, your sacred place, and I fear I have intruded. Why did I not think of this before?"

When Caroline grasped the meaning of what Gretchen said, she embraced her friend. "Because there was nothing to think about. Roderick and I are so happy you wanted to be married here. Our beautiful memories of our happiest days right here in this room will keep multiplying. No more of this nonsense. Come on in. Angel's dying to see you, and I see she's already met Peter."

With the introductions made and initial conversations waning, Lilah said, "Mr. Kornilov, if I could have the keys to your vehicle, Chip is on his way to get your luggage to your suites."

"I would be so grateful, Lilah, if you would call me Peter. I understand all of us here in this room are family, or about to be." He handed her the keys. "And thank you for taking care of our luggage, although I am happy to do that."

"Mr.—Peter, you're our guest here for this momentous occasion, and we plan to treat you royally. Now, Caroline and Roderick will show you to your rooms, and you can get settled. We'll have some refreshments in about twenty minutes. I think Roderick has plans for you gentlemen the rest of the afternoon."

Caroline slipped to Roderick's side and looked up at him. "I'd be most interested in these plans of yours. I have some plans of my own."

Roderick winked. "I've plotted our escape from the house so you ladies can talk all things wedding."

Caroline stood on tiptoes to kiss his cheek. "You make marvelous plans. Is your escape route a secret?"

"Well, Ned and Fred reminded me they've never seen all of Rockwater, and neither has Sam. They've only had the Christmas carriage ride over a small portion of the property. And of course, this is Peter's first visit. So I'm taking them on a drive to see the place. And then later, Chip has the carriage all cleaned up, and we're taking a carriage ride through the hills to a special place for a late-afternoon picnic." He looked down at Caroline. "Does that suit the lady of the manor?"

"Perfectly. You ordered a white Christmas for us, and now you've ordered golden sunshine and a warm autumn afternoon for us to enjoy a picnic. You must have a direct line to the One who gives us those beautiful blessings."

———•———

After Lilah served tea and her famous ginger cookies, the men were out the door. Bella was begging to play the piano, and Karina followed her. Lilah was with the extra kitchen help she had hired, putting together the picnic for their carriage ride and early dinner.

Gretchen followed Caroline and Angel, and the three of them made themselves comfortable in the morning room. Angel propped her feet up on the ottoman and rested her hands across her plump waist. "Now, tell me, Gretchen. I wanna hear everythin', and I mean everythin'—how Peter proposed, where you two will be hangin' your hats and your hearts, and I especially want to hear all about your honeymoon. Caroline's already let a few cats outta the bag, but I want to hear it all from you. No one can tell our own stories as well as we can."

Gretchen began to answer Angel's questions, embellishing everything with her feelings of joy and gratitude and almost disbelief at how everything was coming together—and coming together so quickly.

Finally, she took a breath and glanced at Caroline. "And I could not be more appreciative of Caroline's sharing of Rockwater with us. Some of my most beautiful memories were made right here. Again, I just pray I am not intruding on your 'special memories' place, Caroline."

Caroline responded quickly. "I thought we settled that.

We are honored you would want to share such sacred moments in our home and with us. But I'm growing more curious. Would you tell us more about your honeymoon plans?"

"It is most unusual for me to speak of a honeymoon at my age." Gretchen grinned shyly. "As you know, Caroline, we will spend our wedding night at the Kentucky Castle, and then we must all return to Durham on Sunday. The girls have school, and the bakery must be attended." She paused. "But in a few weeks, we will have a real honeymoon, and it sounds as magical as the castle. Peter wants us to return to Austria."

Caroline almost squealed. "You're going back home to Austria?"

"Yes, we are, but only for two weeks, and then we'll return to make our home in Durham. Peter has a chalet in a small village near Innsbruck." She looked at Angel. "Innsbruck is in western Austria and is a beautiful city where people go for winter sports. His chalet is at the base of the Alps, and he rents it to visitors for most of the year. We will stay there for one week, return to Linz for a few days, and then we may visit my family in Český Krumlov. We phoned them yesterday to tell them we were getting married. They are so pleased. Pappá said it will be as it should have been with Peter and me all along."

Angel cleared her throat. "You look like some starry-eyed girl when you say those things, Gretchen. I'd say that will be a dreamy honeymoon to remember. And you're leavin' Bella at home with Karina?"

"Yes. I must say that unsettles me somewhat, but Karina is good with Bella, and so responsible. She insists for me to make this trip, and I cannot disappoint Peter."

"Nobody needs any more disappointments. I'd say the Good Lord has designed somethin' special for you and

Peter, and you need to honor His blessin' by enjoyin' every minute of it, wherever it takes you. See, Sam told you good things would happen and not to give a moment of worry about those annoyin' phone calls."

Gretchen stammered. "Yes, those phone calls." Her heart sinking, she looked down and said no more.

Angel moved from her relaxed position. "Somethin' you're not tellin' us? Are you still gettin' those phone calls?"

"I hate to even mention it, but in truth, yes, I still get the phone calls." She hesitated. "Peter thinks he may have an answer, and I believe him to be correct.

Angel's tone turned serious. "Well, that beats a chicken swimmin'! How on earth would Peter know anythin' about your phone calls?"

"Because he is getting phone calls from the same person." Gretchen glanced at Caroline. "Caroline, do you remember Iris Brandhof?"

"Yes, I do. She was the woman at the hotel in Melk, the one who had been involved with Peter's brother years ago. And if I recall, Elfi and her doctor friend told you Iris wasn't to be trusted." Caroline moved forward in her seat. "But why on earth would she be calling you, and if it is Iris, why doesn't she identify herself?"

Gretchen nervously twisted her engagement ring. "Peter says she wants money. He went to meet with her in Melk before he came here. She says a journalist will pay her money for information about me. It was the same journalist who covered my disappearance years ago. She has convinced him there is more to my story." She stammered. "She wants the money to hire someone to find Nicolai, and getting this money would help her."

Gretchen watched Caroline rise from her chair and walk to the window. "Oh, Gretchen. You mustn't worry. Peter will handle this. He will never allow Iris to become a problem for either of you."

"He assures me he will take care of everything. She has called him even when he is here, but he does not answer. He has blocked her number."

Angel piped in. "Well, I don't know this Iris, but some woman still carryin' that kind of torch is likely unhappy about being ignored. But she'd better get used to it."

Gretchen responded calmly. "I fear it is more than a torch she is carrying for Nicolai. It is also a grudge against Peter." At their questioning looks, she began to explain.

Angel sat straight up. "That's it. No more talk of this nonsense. You just shut the door on these worrisome thoughts and open wide the door where happy thoughts come from. You listen to me now. Your feelin's are always gonna follow your focus, and you can only focus on one thing at the time. You wanna feel good and happy, don't you? Then forget Iris and all that mess, and focus on this beautiful weddin' and the life you're about to have. You and Caroline have had enough sadness. God has given you two a couple of princes, and you deserve to live in a fairytale for a while."

Gretchen forced a smile. "Yes, a fairytale. You are a sage, Angel, and I receive your words as precious pearls of wisdom. I will do my best to do as you say, my trusted friend."

Still, Gretchen continued to twist the ring on her finger as she recalled the fairytales she had read to Karina and Bella in years past. They always seemed to have a witch, a wolf, or a wizard, but they did have happy endings. She could only hope it would be true for her.

——•——

Roderick had been driving the all-terrain vehicle for over an hour with Sam in the passenger's seat next to him. He looked in the rear-view mirror to see Ned and Peter in the back seat and Fred standing up on the back fender holding onto the frame. Fred's head rose above the vehicle's frame and rotated slowly from one side to the other like a surveilling periscope.

Roderick slowed as they reached the rocky path to Blue Hole. "Sorry, gentlemen. This vehicle is outfitted for four. I hope you aren't too uncomfortable back there. It's about to get bumpy. Hold on, Fred. I'll get us down to Blue Hole, and then we'll trade spots, and you can drive us home. I have a feeling you're like a homing pigeon and a better driver than I am."

Fred said nothing, but the grin on his face was his answer. Roderick knew that Fred liked all things mechanical.

Roderick tried to stay in the worn ruts, driving unhurriedly down the rocky lane that paralleled the creek bank. He pointed out landmarks and told tales of his boyhood days exploring every deer path along the creek banks, of fish he'd caught, and deer he had killed. "We have quite a whitetail deer population on the property, and every now and then, we hear talk of sightings of a mountain lion in the area. I've never seen any signs of one at Rockwater, and word is that there have been no mountain lions since the Civil War, but they are finally introducing the gray wolf back into this area. They've been nonexistent around here for years."

Sam commented. "We've been riding this property for over an hour, and it's all Rockwater?"

"Yes, it is. Most of the land in Kentucky is held by small farmers, probably on the average of less than two hundred acres. The horse farms may have four to five hundred acres to support their business, but we're blessed to have almost twelve hundred acres with running water, rolling hills, caves, and some fine forests."

Ned spoke. "I ain't never seen nothin' like it. You ain't gonna see land like this in Moss Point. And I ain't never in my life seen so many big rocks. I'd say they's boulders."

"And I'm about to take you to the largest one on the property. I'm taking you to the spring at the headwaters of the creek. My mother named it Blue Hole, and it was where we came to swim. In fact, it's where I learned to swim. Mother would not hear of having a pool when we had such a natural one on the property."

Roderick looked again at Fred in the rearview mirror. "Fred, are you still with us? You doing okay back there?"

Ned answered for his brother. "He's doin' fine, Mr. Roderick. You know Fred. He's pauciloquent. Why he wouldn't even say 'Git up' to a mule if it sat down on him."

Roderick kept driving and smothered the laugh that wanted to erupt. He stopped when they got to the path over to Blue Hole and turned off the vehicle. "Well, gentlemen, this is the most beautiful spot on the property. Ned, if you and Fred and Peter want to walk the short distance and climb that boulder, you'll be standing above the most beautiful deep spring you'll ever see. Cool, crystal-clear water of depths unknown." He stepped out and turned to Sam. "Sit tight, Sam. When we get back, I'll drive you up to the next bend where you won't have to climb a boulder, but you'll get a bit of the view looking back this way."

Ned and Fred got out and helped each other to the top of the boulder. Roderick came behind them with Peter and stood beside them when they reached the top. "I don't think I ever come here that I don't want to dive in. That water will refresh your soul. What do you think?"

Peter spoke first. "The rivers of my homeland and the Wachau Valley are all spectacular, but no more spectacular than this. And look at the color on that hillside! How blessed you are to call it home."

Fred mumbled something Roderick did not understand. Ned answered. "I believe that's the clearest water I ever did see. Just like on one o' them beer commercials, but this is for real. Like Peter said, you a mighty blessed man, Mr. Roderick, to own a parcel of land like this one. I do believe this must be the Garden of Eden the Bible talks about. And you got some caves?"

Roderick chuckled. "You may be right about that Garden of Eden, Ned. And yes, if you could see underground here, there are streams of the purest water and caves. We have several small ones on our property, unmapped or charted. I get several requests a year from spelunkers wanting to explore them, but I have yet to say yes. Too dangerous and too much of a liability. I've been in a few of them myself, and I can assure you I have no plans to return. You've never experienced darkness until you've been in a cave."

He patted Fred on the back. "What do you say I drive to the next bend so that Sam can see Blue Hole, and then I'll hand you the keys and we'll be on our way home?" He watched a pleased grin spread across Fred's face.

They returned to the vehicle, and Roderick drove farther up the lane, where he and Peter helped Sam out. They made the short walk to the creek bank. "Look down there. This isn't the best view of Blue Hole, but I'd never hear the last of it from Angel and Caroline if I let you injure yourself climbing a boulder."

Peter took Sam's arm. "And if you injured yourself, who would escort my dear Gretchen and give her to me in marriage Saturday?"

Sam, in a quieter voice than usual, said, "In that case, gentlemen, we will be most careful. Walking canes and rocks don't usually mix very well, and I don't think I want the experience of having three females upset with me. Even one would be more than I desire."

They walked carefully to the water's edge and stood for a few moments of silence, inhaling the beauty and the woodsy smell of the hardwood forest. Then Roderick led them back to the vehicle and said, "Fred, the driver's seat is yours."

Fred got in, turned the key, and revved the engine. Roderick stood on the back fender and clenched the frame.

Ned instructed his twin. "Now, Fred, if you's gonna do something like spin a tire or take a sharp right turn off this here road, would you give us a gardyloo?"

With the roar of the engine to drown it out, Roderick laughed out loud. *Gardyloo?* He must remember to tell Angel that one.

Chapter Fifteen

---◆---

Wedding Spirits

Friday evening, the eve of the wedding, at Rockwater

Caroline and Roderick waited in the library for the others before their departure for dinner at the Kentucky Castle. Sarah dashed through the doorway, dressed impeccably but seemingly flustered.

"Who licked the red off your lollipop, sis?" Roderick inquired. Caroline was relieved to hear Sarah laugh and to see her hands-on-her-hips attitude change as she glided toward the sofa, stopping in front of Roderick.

"I don't even have a lollipop. I'm just wondering how we could be the parents of such a little diva. When Rosita learned we were dining at the Castle again, she insisted on bringing her princess tiara, and she is heels-dug-in determined to wear it." Without her normal reserved manner, Sarah plopped down at the end of the sofa. "I made certain she was dressed and her hair was combed and left George to deal with the tiara and her dress-up play jewelry. Clever she was to sneak that into her bag. We're talking garish and tacky play jewelry, but at least she didn't bring the hot-pink boa."

Caroline couldn't hide her laughter. "Professor George, plastic pearls, and a tiara? Can't wait to see how that turns out."

Sam and Angel were the next to arrive and took their favorite chairs flanking the fireplace. Caroline greeted Ned and Fred and Peter at the library doorway and offered them a seat. It pleased her that they all seemed to have their favorite seats in the library now as though they had been assigned. "Come in, gentlemen. We're waiting on Gretchen and the girls and Lilah. And if I know Lilah, she's in the kitchen. I'll fetch her."

She met George and a bejeweled and crowned Rosita coming out of the kitchen and down the hallway. She stopped and gasped dramatically. "How lovely you look, Princess Rosita!"

"Thank you, CC. We are going to the Castle, and every castle must have a princess. Last time you were the princess. I get to be the princess tonight, and I'm getting a hamburger."

Caroline knelt to face her. "Well, I'd say every girl deserves to be a princess sometimes and to eat a hamburger. Let me see about this." Caroline adjusted the crooked tiara, stood, winked at George, and walked toward the kitchen. "Lilah and I will meet you in the library. We'll be leaving shortly."

Only moments after Caroline had returned with Lilah, they heard steps in the hallway. Bella and Karina entered first, both dressed in pale-blue dresses. Caroline still marveled at their unblemished, porcelain complexions, platinum hair, and their silvery green eyes just like Gretchen's. She watched Peter rise from his chair. Such a gentleman obviously awaiting his bride.

Gretchen entered, elegant in a deep teal dress with her

hair pulled into a bun at the nape of her neck with trailing wisps at her cheeks. Caroline assumed Karina had helped with that.

She watched Peter approach Gretchen and kiss her on both cheeks as though they had not seen each other since last spring. Rosita rushed to Bella's side and was holding her hand within seconds, chattering about her tiara. Karina moved to the side to allow Peter and Gretchen to enter the room together. Caroline wanted to capture these almost magical moments she never dared to dream would happen.

Within the hour, all fourteen were seated at an elegant table set with a white linen tablecloth, white china rimmed with a gold band, and crystal for water, wine, and tea at each plate. Freshly cut grape vines with tags of grapes entwined with other seasonal berries and colorful leaves ran the length of the table down the middle. Votive candles interspersed randomly provided warm light for the autumn colors.

Caroline smiled with satisfaction as she surveyed the tableau, approving what the staff had done with her suggestions. She thought the table a delicate balance of simple elegance and earthiness and symbolic of the autumn season of Gretchen's and Peter's lives.

The dinner was equally elegant: a spicy butternut squash soup, a salad of field greens with sliced pears sprinkled with candied walnuts and dried cranberries, a petite filet of beef and a lobster tail served with a rice pilaf and roasted asparagus. Classic apple pie with cinnamon-laced home-made ice cream was dessert. Everyone's palate was pleased, including the two young girls who had cheeseburgers and tater tots. Sarah and Gretchen had been hesitant about the girls' choices, but Caroline assured them it was a night of joy and not a night to be teaching them about table manners or wrestling with a lobster tail.

When everyone had finished the meal and the plates had

been taken away, after dinner-coffee was served. Bella and the princess were served hot cocoa in pumpkin-shaped mugs. Rosita excitedly said, "*Ayote! Ayote!* I love *ayote en dulce.*"

Sarah tried to calm her. "No, my sweet. This is not *ayote en dulce*, and I know you love that, and we'll make it at home. This is hot chocolate in a pumpkin mug. Do you remember *pumpkin* is the English word for *ayote*?"

"Pumpkin and jack-o-lantern? Now I remember." Rosita giggled. "*Pumpkin* is a funny word."

When things were quiet again, Peter turned to Caroline, seated on his right, and whispered a request to speak. She nodded in agreement and smiled, and he stood at the end of the table and waited patiently until he had everyone's attention. He cleared his throat and began to speak. "I am not a man of eloquent words, but I am a man with a most thankful heart, and I must speak my words of gratitude to you. I am thankful to all of you for being here with us this evening and allowing us the pleasure of hosting this beautiful occasion."

He turned to Caroline. "And Caroline, I am most grateful for your help in making this evening lovely beyond my English to describe it. I must say this castle does rival those along the banks of the Danube. And to you and Roderick, I am most grateful that you opened your home and your hearts to us as Gretchen and I become one tomorrow. God took care of my dear Gretchen and gave her a family, but not just *a* family. You are the most caring, compassionate, and enjoyable people, and you have loved my Gretchen and Bella and Karina. I can only hope you will grow to love me as well as I become a member of this beautiful family. I will always be grateful to you, to each of you."

Peter paused and leaned to pull an apple-box-sized crate from underneath the table. "I have gifts for the ladies." He pulled small satin bags from the crate and distributed gifts to Caroline, Angel, Lilah, Sarah, and Rosita. "These are Swarovski crystal music boxes, and I hope they will cause you to remember this evening and my gratitude."

He then removed two bottles from the crate. "I would not forget you, gentlemen. For each of you, I have a bottle of our finest apricot brandy from the Wachau Valley and a bottle of our choicest white wine."

Roderick responded. "It seems you're giving us a vicarious trip to Austria with these fine bottles. I do remember the apricot brandy. Thank you."

Sam announced. "Yes, thank you, Peter. Sounds like I need to pull out one of my finest cigars to accompany this brandy."

Caroline watched Ned's and Fred's reactions. She assumed that wine nor brandy had ever passed these gentlemen's lips. But Fred's face lit up with surprise and delight. She must remember to have Roderick caution them. She did not want them suffering a hangover on Gretchen's wedding day.

Peter continued and took two velvet bags from the crate. "These gifts are for the beautiful girls who will become my daughters tomorrow. Identical strands of pearls with a green amethyst pendant to match their beautiful eyes. These amethysts are from a mine near Austria." He walked to Karina and Bella, handed them their bags, and kissed each of them on the cheek.

Caroline watched with great delight as the girls opened their bags and helped each other put the pearls around their necks. They rose together and kissed Peter's cheeks and thanked him quietly.

"And the most important gift of all for the woman whom I have loved for my lifetime, my dearest Gretchen." He reached again and pulled out a larger velvet bag.

"Gretchen, this is but a symbol of the real gift." He pulled a frame from the bag and turned it around for Gretchen to see.

Gretchen gasped. "It is the cottage in Melk where I grew up along the Danube. How beautiful!"

"This, my love, is only a photograph. I have commissioned a fine artist from Salzburg to do an oil painting of this photograph. I have hopes that it will be finished when we arrive in Austria later this month. You have carried your home in your heart all these years, and I only hope that you will enjoy the painting as it hangs in our home."

Gretchen rose, embraced him, and said, "It is quite a treasure, but my dearest Peter, you are my home. Wherever you are is my home, but I am very grateful for this beautiful gift, a reminder of where we started and where our love was born."

——·——

Late night on the eve of the wedding at Rockwater

The eve of the wedding day had ended. The halls of Rockwater, filled most of the day with laughter, music, and conversation, were quiet again. Peter had hosted a most memorable evening at the Castle. And now they were all back at Rockwater and in their suites.

Caroline finished brushing her hair, slipped into bed, and curled up next to Roderick. She spoke quietly. "It has been quite a day, topped off with Peter's lovely dinner at the Castle. I asked him how he arranged to have the crate of gifts there."

"I also wondered how he managed that one. I imagine he made some assumptions before he left, but he couldn't have known about our Georgia guests."

"He had made some preparations before he left Austria. But when Gretchen said yes and we planned the wedding, his administrative assistant quickly put together the music boxes, brandy, and wine and flew the crate counter to counter to Lexington and arranged for delivery to the Castle."

"Resourceful man Peter is."

"Yes, he is, and I'm so grateful that in this season of their lives, they have each other. Gretchen deserves a resourceful man." She sighed contentedly. "It has been the perfect wedding eve."

Roderick pulled her close to him. "And you, my wife, are the perfect hostess, making certain everyone is well fed and doing meaningful, enjoyable things."

"Why, thank you, sir. I'll let you in on a secret. I take my cues from my husband, but please don't tell him."

"Our secret. Now close those blue eyes and think beautiful thoughts and sleep peacefully, my precious one. Tomorrow will come sooner than you think. Sweet dreams."

Caroline nestled her head in the crook of his shoulder. She closed her eyes and breathed a long, slow breath, satisfied that tomorrow would come, righting wrongs and fulfilling hopes of people who truly loved each other.

She slept serenely in Roderick's arms and woke early to a spectacular indigo sky sprinkled with stars that would soon disappear in morning light. After grateful thoughts of waking next to Roderick at Rockwater, she thought of the wedding day. She lay quietly with her thoughts, going over her mental checklist. Lilah had relieved her last night after dinner with the news that the arch was safely tucked away in the butler's pantry and would only require a half hour for the florist to finish dressing it with fresh foliage. That meant the wedding party would need to be sequestered at nine thirty to keep the surprise. Caroline smiled at the thought that Gretchen was not even expecting flowers or candles and yet she would be married under an arch that would become a wedding gift for their garden at home.

Caroline had no worries about the ceremony itself. She, Peter, and Gretchen had met with the minister on Friday morning, and with such a small and intimate ceremony, there had been no need of a rehearsal. The minister, seasoned and so congenial, would make certain things happened when they were supposed to happen, and Bella and Karina were well rehearsed.

After all the wedding fiascos Caroline had witnessed as a church musician, she appreciated the simplicity of an intimate and meaningful ceremony where the marriage itself was the focus and not all the wedding trappings. The Scripture, the prayers, the vows, the music offered in love by the girls Gretchen cherished more than life, a lovely brunch around their table to celebrate—and Peter and Gretchen would be husband and wife.

As the fingers of morning stretched into the night sky, these thoughts brought Caroline peace and satisfaction and an anticipation of a perfect wedding day to rival the perfect wedding eve.

She felt Roderick adjusting the sheet to cover her shoulder. "You decided to wake?" she asked.

Roderick responded sleepily. "I don't recall deciding. I think it just happened. My guess is that you've been wide awake for a while."

"A short while, just long enough to see the daybreak and decide it will be the loveliest of days. Everything is taken care of, and in a few hours, the second Rockwater wedding will be history. I really have little to do this morning thanks to Lilah and her kitchen help, but I'm anxious to get up and get at it."

He pulled her closer to him and kissed her cheek.

"There is one thing I need to check on fairly soon in case it needs more attention."

Caroline curiously turned to face him. "And what would that be?"

Roderick teeheed. "Well, I saw this glint in Fred's eyes last night when Peter gave him his bottles of apricot brandy and wine. I don't know the drinking habits of those men, but something tells me I might need to check on them and make certain they're upright."

Caroline sat straight up in bed. "Roderick, no. Surely, they wouldn't. I meant to tell you last night to talk to them and warn them not to drink too much."

"Can you imagine those two sloshed on apricot brandy?" Roderick snickered. "I certainly don't think they would intend to imbibe more than they should, but I do wonder if they know when to draw the line. Do you know if they drink alcohol?"

Caroline rose and put her feet on the floor at the bedside and turned back to Roderick. "I'm not certain, but my guess is the strongest thing that ever passes the lips of those men is a Coca-Cola. They feel obliged to drink it since it was Coca-Cola stock that generated their wealth."

"Let's hope they didn't feel obliged to drink four bottles of these beverages just because they were gifts from Peter—especially the apricot brandy."

She stood. "Now you have me worried. I have no clue about hangovers. I hope you know what to do."

Roderick climbed out of bed. "I can tell you brandy is the worst for hangovers. If there's a need, I'll get Lilah to make a pitcher of ginger tea to ease their stomachs, and we have some sports drinks to get them rehydrated. And they'll need something for probably the worst headache they've ever had."

She began pulling up the sheet and blanket on her side

of the bed. "You must go and check on them soon. Gretchen's wedding day must be perfect."

As was their custom, Roderick assisted in the bedmaking. "I'll go before breakfast. Maybe I should take a thermos of coffee with me. Besides, bringing them coffee gives me a good excuse for knocking on their door so early."

"Whatever you do, don't tell Sam. Ned and Fred would be so embarrassed. Promise them it would be your secret."

"Scouts honor." He laughed again. "Maybe they won't still be green by wedding time."

Caroline didn't even so much as grin. She only raised her right eyebrow.

———•———

Lilah and the extra kitchen help were already busy in the kitchen when Roderick entered. He was pleased the coffee pot was full and reached for the thermos he used for his early-morning fishing or hunting trips. As he fixed coffee and grabbed a couple of mugs, he wanted to explain the possible predicament to Lilah, but he had promised Caroline. He knew thoughts of Ned and Fred hungover would throw Lilah into one of her grabbing-her-apron-and-covering-her-mouth laughing fits.

He whistled while he walked down the lane to the barn. The smells and breezes of autumn made for a feel-good morning, one where a light jacket was needed. He entered the barn. Chip had already fed the horses and was mucking out the horse stalls. Roderick stopped to speak to him. "You're up early, Chip."

Chip stopped what he was doing and walked to the open grille of the stall door and leaned over it. "Yes, sir. Fletcher needs me a little later to help put the wedding arch in place, so I needed to get this done because I'm taking off for a while this afternoon. Got a date for the fall festival in Lexington."

"When do I get to meet this girl that seems to have so much of your attention lately?" He watched Chip's face turn slightly red.

"Hopefully soon. I would like to bring her out some time, if you don't mind."

"Mind? Chip, this is your home. I trust your judgment in your choice of friends and girls." He winked at Chip. "You've never disappointed me. And speaking of friends, have you seen Ned and Fred this morning?"

Chip lowered his head. "No, sir, but I did pick up the four empty bottles just outside the door to the tack room."

Roderick's brow instantly wrinkled. He couldn't really say what he was thinking, so resorted to, "Then I'm thinking this thermos of coffee was a grand idea."

"Sir, do you think they drank the four bottles? I didn't figure them for drinking men."

"They're not drinking men. Never have been and most likely they don't know anything about drinking. But they might have felt obligated to drink these bottles since they were gifts from Mr. Kornilov."

Chip grinned awkwardly like he wanted to laugh. "Let me know if you need any help, sir. The water trough's full of cold water."

"I think we won't go to those extremes. But hopefully this coffee will help. And Lilah makes a mean ginger tea if needed. And I have some aspirin in my pocket."

"Yes, sir. Just let me know if I can help."

Roderick walked to the tack room door and knocked gently. No answer. He knocked again, louder and harder. Still no answer. He opened the door. The room was empty. The beds were made as though a drill sergeant would be inspecting.

Roderick walked quickly to get Chip. "They're not here. Beds are made. Don't know if they spent the night in them or where they might be. Please tell me the all-terrain vehicle's here."

"I'll check." Chip put down his rake, came out of the stall, and walked in the opposite direction. Roderick waited.

Chip came back around the corner. "It's here. Why don't we check the shop?"

"Good idea." Roderick followed Chip. As they approached, he could hear sounds coming from inside the shop. He just hoped the twins were sober and not trying to use the shop equipment in some inebriated state. He was almost afraid to look in when Chip opened the door.

There were Ned and Fred, dressed in their overalls and plaid shirts, working away. Fred was working the saw, and Ned was measuring lumber. Roderick felt relief.

"Good morning, gentleman. You two are up earlier than Chip. I thought you might be, so I brought you some coffee."

"Thanky. A cup of coffee sounds mighty good. We know today's the weddin' day, and we jes wanted to git some of our work done, at least some of the measurin' and cuttin'. And besides, Fred likes this new saw better'n a pig loves slop. He cain't hardly sleep for wantin' to saw somethin'."

Roderick poured the coffee into the two mugs. "It's Saturday and Gretchen's wedding day, and we certainly did not expect you to work, but if that makes you happy, then by all means do what makes you happy." He was reluctant to ask, but he had to. "I noticed the empty bottles next to the tack room door."

Fred stopped sawing, and Ned stopped measuring. Roderick watched as the two men's eyes locked on each other. He remained quiet, waiting for something to happen. When nothing did, he handed them their mugs of coffee.

Ned took the mug and took out his handkerchief to wipe his mouth. "Well, Mr. Roderick, I'm a-guessin' we owe you a good explainin' about the empty bottles." He paused. "Me and Fred just ain't no drinkin' men, but we didn't want to appear ungrateful for Mr. Peter's gifts to us. And we ain't no lyin' men neither, so I s'pose I jes better tell you the truth. We poured it down the commode and flushed it three times, and we set the bottles out so somebody would think we wuz grateful and enjoyed ever' drop." He looked at Fred and then back at Roderick. "We didn't know what else to do. Our ma would turn over in her grave iffen she thought we drank a drop of likker, but she would do the same thing iffen she thought we wuz ungrateful or disrespectful to a man like Mr. Peter."

Roderick put his hand on Ned's shoulder. "Well, Ned. Your ma would be proud of you this morning. You two are some of the finest and most honorable men I know. It is no wonder Sam and Angel have such fondness and respect for you, and why Caroline thinks of you as family. This will be our secret. No need to mention it to a soul. Now, enjoy your coffee, and we'll see you for breakfast in about forty-five minutes."

Roderick left the barn somewhere between pleased and prickled—pleased that Ned and Fred were stone sober, upright, and working and prickled that he'd ever doubted them—and because he would have savored the wine and the brandy.

Caroline was in hand-wringing mode when he opened the kitchen door. "All is well," he was quick to reassure her. "No need, absolutely no need, to worry about wedding spirits."

Chapter Sixteen

———————♦———————

Wedding Images

Saturday, October 2, Wedding Day at Rockwater

After an early wedding-day breakfast, everyone seemed to scatter. Roderick took Peter on a walk down to Blue Hole while Ned and Fred returned to the shop for a couple of hours. Gretchen and the girls went to their suites for showers, doing hair, and dressing. Sarah and George took Rosita for a walk through the forest to gather a basket of fresh leaves for her flower-girl basket. It was no surprise to Caroline that Sam and Angel had shown up for breakfast in their wedding attire and spent the morning in the library reading. Lilah was directing the activities in the kitchen in preparation for the wedding brunch.

After the florist finished the arrangement of fresh willow branches and berries on the arch, Caroline saw to its placement in front of the loggia window while the house was quiet. She stepped back to see it fully in front of the window. Perfect framing. She was pleased.

The photographer arrived at ten o'clock. There had been no mention of a wedding photographer, but it was unimaginable that these moments of sheer gladness would not be captured. On short notice, Roderick had engaged the photographer he used regularly for business, but he cautioned Caroline that he was more of a photojournalist and would need to be instructed for a wedding. She was the perfect one to school him. She wanted just a few staged photos and mostly candid shots. Surely a photojournalist would be adept at that.

At ten forty-five, everyone except Gretchen and Caroline gathered in the loggia. Sam and Angel took comfortable seats with Rosita between them and Sarah and George. Lilah took the seat next to Sarah, and Ned and Fred sat beside Sam.

Bella began to fill the room with music, mostly Chopin and Brahms, favorites of her mammá and Peter. At precisely eleven o'clock, the minister entered with Peter and Roderick to take their places in front of the arch.

Caroline and Gretchen had hidden themselves in the upstairs gallery hallway, which allowed them a perfect view of the loggia below as everyone gathered. Gretchen turned to Caroline and whispered, "I cannot believe the beauty of what I see. This was your idea?"

Caroline whispered back as they began their walk to the staircase. "Yes, it was, my friend. You will see willow branches when you get closer. I designed it with Fletcher's help, and Ned and Fred built it. As our wedding gift, we will ship it to Durham, where you can have it installed in your cottage garden."

"In the shade of the willow tree. That will be its new home. What a lovely gift, my dearest Caroline. Such a meaningful and memorable treasure."

When they reached the stair landing, Gretchen paused, and Caroline continued down the steps. She signaled Roderick to nod for Sam and Rosita to join Gretchen.

Gretchen came down the last flight of stairs to the floor level, and Sam, cane in hand, was there to offer his arm to her. Caroline moved to take her place on the other side of the arch from Roderick. Rosita, minus her tiara, followed Caroline, gleefully tossing the leaves she had gathered earlier, and giggled as they drifted to the marble floor. She took her place next to Caroline.

Sam stood with Gretchen as Karina and Bella surprised them with the duet "Answered Prayer." With such glorious sounds and such full hearts as witnesses, there were few cheeks that had not felt the trail of a tear.

As the last intonement of their harmony reverberated through the loggia, Bella started to play "When Morning Gilds the Skies," a favorite hymn of both Gretchen and Peter, as it was an old German hymn they had sung as children. They wanted this to be their morning hymn of praise from their grateful hearts.

Gretchen and Sam made their way to the arch without hesitation or a stumble, and just as the last chord resolved, Sam gave Gretchen's hand to Peter.

———•———

As Sam placed Gretchen's hand into Peter's, he paused, then announced, "Now, Peter, I give to you the hand of this woman, a good woman. You take hold of her hand, and you don't let go. Sometimes you'll need to hold it tightly, and sometimes gently, but always with a firm grip that lets her know how much you love her."

He returned to his seat beside Angel and took her hand in his.

Lord, I don't know who of us doesn't need love. We all do, and I feel a whirlwind of love in this room right now. I know

Angel wouldn't like what I'm thinking, Lord, but I'm thinking of all Gretchen's been through with Nicolai and then with Ernesto, and then I think about Karina running away and coming home after years of silence, and then Gretchen returning to Austria to find her family. And to her surprise, she found Peter. Well, Lord I know that You've been holding some hands for a long time, and I thank You. And You've answered a whole lot of prayers.

I've been holding my Angel's hand for sixty-two years as my wife, and for sixty-four years if I count our courting days. I knew when I took her hand for the first time that it fit mine, and that she fit me in every way. I was tall; she was tiny. I was brash; she was quiet. I was mostly serious; she was mostly fun. I was dogmatic; she was creative. I was turbulent, but my Angel was tranquil. I was pushy; she was patient.

I needed my Angel. She's everything I'm not.

Lord, I don't know how You made us fit, but You did. I'm grateful, and I'm grateful I didn't have to wait for thirty years to find out like Peter and Gretchen did. I ask you, Lord, to give them many years. They won't have the opportunity of sixty-two years like Angel and me, but Lord, I just ask you to give them full, happy years of being together. You joined their hearts years ago, and now you're joining their lives in marriage. Seems mostly like a miracle to me but then again, miracles are Your business. I ask You, Lord, to keep holding their hands, strong and secure.

---·---

Angel felt Sam gently squeeze her hand and lovingly reflected. *My handsome Sam, strong, sure, and always knowin' what to say! I like the feel of your hand takin' mine. It ties me to this earth when I feel so near heaven. Where has our time* gone, Sam? I remember our weddin' day in unimaginable detail, but most especially how I felt—the excitement, the sheer joy, the love that was ours. Sometimes that feelin' of young love and passion and our hopes for our future return to me like a dear old friend I haven't seen for a while, all so familiar, like it was only yesterday. Those memories make me want to weep as I grieve that those days have passed. But how can I grieve when we are here in the winter of our lives with a stronger and deeper love than ever, and still holdin' hands like two young lovers?

I can only be grateful for each day we have, and for the peace of knowin' that we will hold hands for always. Maybe in heaven, our hands will be young again and our spirits will be burstin' with love. We will be together with the One who made us and gave us our love, and His Word says He is love. But for today, I'm here, holdin' your hand and celebratin' with Gretchen and Peter.

God blessed you and me and allowed us to live most of our dreams, except the dream of havin' children of our own. But oh, what a gift we were given in Caroline and now Gretchen, like the daughters we never had. And Bella is like a granddaughter, a rare one. They warm the winter season of our lives. And somehow, I think they need us. At least they make me feel that they do.

Peter and Gretchen had their spring of young love so long ago, and I'm sure it feels like spring has come again. But they know full well they're in the autumn of their lives and that winter follows autumn, and they know how to appreciate every day. Their maturity and their faith give them hearts of gratitude. And that gratitude will bring such joy.

My Sam knew exactly what to say about that hand-holdin' business. Out of millions of hands, I would know if it was Sam's takin' mine. I think Gretchen and Peter would know each other's hands too.

———•———

Watching as Gretchen and Peter stood hand in hand, Ned ruminated.

I ain't believing that me and Fred's sittin' right here in this room ag'in, and this time it's Miss Gretchen gittin' hitched. Why, me and Fred's like gubbins sittin' here with all these fine folks. Maw wouldn't believe it, neither, us sittin' here in fancy chairs on a marble floor.

Before Miss Caroline's weddin', we ain't been to but one weddin' in our whole lives. That was when Cousin Tabor got married in the next county forty years ago, and Paw said there was a shotgun behind the door at the church. And now we's aflyin' in a private jet and eatin' the tail of a lobster in a castle. I ain't ever even seen a whole lobster, but it was good. And then we got presents and didn't git them a thang. Mr. Peter is a generous feller, and I do hope Mr. Roderick'll keep our secret about pourin' the likker out. We got to git our heads together about a weddin' present for Miss Gretchen and Mr. Peter.

Me and Fred ain't good fer much, but we can build things. I like what that flower lady did to the arch we built, all them leaves and willow branches. Miss Caroline knew what she wanted, and she knew it would be just right for Miss Gretchen. And now Miss Gretchen's gonna take it to North Carolina. I hope she'll remember us once in a while when she looks at it.

It mighta been nice if me or Fred wuz married, but not many women coulda put up with one of us, let alone two of us. We's set in our ways, but we got each other and some mighty fine friends. We look after them, and they look out for us jes like we's family.

Them two girls look just like Miss Gretchen, like some angels got lost and fell outta heaven. And they sound like angels too, beautyful. It's all beautyful, just downright supernal.

———.———

Roderick looked across at Caroline, his heart full of gratitude for the woman standing there.

Radiant. How could you be more beautiful in this moment than you were on our wedding day, Caroline? I didn't have to wait as long as Peter did, but I had convinced myself that finding the right woman to do life with was not likely to happen for me and that I was more likely to end up an old curmudgeon of a bachelor. And then, a phone call out of the blue about a piano I had purchased, and the rest is history— beautiful, bumpy history. It was your piano that pulled your heart strings and brought you to Rockwater, but from the very first sight of you, you pulled mine, and you still do.

Just thinking of Gretchen's and Peter's long journey to get to this day makes me know I've made the right decision in selling Adair Enterprises and giving my life to you and to creating a legacy that will make a difference in the lives of many people. I live to make you smile and to make you proud of me.

How I wish my mother was here to know how fulfilled I am and to witness Rockwater full of life again, and how I wish she could have known you. You are so much like her, my blue-eyed beauty. And my father—how I wish he knew I took what he built and increased it, and that you and I together will use it well.

I can only hope that these two will be as complete as I am with you, Caroline. I hope they will take joy in each other and in every day that they are together. If anyone deserves anything, these two deserve these coming years of happiness.

———.———

From her seat in the loggia, Sarah smiled as she recalled the history that had brought them to this moment.

Another simple but grand occasion to celebrate love at Rockwater! I was almost certain these halls would remain silent forever, but Caroline brings life back to this place. Not only her presence and her love for my brother, but then she brings this wonderful group of her eclectic friends who feel like family to us now.

And when she discovered Bella and Gretchen and asked me to help? I know my brother used me to keep his acquaintance with Caroline, but his happiness means so much to me and what a gift Caroline is as the sister I never had! How could I ever have imagined that she and Roderick would fall so deeply in love and that their love would bring me and George to a place where we could become parents? Amazing that the change in one life could bring so many ripples and changes for so many.

And there is my little princess standing next to Caroline. How her life and future have been changed. We can never, ever forget she saved Caroline's life as they both were trying to survive a mudslide in Guatemala. I wonder if she might want to marry right here at Rockwater someday. I must cherish every day with her. Her wings will grow and become strong, and one day she will fly away on her own strength. My job is to raise her not to need me and then be satisfied that she doesn't.

I'm hoping Peter and George can become close friends. As new fathers who didn't really plan on being fathers, they could use each other's company, sharing their daughter stories. Besides, George needs some friends who aren't part of the university family. They get so cerebral and stuffy sometimes.

I look at Bella and Karina, remarkably beautiful girls with such musical talent. Who knows what is ahead for them? Fortunately, they will have Peter and Gretchen, and Caroline and Roderick and us. Bella is such a rare human. I hope Peter can cope with her limitations and her tremendous gift. Their love is strong and as rare as Bella. They will be fine.

Springtime of the Song

———•———

Across from Sarah, Lilah had similar thoughts as she remembered and acknowledged God's hand in what was unfolding before them.

This old house has a heartbeat again, like it's been holding its breath until life and love returned, and now it's breathing again. We can thank God that He brought Caroline to Roderick to do just that. And we didn't just get Caroline, we got her whole family and her host of friends who are now family. And then we got her music that comes from a special place that not many folks have. I don't know if you can look down from heaven, Miss Angeleah, but your boy is happy—happier than I've ever seen him.

And you would love Caroline. She's so much like you. She loves Roderick, all of him, and she loves this house like you did. Look at what she did with that arch. Who would have thought of such but a woman who appreciates the beauty of what God made, just like you did?

And she's fiercely loyal to those she loves. When I think of Gretchen's story and how God used Caroline to lift her out of that miry pit she lived in, I realize it was a miracle. And then how Caroline's piano and Bella brought Roderick and Sarah into her life. Nobody can tell me God didn't have a hand in that. And to think how Roderick and Caroline took Gretchen to Austria to find her family, and she found them and Peter. And she found Peter when she wasn't even looking. Now who's going to tell me God didn't orchestrate all of that? I'm just glad Caroline was His instrument and that Sarah and George are part of that music.

Family and friends are Caroline's lifeblood, and music is the air she breathes. I'm hoping I live to see Roderick and Caroline having children of their own, and the next generation of Adairs standing right here in this hall to celebrate their love and marriage.

———•———

Karina gazed up at her mother, her heart full.

Mammá is the happiest I have ever seen her. When I look at her standing there next to Peter, it is as if she is twenty again. Her face is so beautiful and radiant. And I sit here next to Bella, my own daughter who looks like Mammá and me. How different our lives are now.

Bella and I have so many advantages because of the hard choices Mammá made. Her life has been one of endurance, and now Peter, her love, has returned. I knew growing up there had to be more to life and love and marriage than what Mammá had. She endured, but I could not. I ran in search of something that I felt existed, but oh, how sorrowful I am about the places where I looked. I would never find what Mammá and Peter have in those places. I am so grateful they both endured.

I can never repay Mammá for loving Bella the way she does, and for loving me and accepting me after I ran away and returned after all those years. I will try to repay her by being the daughter she taught me to be—and if God wills it, to be the best mother I can be and to accept the responsibility that was given to me at Bella's birth. But I will respect Mammá's wishes.

I hope someday I will find the kind of love I see in this room—Mammá and Peter, Caroline and Roderick, Sam and Angel, and Sarah and George. I am beginning to wonder if I might have that in Brandon. I will patiently wait and pray and see. Until then, I now have a father, a real father.

———•———

Springtime of the Song

Sitting next to Karina, Bella sensed the excitement in the air.

Mammá is pretty. Her face is happy like Karina's. Peter's face is happy. I hope my face is happy. Everybody's face is happy. I played Chopin. Karina sang a song. I did too. Rosita made a mess. She dropped her leaves. I will help her pick them up. Not now. I must play the piano when Mammá and Peter turn around. Happy music. No more Chopin.

Mammá says Peter will be my pappá. I never had a pappá. I like Peter. He makes Mammá smile. Happy music. Then I call Peter Pappá. We go back home tomorrow. It is Peter's home, too, Mammá said. Pappá's home. I play Chopin. Not now. At home, for Pappá.

—•—

Standing in front of everyone, Peter gazed into the face of the woman he had loved for decades. Thinking back over those years, his heart full, he made a plea and a promise.

I am overflowing with joy and gratitude. The face I thought I would never see again is looking at me as we proclaim our love and take our vows here in the presence of friends who are like family. We are promising to love and cherish each other for the rest of our lives. That is the easiest thing I have ever done. Your face is the one etched on my heart from my youth. And now I will wake to see it every morning.

I am sixty years old, and yet, God, You have returned Gretchen to me. And You have given to me Karina and Bella, who are now my daughters. Oh, Lord, I ask you to make me a husband worthy of Gretchen and to make me a father worthy of Bella and Karina. Teach me how to love them best and to support and encourage them every day. Help me rise every morning with a purpose to make their lives everything You desire for them. Give me wisdom, I pray.

As Sam said, I will hold your hand, dear Gretchen. I will hold it as we walk, as we sit in the garden under the willow tree, when it is covered with bread dough, when we sit next to each other in church, and when we say our nightly prayers and sleep peacefully together in the palm of God's hand. I will wake holding your hand in mine.

———·———

Looking up at the man who was finally to be her husband, Gretchen acknowledged how she came to be in this place with these people she loved so much.

Here I stand, underneath the willow branches, holding the hands of my dearest Peter. All those years I lived day to day and prayed for help . . . I never would have prayed for this. And yet, I am given this blessed gift without even asking. I prayed for Karina to return and never lost hope, but I forced thoughts of Peter from my mind. But they never left my heart. My family is complete now, and my heart is full.

It is my wedding day, and I should be thinking of the future, but I find myself retracing the past few years. And Caroline has been such a part of it all. The day I bolstered my courage to approach her in the grocery store in Moss Point seems a lifetime ago. My desire for someone to acknowledge Bella's gifts emboldened me, and God led me to Caroline. And she brought with her Sam and Angel. Her search for her piano brought her to Rockwater and to Roderick and changed her life. Her discovery of Bella's gifts and the direction she and Sarah gave to us changed our lives. Karina returned to me and to herself, and we have satisfying lives in Durham. And Caroline took me back to Austria to find my family.

Caroline has been there for it all, And now, because of her gracious goodness, Peter and I are getting married here under the willow branches in her home.

Because of God's blessings and the help of so many friends, I have a future that I can look forward to with Peter.

———•———

Caroline fought to keep her tears at bay. Not tears of sadness but of gladness as she remembered all the changes that had brought her to Rockwater.

How intimate and simple and real this moment is! The way weddings should be. This room and these windows looking out on these Kentucky hills are becoming a sacred space, where love is proclaimed and promised. This love story proves that love truly endures. Peter and Gretchen have endured unspeakable sorrows and hardships, but now they're looking forward to a future together.

I know about unspeakable sorrow and indescribable joy. My Roderick and his love filled the cracks of my heart that had been broken and shattered. I looked at my parents and then Sam and Angel, and I had given up on ever having what they have—an enduring love. I could not bear to think of my future, for all I saw was more of the same—a monotonous, rhythmic life without passion or purpose, just existence. But Roderick brought passion and hope and meaning. And now we are about to embark on an adventure I've hardly had time to think about.

Life changes. The changes in my life over the last ten years would make a long list. Angel's right. Things never settle down. There is no real settling if you only consider the circumstances. Who can settle into those as fast as they change? But like Angel said, I've settled on the things that will remain constant: my faith, my love and commitment to Roderick, my values, and my family. Those things will keep me grounded and settled when seasons and circumstances change.

Gretchen and Peter are settling some things this day, right here at Rockwater. Lord, may this settling be their anchor for their future. Give them many years of joy to make up for what they missed. And like Sam said, let their hands and their hearts be bound together forever.

———•———

As the simple service came to an end, the minister said the last amen and announced, "The prayers have been prayed. The vows have been made. And what pleasure I have in presenting to you Mr. and Mrs. Peter Kornilov."

Peter and Gretchen turned to face their friends. Tears of joy. Applause. Sighs. Clicks of a camera. Then came the sudden burst from Bella. "Peter. My pappá!" followed by a fanfare of joyful sounds from the piano and roaring laughter from the wedding party.

Caroline took Roderick's arm and followed the bride and groom as they went to greet their friends and families. Her heart was full and satisfied. It was done and done well. Gretchen and Peter were now husband and wife.

Chapter Seventeen

Plans and Passions

Monday morning, October 4, at Rockwater

By Monday morning Rockwater, which had pulsated with people, music, and wedding excitement the past few days, was back to its normal state of tranquility. The Durham guests were all safely back home—Gretchen and her family to start a new season in their lives as they learned how to be family, and Sarah and her family to start a regular week as the family they were becoming.

After breakfast, Ned and Fred returned to the shop for more measuring, sawing, and loading the all-terrain vehicle with tools and lumber to start the gazebo. This quiet morning Roderick intended to take advantage of his first opportunity to have a meaningful conversation with Sam and Angel about his new plans. He invited Lilah to join them. Explaining his decisions and plans to others was new to him, but he felt these people deserved to know, and he didn't want to tell the story more than once.

At the far end of the room from the breakfast table, the morning room offered comfortable seating arranged for conversation around the fireplace. Natural light flooded the space through windows that flanked the fireplace and opened to forested rolling hills aflame with the blush of autumn. With chairs and windows positioned as they were, everyone had a view of gardens or hills. Roderick's mother had seen to that when she designed the house. This was his favorite room.

Sam and Angel settled on the sofa facing the fire. Angel grabbed the fluffiest of the pillows, put it in her short lap, and rested her arms. Lilah and Caroline took places on the love seat, and Roderick took the wing chair next to the hearth.

Roderick sat on the edge of his chair and began. "I'm most certain all of you know by now that there are about to be some significant changes in our lives. Angel, Caroline has told you, and I am assuming you told Sam. And of course, Lilah, you knew from years of experience that something was brewing, and you and Caroline have talked. But out of deep respect for each of you, I wanted to give you my reasons for doing what I have done and my ideas for the future."

Roderick continued as he retraced the of history of Adair Enterprises, starting with his grandfather and continued through his father's death when he had taken the helm of the family business. "As a single man with a single purpose, which was to see Adair Enterprises flourish and to increase the wealth left to Sarah and me by our parents, I have been driven solely to succeed the last fifteen years. And I'm blessed my focus on my work has paid off. I think you understand that work was my life. One merger brought on another, and yet it never seemed to be enough. But then came Caroline." He turned to her and smiled.

Sam chuckled and repeated Roderick's words. "But then came Caroline. Now that is one power-packed statement if I ever heard one, and believe me, I've heard many during my years on the bench. I imagine Caroline might look at her adult life and say, 'And then came Roderick.' You two were like gale-force winds of change in each other's lives. Fortunately, those winds breathed new life and love into both of you."

Caroline replied. "Gale-force winds followed by a tsunami. But I think it would have taken that for both of us to realize what was happening. We both were so guarded about feelings."

Roderick continued. "Agreed. I can tell you, after her first visit to Rockwater to play the parlor concert on her childhood piano, I was in turmoil—a changed man in turmoil."

Lilah laughed. "Why don't you just say it, Roderick? You were obsessed."

Roderick nodded to Lilah. "Lilah's right. She usually is. One encounter, and I could not imagine my life without Caroline. But this was a kind of merger I had no experience navigating. I was not known for caution in the business world, but I can assure you I was more than cautious with Caroline, not wanting to make a mistake. And honestly, I was afraid she would never feel the same way about me. But by God's grace, she did, and here we are. With Caroline, it's been one adventure after another, and now comes the next one." He paused. "I watched her as she built the Guatemalan Children's Choir from nothing, organizing, planning, gaining indigenous support, and I must tell you I was impressed."

Roderick went on to describe how he had observed so many communities where he owned businesses—communities dealing with identical problems, trying to financially support the many help agencies and connecting them to the poor and the working poor who needed their services. "I have some ideas about streamlining the efforts of these nonprofits, cutting costs, centralizing the administrative work, and yet making it easier for the people to know about and get the support they need. And I have ideas about programs that would prevent some of the issues these community leaders must address every day, be it healthcare, education, crime, or childcare. My goal is to start with a couple of communities, meet with the leaders, establish a plan, and create a model. We will learn from our successes and our failures. Then, if the venture is measurably successful, it could be improved and replicated around the country."

Angel squeezed the pillow she held across her middle and retorted, "Sounds like big ideas you have. Any ideas about where you intend to start?"

"Still doing research on that. Designing for success from the beginning is critical, so I need to start where I have friends who are like minded and who are willing to stick their necks out politically. It'll make the work easier. I think we'll start somewhere close to home." He turned to Caroline. "And I'm counting on my wife to help me. I'll need her to use her discernment, her wit, her people skills, and her ability to rally folks and organize them. And if that doesn't work, I suppose she'll just have to sing them a song and charm them."

Caroline breathed deeply. "Those are big shoes to fill, and I feel my feet are much too small. But you know I'll do my best to support you." She paused. "My daddy would say that it's all about stewardship, whether it's the money we give to the church or what we give back to our community. He taught me that whatever God has entrusted to us, we have responsibility to use it wisely for the greater good and not just to feather our own nests. I just could never have imagined having this kind of responsibility."

"Now you know why I was obsessed with this woman." Roderick winked at Sam. "And it doesn't hurt that she's beautiful too."

Sam agreed. "Sounds like you've seen something beyond her fragile beauty." He cocked his head as he often had on the judge's bench when he was about to make a pronouncement. "So, you're planning to give yourselves and your fortune away for the good of others. For ordinary folk, that sounds like the dream job, but for those of us who have borne the weight of responsibility for the lives of others, we know it's difficult, sometimes heartrending work. You'll be trying to engage some folks whose hearts are calloused and jaded, and then you'll be stepping into people's lives where they hurt. You're likely to see things and be in situations that are beyond your realm of experience."

Roderick eased back into his chair, relishing Sam's wisdom and understanding. It was as though Sam was reading his mind. "You're right. I've already experienced a bit of that. That is one of the reasons I can no longer just acquire wealth. I believe I have a responsibility—or as Caroline said it so beautifully, I must be a responsible steward of our blessings and try to help relieve some suffering."

"Did you consider usin' your fortune for anything like medical research or education?" Angel asked, almost hesitantly,

"Excellent question, and I did consider those options and more, but I find myself wanting to be involved and be more than just a check signer. I want to get my hands dirty, so to speak. Oh, we will still make our regular contributions to medical research and education, but I want to try something new, something that to my knowledge hasn't been done before."

Sam quickly retorted, "Well, you must be a good steward of that entrepreneurial spirit too. I'll look forward to some more conversation about all this. It'll be interesting to see how it develops. Unless you decide to run for office."

"Oh, Caroline told you about that too?" Roderick hesitated. "You know, at this point, I have little to no interest in politics, especially Washington politics. I think I'd be frustrated to the point of being an utter failure. Caroline and I will have conversations about a potential political future over the next few months, but right now, my dreams and passions are all about working with her and trying out my ideas in these communities. None of that requires someone to vote for me, and I don't have to work inside a contaminated, diseased, and inefficient bureaucracy."

Sam sat up. "Well said, Roderick. You nailed it. Follow your passions, ones that don't require someone else's permission." He chortled. "Well, maybe except Caroline's."

"I do believe I have that part straight now. I'm a slow learner in a few areas, but once I have it . . ." Roderick winked at Caroline.

Angel moved the pillow she'd been holding tightly and sat up straight. "Well, I've been listenin' and I've been quiet as long as I can be quiet. And if you don't mind my interruptin', I thought I might save you a bit of time and tell you I have it all figured out."

Sam shook his head. "Okay, here it comes. Listen up."

"Yes, you should listen to me. You'll start in Moss Point. There is no better place. You'd have Sam to help you build alliances in the community. No one knows the community and its institutions and organizations better than Sam and his cronies. And you did marry the town's darlin', and bringin' her home to do something like this would garner you more good will than you know. Then you have Ned and Fred and their fortune, and I do believe they could be persuaded. So, when do we get started?"

Sam led the laughter as he took Angel's hand. "This

little woman may be no taller than a fire hydrant, but she's power packed and never had trouble speaking her mind. And for the most part, her mind has always been good. And she didn't even mention that this would mean we'd get to see you two more often, but I'd bet my old fishing hat that was her first thought."

"I can tell you, her mind is resonating with mine," Roderick responded. "Actually, I was hoping that Moss Point would be one of our first models for the very reasons you mentioned, Angel."

Angel nodded. "And, Sam's right. It would mean we'd be seein' more of you, and it might mean that Sam's easy chair would last longer because he wouldn't be sittin' in it fourteen hours a day. He needs a project, and this one's right up near his judge's bench."

"This all sounds too wonderful. My mind's buzzing." Caroline smiled at Roderick. "I've taught most of the children whose parents sit on the very boards of the organizations and institutions you'd need to align with you. Do you really think Moss Point would be a good model?"

"I've done some initial research, and I think it just might. I was hoping to spend some time with Sam. My guess is that he's a walking answer book to most of my questions, especially the ones regarding the community's leaders. Having the right folks involved will be crucial to the success of the project."

Sam cleared his throat. "I can certainly help you there. And I can most certainly tell you the ones who will be first in line for the bandwagon, but they're the ones you'd better kick to the curb in a hurry."

"Sam! Don't you think that's a bit harsh?" Still, Angel snickered.

"I most certainly do not. And you know the very ones I'm talking about, and Miss Blue Eyes over there does too.

We don't have time for that kind of nonsense. I'm eighty-eight years old, and I've wasted years of my life sitting in boardrooms and committee meetings where next to nothing got done because of the inertia of one or two disgruntled pinheads. I'm done with spending my time like that. Roderick's my kind of man. He knows what he's doing. He knows how to make a decision, and I plan to direct him to men and women who will follow his lead."

Roderick felt a sudden baptism of affirmation. Since his father's death, there had been no father figure to offer the blessings he so needed, but Sam had become the one. "Thank you, Sam. You just got yourself appointed to chair that committee if that's how we decide to structure the governing group. We can talk later about how best to create that structure." He paused and slapped his hands to his knees. "Now, what do you say to taking a ride out to the pasture to see if Ned and Fred are making some progress? We'll give the ladies time to talk or do whatever it is that ladies do when men aren't around."

Sam pulled himself up from the sofa and grabbed his cane. "Lead on, sir. I'm right behind you." He took a few steps and stopped. "Just so you know, the minute we're out of the room, these two will be talking about what remarkable men they married." He snorted and kept walking.

Roderick turned to Caroline and took pleasure in the satisfied look on her face. "I trust you to speak truth, Sam. We'll be back in time for lunch, ladies, and we'll bring Ned and Fred with us."

———•———

Sam climbed into the passenger's side of Roderick's truck and propped his cane on the seat. "Ten years ago, I would have saddled one of your Kentucky thoroughbreds to ride through these rolling hills. When I was a boy, my dream was to ride in the rodeo."

Roderick cranked the truck and put it in gear. "And ten years ago, I had given up horseback riding, so you would have ridden alone, my friend."

"Too busy building your empire?"

"I was busy, but that wasn't the reason. I grew up with horses. Both my parents were excellent equestrians, and my mother had me on a horse soon after I could walk. We would take long rides all over this property. That's how I got to know every hill, valley, and stream."

Sam could always smell when there was more to the story. "So, you kept the stables and kept breeding horses, but you gave up riding?"

"I thought maybe Caroline might have told you why."

"If I know Caroline, and I do, she rationalized that it was your story to tell and not hers. But she has told us that you've been taking her horseback riding. So, for whatever reason, I'm glad to know you're back in the saddle."

Sam noticed the tightening muscles in Roderick's face. Years on the bench had taught him to read faces for things unsaid.

"Ten years ago, I couldn't have told you this story either, but I'll tell you now. My mother died from a tragic fall from her horse during a thunderstorm. Afternoon storms can come up quickly in these hills in the summertime."

Roderick paused. Sam remained silent. He had learned that lesson from the bench too. If he waited, more of the story would come. It always did.

Roderick continued. "I was only ten. The two of us were out riding, not realizing a storm was brewing behind us. When it blew in, it was a quick and fierce one. We galloped, trying to make it to the covered bridge my father had built for such times, but we didn't make it. Lightning—close lightning—and Mother's horse bolted, catapulting her into the boulders of the creek bank. She died in my arms, making me promise I wouldn't leave her. I watched the blood from her head wound washing away with the rain until there was no more red. I wanted to ride for help, but I kept my promise. I stayed through the storm until the stable hand found us."

Sam waited again, but Roderick didn't speak. "I'm sorry, Roderick. That's something no ten-year-old son should ever experience. I can tell how much you loved her, and it certainly explains why you chose not to ride again."

"The doctor assured us that with her injuries she would have died anyway, but I still felt responsible. I didn't utter a word for a year. All the life left Rockwater when my mother died. In his grief my father was never the same, and Sarah was left to mother and sister me. She was my comfort and my voice when I had neither." Roderick slowed the truck. "I think her experiences with me motivated her to become a child psychologist."

"But that wasn't the end of the story."

"No, Sam, it wasn't, but I thought it was. Rockwater is full of life again because of Caroline. And I'm riding again and teaching her to ride. But you know, I'll give my life to protect her."

"I know, and I believe you. Your love for our dear Caroline is a gift not only to you, but it's a gift to Angel and me too. We wondered if Caroline would ever smile again. Oh, she tried, and she did make some beautiful music. But we knew the music was no longer in her like it had been. But it returned with her love for you."

"Yes, sir. Neither of us take our love for granted. And I know how much she loves you and Angel, and I wanted Ned and Fred to build this gazebo to remind her of you and the gazebo in the park you gave to Moss Point." Roderick pointed in the distance. "See that big oak on that rise straight ahead?"

"I do. Looks like that one's been around for a while."

"A few hundred years, and Caroline's gazebo will be nestled in its shade." Roderick drove on a few hundred yards and parked in the shade of the oak. "This is Caroline's iris garden I had planted for her last Christmas. It was something this spring and will just get better as the years go by. Let's see how much progress Ned and Fred have made."

Roderick got out of the truck and came around to help Sam. Approaching, Sam heard Fred whistling as he sawed a board between two sawhorses. Ned stopped his hammering and met them.

"My goodness. We didn't expect to see you this mawnin'."

Sam put his hat on. "Roderick had to come and see what progress you've made."

"Now, I kin tell ya that this here foundation made our work easy. We justa buildin' the framework to hide the foundation now, and we might git the railin' up this afternoon."

Sam walked closer to see the foundation. "Something tells me there's a story in this."

"You know how Mr. Roderick is. Ain't nothing too good fer Miss Caroline. I sent 'im the plans and the measurements, and I kin tell ya, they was rough, hand-done plans. And Mr. Roderick showed 'em to somebody who could figger 'em out. Then somebody poured the foundation and filled it with river rock from the property. That floor is somethin' all right. So now, we're just coverin up the ugly with some of this good wood. That's what Fred's cuttin' over there."

Sam noticed Fred never looked up. He just kept sawing and whistling.

Ned added, "We changin' a few thangs to make it differ from the one in the park and to make it special fer Miss Caroline. And Fred? Why he's just plain gobsmacked at havin' all these tools. I ain't sure you're gonna git rid of 'im, Mr. Roderick. He's done asked me if you have anythin' else we can do and just stay fer a while."

Sam laughed. "You can forget that notion, Ned. As soon as the last coat of white paint's on that gazebo, we're flying home to Moss Point. We all have work to do." He gave Roderick a questioning look, and he liked it that Roderick understood and spoke.

"Sam's right, Ned. You'll be seeing a lot of Caroline and me in the months ahead, as we'll be starting a project in Moss Point, and we will need your help there. I think you asked to have a board meeting while you're here. Caroline and Sam will tell you all about it then."

"Well, I guess I'll jus' be gobsmacked too. I hope it's a big project and'll keep you there till Fred and me go home to heaven."

Sam smiled. "What Roderick's planning will hopefully outlast us all. He's a man of passion and plans." He patted Roderick on the back.

"But I don't have a plan for keeping this surprise from Caroline until Christmas." He gestured at their work. "She's already asking to see the gazebo, but I don't want her to see it until Christmas. So, Ned, if you have any ideas about that, I'd like to hear them."

Ned retorted, "I'd say keepin' Miss Caroline away fer that long is 'bout like keepin' Diesel from chasing coons."

Sam chuckled when he saw the look on Roderick's face.

"Diesel, you say?" Roderick asked.

"Yeh. Diesel's my coon dog, and he's got . . ." Ned looked puzzled. "What was that you said, Mr. Sam, about passions? Well, ol' Diesel's got passions, too, and they got rings 'round their tails."

Chapter Eighteen

———— ♦ ————

Schemes and Scraps

Monday afternoon in Melk, Austria

Iris was at her desk pouring over the hotel receipts records when her phone rang. She answered. "Iris Brandhof, how may I help you?"

A gruff voice barked. "Ms. Brandhof, Herbert Wurm here again."

Iris's pulse quickened. Her voice was not warm, nor was it sure. "Yes, Mr. Wurm. I have been expecting to hear from you since I deposited the funds into your account. Do you have the information about Nicolai Kornilov that I am seeking?"

"I do not have all the information as of this moment, but I am narrowing my leads. I will engage the services of one of my associates in Germany to do the follow-up, but that will require more funds."

Iris felt lightheaded and queasy. Mr. Wurm was such a despicable man, and his name suited him. She concluded that he either knew nothing and was taking advantage of her because he could, or he had more information than he was letting on.

She had spent the afternoon working on the hotel's financial records, wondering how to juggle the reports to cover the money she had taken from the hotel receipts days ago. She was in a suffocating bind, and the bind was growing tighter. She had already committed grand larceny. Peter was not answering or returning her calls, and she did not have the funds personally to cover her theft. Seeing no way of acquiring more funds, she answered him hastily. "Mr. Wurm, there will be no more money until I have information. If you have leads, then I think it is only fair that you provide me with that information in return for the money I have already given to you."

His voice was gravelly. "That is not how this works. You gave me nothing. You pay me for results, not leads. I will get the job done, and the follow-up to complete this job requires more money."

"If I am paying you for results, why are you hiring someone else to do your work? Why not go there yourself?"

"Do you want this done quickly, madam?" She heard the disdain in his voice.

"Of course, I do."

"Then this is the quickest and surest way to find Mr. Kornilov. My contact is in country, has connections, and will cost you less than sending me there."

So, Nicolai is not in Austria. "I see. But how much?"

He told her. Her queasiness quickly turned to nausea, and her brow and upper lip broke out in perspiration—the kind of perspiration only shock and fear can bring. "I will give this more thought and get back to you in a couple of days."

"In a couple of days with proper funds, I could have your precious Nicolai located, and my job would be finished."

She wanted to believe him. "I understand your position, but you must understand mine. I am a single woman without unlimited funds. I would need to make arrangements, and that takes time."

"Your time. Your decision. I will call again for your answer in two days." His statement was followed by an abrupt click.

Iris held the phone, gripping it tightly, squeezing it as she would like to squeeze Herbert Wurm's neck until he no longer had breath. After a moment she slammed the phone onto its cradle and rose from her desk. She made her familiar stride to the window overlooking the hotel restaurant and gardens, staring as though she might find an answer among the tree limbs and canopies.

No answer was to be had. Her biggest problem now was to get the money to replace what she had embezzled from the hotel. With no response from Peter, that left only one option—approaching her husband's children who had inherited his wealth and who despised her. What story could she concoct that would persuade them to give her the money she needed? She had vowed never to speak to them following the settling of the estate and their heinous accusations of her. Where had they been the last three years of their father's life when he required constant care? She had looked after him, but they got the money that should have been hers. After skulking since the reading of the will, she could not see approaching them as an option.

Maybe there was another way. Since she had not deposited the stolen money into her account, there was no way it could be traced to her. She had been careful about that. Only she and two other employees had access to the receipts. Finn worked the front desk, and Isla took care of restaurant receipts, which were mostly cash. Neither of them knew the total amount, only what they each delivered to her daily, sometimes twice a day.

Iris reasoned she could report the discrepancy as though she'd discovered it, implying that someone else had taken it. She would insinuate that Isla was the thief. She was young and single. Finn had a family and needed his job. Maybe the owners would want to keep the crime quiet and allow Isla to repay the funds rather than prosecute her.

Iris paced from the window across the room to her desk and back to the window as she often did when her thoughts were fermenting. Her plan might work, but it would take some intricate book work. Perhaps there was an easier way—

A robbery. She had lodged past complaints to the owner about acquiring a safe for the daily receipts when going to the bank over the weekend or holidays was not an option. The only current protection for the money was a brown leather bag placed inside her locked desk drawer. A robbery could really work.

Iris had just finished tallying the receipts from the weekend before Wurm called, and she knew those funds would more than cover what she had taken. She could use the stolen funds to replace what she had taken earlier and use the rest to pay Wurm the next installment. Her mind was a centrifuge, spinning and separating ideas until she had refined the plan.

She would call Finn into her office for some other matter at the end of her workday before she left to go home. While he was there, she would make certain he saw her place the leather pouch holding the cash into her bottom desk drawer and lock it, explaining that it was late and the bank was closed. Then she would casually talk about occupancy and mention that she had noticed a certain man frequenting the hotel garden restaurant over the last few days and inquire if he was a hotel guest or if Finn had noticed or seen him. She would describe him as a seedy character that made her uneasy. That should set the stage.

The boutique hotel was quiet after midnight, especially on Mondays when occupancy was usually low. She would return through the back entrance of the hotel and take the back hallway into her office unnoticed. She had tools that could easily make her office door appear tampered with, and a claw hammer to pry open the locked desk drawer holding the cash.

She would arrive the next morning find the break-in, and her response of shock and fear would leave no doubt this was a criminal act—the cash bag gone, the opened file drawers, strewn papers, a few personal items taken. The local newspaper would carry the story of a robbery at the Hotel zur Post. Surely they would quote her, allowing her the opportunity to hint at the suspect.

The local authorities would search for the phantom criminal while Herbert Wurm's associate was locating Nicolai. All her problems solved.

As planned, she called Finn to her office on some pretense and made sure he saw her lock the bag of cash into the bottom drawer. After he left, she looked at the paperwork on her desk. No reason to tidy up since she would just return to create a staged mess of things in a few hours. Instead, she went to the restaurant for a coffee before leaving the office. "Good evening, Isla. I will take my coffee to go. I am so very tired, and I am hoping this will give me enough energy for my walk home. There is so much work to be done on Monday that it makes the weekend not worth staying away."

"Yes, I will prepare your coffee just as you like it, Ms. Brandhof. I believe we have leftover potatoes that we did not use at lunch. If you would like them for your dinner, I will put some in a box."

Iris did not hesitate. "Yes, please. That will make for an easy dinner after such a hard day." Actually, it relieved her not to think about dinner, and she was not certain with the queasiness she still felt that she would be able to eat anyway.

She took her coffee and the box from Isla and thanked her, expressing more gratitude than usual for Isla's hard work and diligent management. Then she strode through the hotel lobby to make certain she was seen before she left. "Good night, Finn. It is so late I thought you would be gone."

"Yes, ma'am. I should be, but the night clerk had car trouble and is running late."

"Karl, again?"

"Yes. He seems to have more than his share of troubles."

"I am sorry to hear that. I will see you in the morning." She walked through doors of the hotel onto the sidewalk and made the turn up the hill to walk to her cottage. She was relieved. With what she knew of Karl, he would be asleep at the front desk by midnight. She walked, sipped her coffee, and went over the details of her plan.

Iris's obsession to find Nicolai and her feelings of not being appreciated or paid sufficiently eased what little conscience she had left. She was always the victim. Her husband had died and left her little. Peter had refused to help her and Nicolai years ago, and Nicolai could not bear to return to Melk after his prison term and so had disappeared from her life. Peter ignored her calls. Her employer treated her as less than she deserved. And now Herbert Wurm, her closest link to finding Nicolai, could be taking advantage of her.

No more being the victim. Her plan would work, and neither Finn nor Isla would be implicated. The amount of money she would take was a serious crime, but the money was not significant money to the owner. She had devised the perfect way to cover her previous theft and get what she wanted most: Nicolai.

———•———

The early evening clouds drooped low on the horizon as Iris reached home. Usually, the walk home cleared her head, but not this evening. She balanced her coffee and box of potatoes as she unlocked the deadbolt, entered, and then closed and relocked the heavy wooden door and leaned her back against it, breathing deeply the relief of being within her cottage walls. The place was meager, but it was comfortable, and it suited her.

She removed her green jacket and plaid scarf and hung them in the hall closet. While there, she shuffled through the garments until she found her black raincoat. No need for a scarf since the coat had a hood. She took the coat off its hanger and draped it over the back of the chair near the door, ready for her night's covert work.

She changed from her business attire into dark-gray pants and a sweater and headed to the storage closet on the back porch to look for the tools she needed. The claw hammer hung between two nails on the post, and the crowbar sat in a barrel in the corner. They and sundry tools had been left in the closet by the former owner.

When she'd gathered all she needed—determining that a hammer and crowbar could be easily concealed under her coat so that she had no need for a bag—she returned to the kitchen and placed the tools on the small kitchen table next to the window. Her walk home from the office in the fresh air had not cleared her head but had cleared her queasiness, and she found herself hungry. She fried two pieces of bacon, removed them from the pan, and added the leftover potatoes

Isla had given her with a handful of chopped onions. After letting them cook and brown a bit, she plated the potatoes, topped them with the crumbled bacon, and was about to crack an egg when her front bell rang. No one ever visited her, and she was certainly not expecting a visitor tonight. She removed the skillet from the stove, wiped her hands, and went to the door. It was her neighbor from down the lane.

"Good evening, Iris. I am sorry to come unannounced so late in the day. I was watching for you to come home."

Iris forced a smile to cover her frustration. "Your visit is not a problem. Would you like to come in?"

"Only for a moment, for it is growing dark earlier these days, and I felt a few sprinkles on my walk here. I must return home to finish preparing dinner for my husband." The woman pulled an envelope from her jacket pocket. "This was delivered to me by mistake today. I was simply bringing it to you. Our new mailman is making fewer mistakes these days than when he started a few weeks ago."

"Yes, he is." Iris took the envelope. "Bringing the letter is most kind of you. Thank you."

Her neighbor turned toward the door. "You are welcome." She stopped, looking in the direction of the chair. "You must be going out, and I do believe you will need this raincoat, for the showers are coming."

Iris fumbled for an answer. "Oh no, I am not going out this evening. I have it out for my walk to work in the morning in case it is raining. Tonight I will have my dinner and retire to read. I have an early day tomorrow. The first few days of the month are always the busiest at my office." Iris reached for the doorknob and opened the door.

"Ah, yes, I understand. Good evening, Iris."

"Good evening, and oh yes, it is beginning to drizzle. Thank you again for bringing the letter."

Iris closed the door and leaned against it again, this time in irritation at herself. She convinced herself it was nothing. People left their jackets out all the time. She could only hope her neighbor had not seen the hammer and crowbar on the kitchen table.

She returned to the kitchen and quickly fried an over-easy egg to top her potatoes. A plate of potatoes, a serving of mountain cheese on top, a slice of crusty bread, a piping hot cup of tea, and her dinner was complete. She ate in silence, walking through every step of her intended robbery, replaying it like a movie in her mind. She decided to call Finn to make certain Karl had made it in to work. Finn was more diligent in making rounds through the hotel hallways overnight, never sleeping on the job. Karl was not. She could only hope Karl would answer the front-desk phone. Checking on the hotel and employees in the evenings was not unusual for her and should not raise any suspicions.

Iris cleaned her dishes and looked at the clock on her small desk in the corner. Ten after eight. At least four hours before she could enact her plan. On her way to her desk to call the hotel, she walked to living room where her black raincoat lay draped over the chair. She put it on, tied the belt tightly, and confirmed the foot-long crowbar would fit in her sleeve and the hammer in the inside pocket. They did. No need of the encumbrance of a bag, which would only raise suspicions if anyone saw her.

She sat at her desk and rehearsed again every detail from turning out her lights around ten o'clock as though she had turned in for the night to dressing and leaving in the dark. If she left shortly after midnight, with a fifteen-minute walk to the hotel and no more than fifteen minutes to do the deed, and then another fifteen-minute walk home, she should be safely in bed by one o'clock. No. That was too early. The hotel would be quiet for certain, but her neighbors could still be up and might see her. She would wait until one o'clock. Home by two with enough cash to solve her problems and then some.

Iris picked up the receiver, dialed the front-desk number, and held her breath. Five rings and no answer. That was not acceptable as hotel business practice, and it was most annoying at the moment.

Sixth ring. Karl answered. No less irritated, she easily played her role as a concerned supervisor, having lived in pretense most of her adult life. "Good evening, Karl. I was calling to make certain you were able to get in to work or if I needed to return to relieve Finn for the night shift."

"Yes, Ms. Brandhof. I am here, and all is well. The hotel is quiet. Finn left an hour ago."

She refrained from asking him why it had taken so long to answer the phone if the hotel was quiet. "Very well. Then I will ready myself to retire for the evening. I have an early day tomorrow to finish the reports. Good night."

"Good night, Ms. Brandhof, and have a pleasant evening."

A pleasant evening? No. But an evening that would change her life and fortune.

An attempt to sleep would be futile. Her mind raced. It was as if someone kept hitting the replay button on the film reel of the entire act in her mind. She could see every detail from slipping unnoticed into the back hallway to using the crowbar to pry open her desk drawer. Her pulse remained rapid and her breathing shallow as though she were actually there.

For distraction, she went to her bedroom, picked up the book on her bedside table, and returned to her chair. This was not a night for the distraction of television. She craved silence. She opened the book, tried to read, and found herself rereading sentences and turning pages without knowing what she had read. The hum of the refrigerator, usually unnoticed, sounded more like a hive of bees, drowning out the sound of the rain on the clay-tile roof. Her senses were heightened. For the next two hours, she glanced from the pages of her book to the clock on the desk, only getting up to make herself a cup of tea to settle her nerves. She turned out the lights at ten and sat in the darkness next to the window, mesmerized by the raindrops trickling down the windowpane, joining the other droplets until they became small, determined streams.

At half past midnight, she could wait no longer. She put her teacup on the kitchen counter and picked up her keys off her desk. She put on her raincoat, galoshes, and made certain the hammer was secure in the inside pocket of her raincoat and the crowbar was comfortably up her left sleeve. An umbrella would be an encumbrance she did not need. She opened and closed the door quietly, locked it, and looked up and down the street for any activity.

Nothing.

She started her walk up the hill, committed to plans and hoping that she would go unnoticed by her neighbor's dog. She walked with deliberation, and in ten minutes she was in town. No one was out this late on a rainy Monday night. As she neared the hotel, she took the back alleys to reach the rear entrance so as not to be seen by anyone in the lobby. Her hands steady, she inserted the key into the back door and stepped inside, leaving the door unlocked so that she could escape quickly. She pushed the raincoat hood back and wiped the rain from her cheeks. She was aware of every breath and every step as her galoshes left watery prints on the wooden floor leading to her office.

Iris had just rounded the corner and was only twelve feet from her office when she heard whistling. Whistling? It was one o'clock in the morning. Who would be whistling?

She was totally exposed in the hallway without a place to hide. Nowhere. And out of nowhere came Karl around the corner, almost bumping into her.

He jumped back. Startled, he gasped. "Ms. Brandhof? Is that you?"

Although more surprised than he, she said calmly, "Yes, Karl. It is I."

"But it is one o'clock in the morning. I was making my rounds as you have instructed me to do three times during the night. Are you coming to check up on me?"

Her thoughts gyrating, she answered, "Of course not, Karl. I trust you to do a good job. I could not sleep, and I have so much work to do that I thought I would come in and work a couple of hours. I was just on my way to find you and let you know I would be in my office. The winter will be upon us soon, and there will be no more late-night walks. I do not mind the rain, but I cannot abide the cold and the snow."

"Yes, I do understand about the cold." He approached her. "Let me help you remove that raincoat. You are dripping."

She jerked away. "Thank you, Karl, but I think I shall keep it on until I warm up a bit. Continue your rounds. I will be in my office working for a while."

"Yes, I will do just that. Could I bring you coffee or tea?"

"No, thank you, Karl. I prefer not to be disturbed while I am working."

"Yes, Ms. Brandhof." Karl continued his walk down the hall and returned to his whistling.

Iris used her keys to open the door. She closed it quietly and locked it even though she wanted to slam it and scream. Then she slid out of her coat, letting it, the hammer, and crowbar drop to her ankles. The heavy objects made a dull thud against the wooden planks. Angry, frustrated, desperate tears filled her eyes. Her teeth and fists clenched, she paced in silence, screaming on the inside.

My plans. My perfectly devised plans to solve all my problems thwarted by that half-wit, Karl. Why this night to slink the hallways making his rounds when most nights I know he sleeps? He just robbed me of my way out. Now I have no way to replace the money I took, and no money to pay Mr. Wurm to finish his job. No way to get to Nicolai. I cannot plan another robbery. I am already a day late with the deposit. And I am stuck here for at least an hour pretending to work. Why is it the world and fate are so cruel to me? First it was my parents, then Nicolai and Peter. And even though I lived in luxury for a few years, they were wasted years playing nursemaid to a sick old man who left me little more than destitute. What have I done to deserve all this misery? My life is the scraps brushed from the tables of everyone else's feasts.

She sat in her desk chair and looked at the financial report. Her eyes moved from her desk to the locked drawer beside her right knee—the drawer holding her answer.

If Karl did not exist, I could have the money.

Chapter Nineteen

———◆———

Stirring the Pot and
Doing Business

Late Friday afternoon, October 8, in Melk

*I*ris stood at her stove stirring the pot of potato soup. Isla had given her more leftovers from the restaurant, and she could not bear another plate of potatoes, cheese, and bacon. She had stopped at the market for fresh bread and vegetables. The soup would last the weekend. With all the events of this week, she had little interest in cooking and less interest in eating alone in a restaurant. She ate to survive, and only her obsession with finding Nicolai made her want to live.

Her late-night attempt at a robbery on Monday had been the perfect plan until Karl decided to do his job and ran into her in the hallway after midnight. He'd given no indication that he was suspicious, but Karl was not smart or crafty. Fretting all week, she had continued to alter the receipts reports to cover her earlier theft, but she knew that she could not keep it up. That much money would eventually be missed. At least she had not added murder to her crimes.

When Wurm called on Thursday, she asked for more time and begged for information. All he would tell her was that Nicolai was in Berlin. She knew she had little to no chance of finding him in a city of nearly four million. Wurm was right. Locating Nicolai would require a local with knowledge of records and documents. And for all she knew, Nicolai could have changed his identity. But, Wurm had convinced her that Nicolai would be found. Believing that fact was all she needed to keep pursuing a way to get the funds.

Iris had left the hotel early for her Friday-afternoon stop at the bank. After making the deposit, she spoke with the clerk about a personal loan. Her bank account was at another bank, but she thought she would ask, not wanting her own financial institution to be aware of such a transaction. Melk was a small town.

Her inquiry produced six pages of information and forms to be completed. The clerk made it clear that a personal loan would require collateral and indicated Iris would likely be approved if she owned her home and had a job with a stable job history. There was hope. The loan would get her what she wanted: a clean slate at the hotel and Nicolai.

She continued stirring the soup until the carrots and onions were tender, knowing that cream did not always rise and that it often stuck to the pot if left unattended. She poured herself a bowl and sat alone at her table on Friday evening with a stack of bank forms and a box of photos for company. Photos of Nicolai and her. Photos of the happiest days of her life. Determined and resolute, she would stop at nothing to find that happiness again. The thick, creamy soup warmed her stomach but did nothing to thaw her frigid spirit.

Late Friday morning, October 8, in Durham

Gretchen was stirring the pot of Austrian garlic soup when she heard Peter come through the front door. Married almost a week, knowing Peter entered her front door as her husband still caught her in the realm of disbelief. She washed her hands, dried them quickly, and met him with a kiss when he entered the kitchen.

Peter returned the kiss and ran his finger down her cheek. "Mrs. Kornilov, you have a way of making me think that you missed me and are happy to see me."

"I am most happy to see you. And yes, I did miss you, Mr. Kornilov. Lunch is almost ready."

Peter put his papers down on the kitchen table and removed his jacket. "I could smell the garlic when I opened the gate. You are spoiling me preparing all my favorites. You won my heart three decades ago, so there is no need to indulge me with these delicious meals."

"What makes you think the soup is for you? Garlic soup is my favorite. The girls do not like the pungent odor or taste, so I never make it. I am glad to have someone to share it with, and I am most happy that it is you, my love." She pulled the toasted croutons from the oven. "Did you have a productive meeting with the attorney?"

Peter sat down in the chair that had now become his at the end of the table. "Yes, I did. I am most grateful for George's recommendation of this attorney. Mr. Reynolds is familiar with the bakery since he helped you set up the business, and we are blessed that he has a partner with knowledge of immigration law because of his work with foreign students at the university. This firm will be helpful with the bakery transaction and with my citizenship."

"If your meeting was successful, then I feel better about our being apart this morning. It was the first time since we were married last Saturday that we have been apart." She continued plating their lunch: sliced pears and figs with crumbled gorgonzola cheese on a bed of greens topped with chopped walnuts, a bowl of steaming garlic soup with homemade croutons, and a slice of bread.

"My plan is that we are never apart now that we are life partners. But I must ask you one last time, are you certain about being business partners?"

She put the plate in front of him. "I am most certain. You are a successful businessman, and I am a simple baker. Karina has been helpful in assuming many duties with the business, and she has creative ideas, but honestly, I do not see her running the bakery as her profession. I hear the words of her heart, and I think she dreams of being a teacher. I want her to do whatever would make her happy, and to have you guiding the business and choosing staff will be welcome for both of us. It will free her to pursue a teaching career. You heard her excitement Wednesday night when we spoke of the possibility of your help with the bakery."

Gretchen sat down at the place to Peter's left. He automatically took her hand, thanked God for the meal and being able to share it together, and kissed her hand after the amen.

He inhaled the steam from the garlic soup, picked up the slice of crusty bread, and reached for the butter. "You have made more bread this morning."

"Yes. I enjoy bread making, and there is nowhere in Durham to buy this kind of bread—the bread we enjoy at home. People in the south prefer softer breads."

He wiped his mouth after the first buttered bite. "Then you must teach our bakers to make this bread and allow us to introduce it to our customers. This is the way we expand our offerings for your customers. And then come the cheeses and the condiments—things I know from my import-export business."

"As Karina reminds me, ideas like that will make our bakery different from the other bakeries in town. I have given myself this week to be at home with you, but I must get back to the bakery on Monday for a few days before we leave for Austria. I fear Karina is working much too hard."

He laid his spoon down gently and wiped his mouth. "Gretchen, above everything, I want you to be happy, but my idea of being together is not getting up and working at the bakery every day. Yes, we will own it, and we will make certain it is run properly, but I do not wish you to rise before dawn to bake pastries every morning."

She stirred her soup. "I agree. We will spend our time together, but I must not forsake Karina. She has hired more help because I am not there."

"Karina is doing an impressive job, and she is doing it smartly. Hiring more help is the way she can grow the business. She is hiring students from the university who need jobs and training them to do the baking. And she says the early-morning hours are good for them. The full-time, experienced help can work longer hours and can handle the front after the others have gone to class. This plan will work."

"Now that you explain it, I believe Karina's plan will work. And to think my Karina is helping other students by giving them jobs."

"And do not overlook the job and life skills she is teaching them as they learn to bake." He picked his spoon up again. "Enough said about work. Let's talk about our trip."

"Our trip to Innsbruck. I feel like it is springtime in my soul, but will it be cold there?"

"It will be cool and colorful. We begin our springtime in October, the most beautiful month of the entire year in Innsbruck. I shall take you on the short drive over to Tyrol. I go there every year for their festivals as the cattle return from the alpine country. They celebrate with food and music and wine. You will want to return every October. There will be crowds but not like in Innsbruck during the winter ski season."

Gretchen swallowed the last spoonful of her soup. "It is a relief that I will not need to shop for heavy winter clothing. The weather sounds much like it is in Melk and the Wachau Valley this time of year."

"Yes, it is. You will only need a light jacket, a couple of sweaters, and comfortable walking shoes. Let us plan to travel light. If you would like something new, we shall shop in Innsbruck, and we will leave those clothes there for our return."

"For our many returns."

"Yes, in the winter, in the spring, and in the summer. Dining in the restaurants in the evening is quite casual, and I plan to take you to some of my favorite cafés where the food is only surpassed by the magnificent views. I have walked into these places through the years, always to sit alone at my favorite table. It will make me so happy to enter with you on my arm and introduce you as my wife to my friends there."

"To be in all those lovely places with you and to see my family again—how can it be? Oh my, how God has blessed us! I was so excited to receive an email from Elfi this morning. We will not be traveling to Český Krumlov after all. They have made plans to meet us in Melk, and Pappá has requested that we attend services at the church on Sunday. He has already asked Pastor Tobias to have a prayer of blessing for our marriage after the service, and Jana, Elfi's doctor friend, wants to have a celebration dinner for us while Elfi and Yannick and the girls are there." Gretchen felt herself beaming as she imagined what it would be like to return to her homeland as a married couple. "I do hope that you are as happy about these plans as I am."

"How could I not be happy seeing the smile their plans put on your angelic face? Yes, I am more than happy." He took her hand and brought it to his lips for a tender kiss. "Finally, we are family as we should have been from the beginning."

She whispered his words. "Family as we should have been."

———•———

Friday afternoon at Rockwater

The week after the wedding had passed quickly at Rockwater. While Ned and Fred worked long hours to finish the gazebo, Caroline had enjoyed her private time with Angel and was pleased that Roderick had spent those same hours with Sam, using Sam as a sounding board for some of his ideas for the Moss Point project. As important as Roderick's new venture was, she was determined not to allow it to consume all their time and conversations. There would be time for that in their future trips to Moss Point. But the gazebo was now finished, and they would be flying Sam and Angel and the twin brothers back to Moss Point on Saturday.

Lilah had left early for her grandson's football game, but not before she almost finished preparation for their evening meal. Caroline was alone in the kitchen. She stood at the stove, stirring a pot of navy-bean soup Lilah had made special for Ned and Fred. Angel had told her it was their favorite soup. The salad was made, the cornbread was in the oven, and Lilah's Kahlúa mocha layer cake was waiting to be cut for dessert.

They would gather around the table in the morning room for their last supper together and a board meeting—the meeting Ned had requested—to follow. She wondered if Ned even knew what transpired at a board meeting, but since he had requested it, she was obliging. Only the official meeting would be around the supper table after dessert.

Although there had been discussion about Roderick's new work every evening after supper, Ned and Fred had listened but had little to say and asked no questions. They usually excused themselves not long after the evening meal. They rose early every morning and worked all day, and an early bedtime suited them. Or maybe it was the big-screen television in the tack room that called their names.

Ned and Fred, in clean clothes with hair slicked down, knocked on the kitchen door at exactly six o'clock just as Caroline knew they would. They joined Sam and Angel in the morning room while Caroline plated the food and Roderick helped get them to the table. It felt homey for Caroline to walk into the room and see the food on the table and hear Ned telling Angel and Sam about their last day of work.

She wished Lilah could have heard Ned. "That Miss Lilah. She's really somethin'. She warshed all our clothes and ironed our pants and shirts. Why, them pants and shirts ain't never see'd no iron b'fore! What in the world is the use in ironin' a shirt unless you gonna wear it to church? Her goodness nearly takes the door off the hinges."

Caroline giggled as she put the plate of cornbread on the table. "Well, I can tell you, Ned, if you think Lilah's doing your laundry took the door off the hinges, wait until you see what she's prepared for your supper—your favorite navy-bean soup and cornbread and a chocolate cake like you've never had before. It's Roderick's favorite and soon to be yours."

Ned cackled. "Fred, we better git our tools ready to put the door back on the hinges if that's what we's having fer supper. How in the world did Miss Lilah know navy-bean soup is our favorite? Mama made it all the time. Her secret was a ham hock. Don't nobody cook like that no more."

Having been there for almost two weeks, they all took the same seats for every meal. Roderick invited them to the table and seated Angel and Caroline. "Lilah does. We eat a lot of ham around here just so Lilah can make soup. I'm looking forward to this bowl myself."

When they finished the meal, Caroline served coffee with the cake and glasses of milk to Ned and Fred, ice cold just like they liked it.

Ned sighed. "Now Miss Angel, you do know we like yo'r cakes and all them sweets Hattie makes, but this here chocolate cake ain't nothing like I ever had. I know there's somethin' secret and special in this cake, ain't there, Miss Caroline? I know it like I know when it's time to plant peas."

Caroline grinned. "You'd be right about that, Ned. No secret, just special. It's fine dark chocolate with about a half a cup of Kahlúa."

"I don't believe I know what that is. Where does it grow?"

Caroline watched the grin spread across Angel's face. "Well, to answer your question, I'd say it's most likely grown in Brazil—the coffee beans for the coffee flavor and the sugar cane that makes the rum."

Ned's eyes blared as they met his twin's equally wide eyes. "Rum? You mean like likker?"

Roderick rescued Caroline. "Kahlúa is a liqueur. But

you can think of it like the vanilla flavoring Hattie puts in her pound cake. Kahlúa just gives the cake and frosting its flavor of coffee."

"It's mighty fine, ain't it, Fred?"

Fred smiled and nodded in agreement.

When everyone had finished and Caroline had returned from clearing the table, Sam spoke. "I suppose it's time to convene this board meeting, and Ned has asked me to call the meeting to order. All the board members are present, and Roderick, you and Angel are invited guests." Then he turned to Ned. "Ned, you asked for this meeting, so I'm turning it over to you."

Ned cleared his throat and sat up a bit straighter. "First of all, I want to thank you for invitin' us and allowin' us to build Miss Caroline's gazebo. We tried to do our best. But I'm thinkin' I'm gonna have a time winklin' Fred away from the tack room. He's done gone and feathered his nest in that comfortable bed, all propped up watchin' that big-screen television."

He looked straight at Caroline. "But you cain't see the gazebo till Christmas or whenever Mr. Roderick decides to take you to see it. You gotta promise you ain't gonna be sneakin' and peekin' like me and Fred use to do around Christmas when Ma put somethin' under the Christmas tree. Then you can let us know if we need to come back and do a better job."

Caroline shook her head. "If you two built it, I know it's perfect and it will last for generations. That's just how you do things. But I do have a few other things in mind for you to build around here if you'd come back."

The grin on Fred's face said he was ready to return.

"Yes, that is why I asked you," Roderick added. "You are the best, and I wanted nothing but the best for my wife."

Ned spoke again. "Like I said, we tried to do our best

like Pa taught us." He hesitated. "Now I got Mr. Sam to check on things at the bank b'fore we left. Our money for the scholarships jest keeps pilin' up. We gotta do somethin' about that. Me and Fred don't need no more money. We been listenin' to all Mr. Roderick's and Mr. Sam's talk about this new thing you gonna be doin' in Moss Point to help poor folks. We wanna help. So, Mr. Roderick, you jest tell us what you need, and it'll be comin' yo'r way."

Caroline took Roderick's arm as he spoke. "Ned, that is quite generous of you, but right now I cannot tell you what we need. And besides, Caroline and I have the funds to cover those needs. Your money does so much good in educating students."

"It ain't right. Moss Point ain't even yo'r town. We take care of our own in Moss Point. Me and Fred know what it's like to be poor. When Ma made navy-bean soup, it didn't have nowhere near the ham we had in the soup tonight."

Sam interrupted him. "But Ned, you're far from poor."

"I know that's true," Ned retorted. "But we know some folks who are, and we aimin' to help 'em. And tryin' to talk us outta this is about as useless as talkin' about friendly fire ants. So, we gonna take a vote right here and now. Whenever Mr. Roderick does his figurin' and knows how much he needs, we gonna give it to him. That's what Ma and Pa would want us to do. They gonna be smilin' down from heaven knowin' me and Ned done somethin' good to help somebody." He turned to Sam. "So how do you take a vote in this board meetin'?"

Sam smiled broadly and spoke like the judge. "All in favor, raise your hand." Everyone in the room raised a hand, even Angel and Roderick, who weren't board members. "Motion passed, and I'll write it up to go in the minutes of the meeting when I get home."

Ned turned to Roderick. "I don't quite git whatcha

gonna do, but me and Fred trust you to do it."

Caroline bit her quivering lip and spoke with a voice stirred by deep gratitude in being reminded that good and honorable men still existed—men like Sam and Roderick and Ned and Fred. "Gentlemen, we are honored that you would partner with us to work in the Moss Point community. We are most grateful for your help."

Ned looked at Fred. "Thanky fer lettin' us do this and fer lettin' us build that gazebo." He paused. "One more thang. Iffen there's any o' that bean soup and cake left, me and Fred surely would like to take some home with us."

Caroline rose from the table. "I'll see what's left in the pot and make sure it leaves with you." And she was determined that a big-screen television would be delivered to them on Monday.

Chapter Twenty

Renovation

Tuesday morning, October 12, in Moss Point

Sam, Angel, and Hattie sat at the breakfast table finishing their second cup of coffee when there came a sharp rap on the back porch door. Angel spoke. "See who that is, Sam."

"You know who it is." Sam took his cane and slid the yellow gingham café curtain to the side to look out the window and confirm. Ned and Fred stood there like wooden soldiers, side by side like they always did. Sam stood and winked at Angel. "Just as I expected. The twins. Hattie, we may need another pot of coffee."

Angel shook her finger at Sam. "Don't you let on that we know anything, you hear? Can't wait to hear this story."

"Yes, my little darlin'."

Sam walked through the kitchen onto the porch and lifted the latch on the screen door and invited them in. "Good day, gentlemen. You're out early this morning. Come right on in. The coffee's on, and Hattie's made coffee cake."

Ned took off his ballcap. "We know it's early, but we couldn't wait no longer, Mr. Sam. You ain't gonna believe this."

Sam grinned big on the inside, knowing exactly what they were about to say. "Well, if it's something that big, maybe you should come on in so that Angel can hear this too." He led the way to the kitchen door and stood to the side while Ned and Fred filed in, holding their ballcaps to their chests. "Look who's here, Angel. They must have smelled that fresh pot of coffee." He paused. "Hattie, they said they have big news. You should probably hear this too."

Hattie was busy slicing coffee cake. "Mighty fine to see you gentlemen. Seems like a coon's age since y'all went to Kentucky, and I ain't seen you since. That was a mighty long trip. I heard about how Lilah done gone and spoiled y'all with her cookin', so I baked a fresh apple-cinnamon coffee cake this mawnin'. It just might make y'all forget about Lilah and remember old Hattie can bake too." Hattie put slices of warm coffee cake in front of them and poured two fresh cups of coffee for the twins and one for herself and joined them at the table.

Ned stumbled for words and cleared his throat.

Sam was impatient even though he knew what was coming. "Out with it, Ned. You got us hovering like cats waiting for milk to be poured in the bowl."

Ned took a sip of his coffee. "Now, Hattie, I don't want you thinkin' I'm not interested in this coffee cake, but my news won't wait. Mr. Sam's done said so." He looked at Fred sitting beside him. "Me and Fred been up all night watching shows on our new big-screen TV. We jes' couldn't turn it off."

Sam laughed. "What? When and where did you get a big-screen TV?"

Ned rubbed his hands together. "Yestiddy when me and

Fred got home from mowing at the park, there was a delivery truck from Singleton's Electronics in the driveway. This young feller got out and said he wuz delivering a new TV and he was s'posed to git it set up and runnin' b'fore sundown. I told 'im we ain't ordered no television. Mine and Fred's heads was spinnin' like tops tryin' to figure that out."

Sam inquired, "Well, did you? Figure it out, I mean?"

"Didn't have to? That young feller handed us a card and said it was a gift from Mr. Roderick and Miss Caroline. A thanky gift for buildin' the gazebo. Why, it was the best vacation me and Fred ever had, and they a'thankin' us for what we did. I'm here to tell you somethin'. Seventy inches of television makes Sheriff Matt Dillon a big man. Why we had to move two chairs and a table to make room fer the table the young feller brought. That TV's settin' up there on that table like it owns the place."

"Well, then, I can't wait to hear what you'll say about the girls on *Gilligan's Island*." Angel chuckled. "You gentlemen deserve the gift, and I'm sure that Caroline and Roderick were pleased as punch to give it to you."

Ned swallowed his first bite of coffee cake and spoke. "We's here to git you to call 'em and let 'em know we got it and it's the best present we ever got."

Sam rose from the table to get the phone. "What if I call them and you tell them yourselves?" He watched Fred's face blanch and Ned get the elbow from the silent twin.

"All righty, Mr. Sam, if you think that's the thang to do, I can tell 'em. I ain't ever had no trouble sayin' thanky."

Sam punched in the numbers and handed the phone to Ned. As he listened, he could only be grateful for these simple and honest men. He knew if anybody—*anybody*—ever slung mud at the twins, it wouldn't stick.

Eventually, Ned said goodbye and handed the phone to

Sam. "There. That's done. Now me and Fred can git on with our other business."

Sam asked, "You have other business in town today?"

"Yessiree, we do. Right after we finish Hattie's coffee cake. You told us we weren't poor, so we goin' to that fancy furniture store on Broad Street, and by sundown, two big ol' proppin'-back chairs will be in front of that fancy new TV."

Sam smiled. Simple men. Simple pleasures. He doubted if they had ever purchased a piece of furniture. "I might give you a piece of advice. Don't be skimping on the chairs. Get the biggest and best and most comfortable they have. Something that won't embarrass that fancy television."

"Yessiree, we will. Two proppin'-back chairs jes' alike, like me and Fred."

———.———

Wednesday afternoon, October 13, at Rockwater

Caroline turned off the road and drove through the gate coming into Rockwater. She stopped the vehicle, making sure the gate was closed before she drove on. Even though the gate had never failed to close, she wanted to be sure. As she waited, she surveyed the landscape of color across what seemed like miles of rises and falls against the late-afternoon horizon. After nearly a year, she still could hardly believe she was driving home.

She and Roderick had married at Christmas with the hills blanketed with snow. She had watched the snow melt into the springtime panorama of wildflowers and his mother's fields of daffodils. But the spring's dazzling colors had nothing on the warm, intense shades of autumn across these hills and valleys. Her first autumn at Rockwater.

Driving alone outside Rockwater was rare for her. She

and Roderick went to church together, dined out on occasion, and then rode to the airport together. Lilah did most of the grocery shopping. There had been so much travel since January and so little need for her to go to Lexington that she stayed home when she could. But she'd wanted to make the trip alone today. She knew if she mentioned shopping Roderick would be easily persuaded to stay at home.

She pulled into the garage, got out, and made certain the garage door closed. Roderick met her at the back door. "Where are all your packages?"

"Packages?" She handed him one bag.

He kissed her cheek. "I thought you went shopping, and you only have one bag?"

She searched for an answer. "Do you remember a few weeks ago you gave me a project of renovating the cottage out back? The holidays will be here in a few weeks, and I'd like to get it done before Thanksgiving."

"Yes. But I thought you'd hire a decorator. I never expected you would do it all by yourself." He put the package on the kitchen counter.

"And I might call your decorator, but I wanted to look around at fabric and furniture and bed linens to get some ideas. There are a few fabric samples in the bag for you to see."

"Oh, so it was shopping in a sense."

She wasn't lying; she just wasn't telling him the whole truth about why she'd gone to Lexington. "Yes, and this kind of shopping is more like work. I think I'll brew myself a cup of tea and prop my feet up for a while before dinner. I do hope Lilah left something in the fridge. I think I'm too tired to prepare a meal."

"You sit, and I'll make the tea and join you. The morning room or the library? Breakfast tea or Darjeeling?"

"Darjeeling with milk and sugar in the morning room. It's nearer." She left him in the kitchen and went straight for the sofa, lay down, and propped up her feet.

She was almost asleep when Roderick joined her with a plate of cookies and cups of tea on a wooden tray. "Lilah made ginger cookies today and got out the dishes she likes to use in the fall." He handed her the cup and saucer. "Here, madame, just as you like it. And here's the best ginger cookie in Bluegrass Country." He took a seat at the end of the sofa, picked up her feet, and put them in his lap.

"Thank you. So, tell me about your day." She inhaled the steam from the tea and took a sip.

"I've been making some phone calls to some friends in the area. Thinking about putting a focus group together to check out some of my ideas. Then the afternoon was perfect for a ride, so I went to see your gazebo."

"Without me?"

"Most certainly without you. If you see it now, what will I ever do for you for Christmas? The ride was spectacular. Cool breezes and bright colors. I did miss you, though, and Magnum had a sad face when I rode away from the barn."

"That certainly sounds more enjoyable than listening to sales ladies tell you exactly what you want and should purchase." She took another bite of the cookie. "You're right about these cookies. I think I'll have another."

"Don't move. I'll get it, but don't spoil your supper. Lilah left lentil soup and homemade pimiento cheese for grilled sandwiches. By the way, I'm certain you can handle a pushy sales lady. Remember, I saw how you handled Liz, the assistant with the red shiny claws."

She saw his playful grin. "I had no choice but to handle Liz until you issued her walking papers. And despite the sales lady, I did come home with some ideas." She didn't want to tell him ideas about what just yet. "Oh, and I don't think I told you about my call from Gretchen before I left this morning."

"No. What's up with them?" He put his empty cup on the tray and began to rub her feet.

"Peter has seen the attorney, and they have begun the paperwork to give part ownership of the bakery to Peter. Gretchen said that Karina is really excited to have Peter's help, especially with his knowledge of certain food items they can import to give the bakery a distinct European edge."

"That's smart and clean. Probably the best for his citizenship and for the running of the business."

She felt a sudden warmth come over her. "But the best news is that they're leaving on Saturday for Innsbruck, and they'll be gone for two weeks."

Roderick rested his head on the back of the sofa and sighed. "The delayed honeymoon."

"Yes, delayed for thirty-three years, but finally their honeymoon. They'll spend a few days in Innsbruck and then go over to Melk. Elfi and her family and Gretchen's pappá will join them there. And Pastor Tobias will have a special prayer for Peter and Gretchen at the end of the service next Sunday. Her family will be there, and Jana is throwing a party for all of them."

"Sounds perfect."

The warmth she had felt suddenly turned to a chill. "I hope so. Seems Iris is still looming out there like a bad odor that won't go away. Where's a good fumigator when you need one?"

Roderick laughed. "Why, Mrs. Adair, I think that may the unkindest thing I've ever heard you say. You must think Iris is up to something. What do you think it is?"

"Only Iris knows that, but she keeps calling Peter.

When he blocked her calls on his cellphone, she started calling the office and leaving messages." She watched Roderick's playful expression fall. "Either way, he's ignoring her."

"Then she's up to something, and I don't get the impression that Iris is a woman to be ignored. Guess they'll find out when they get there."

Caroline sat up and put her feet on the floor. "Oh no, they will not. Gretchen says there's no way Iris could know that she and Peter are married or that they'll be returning to Melk. Their plan is to avoid her, to stay away from her stench."

Roderick slid down the sofa to sit next to Caroline. "You really dislike this Iris, don't you?"

"I prefer not to think that I really dislike Iris, especially when I don't even know her, but what's to like about someone who just seems to spread and smear misery? She's had some hurt and disappointment in her life, but a commitment to bitterness is her choice. I just hope she'll forget about Peter and Gretchen. They deserve their springtime even if it is autumn."

Chapter Twenty-One

Rivers of Hope

Saturday, October 16, in Innsbruck, Austria

Somewhere in the skies before landing, Peter squeezed Gretchen's hand and looked over her shoulder to view the Alps. "There is no place like our homeland, my love. Such rugged beauty."

Gretchen continued her gaze out the airplane window. "Yes, indeed. I miss the mountains, although Durham is only a couple of hours away from the Appalachians. They have their own beauty, but they do not rise as majestically as do the Alps."

"You make the Alps sound like poetry."

Gretchen giggled softly. "I just read those words in that magazine."

Peter smiled, relishing her honesty and the feel of her soft platinum hair against his cheek as he leaned over her. "I long for you to see our chalet and to walk the trails that I have hiked alone all these years. We shall make picnics a daily outing. I have a friend in town who owns a sandwich shop, and picnic baskets are his specialty."

"Do you remember the long walks and the picnics we would take along the Danube?"

"Yes. Those memories have been with me all these years. We shall recreate them. Best to buckle up now. The winds and currents through the mountains can at times be brutish. But it will be a short descent. We could have flown into Munich and driven a couple of hours to avoid this landing, but I knew we would be tired after the long flight, and I want to spend our first night in our homeland in our chalet."

Gretchen turned in her seat and reached for the seat belt. "I am quite happy not to ride two more hours."

"The property manager brought my car to the airport, and we have only to drive about fifteen minutes to reach our chalet." Peter warmed inside to say the word *our*. He used it often. "We have no need even to stop for food. He and his wife left food there for us, and we will be lighting the fire in our home in about an hour. I regret that the sun has slipped behind the mountains and it will be almost dark when we get there. But tomorrow, you will see it all in its splendor, and I will see it again through your eyes."

Gretchen rested her head on his shoulder and laced her arm into his. Her mother tongue returned to her as she spoke to him. "Peter, please tell me I am not dreaming. You and I together, returning to Austria as a married couple with such a blessed future stretching out before us like a river of hope and joy."

The plane jolted, and its wings seesawed in the strong wind. Peter held tightly to Gretchen's arm entwined with his. "The aircraft just answered. You are not dreaming. Yes, it is all real—the realest thing there is."

The wind shear calmed, and the plane descended without further jolts. Peter continued. "Tonight, we shall sleep peacefully in the clean, cool air of the countryside, and rise tomorrow for an adventure. I will take you to *Altstadt*, the oldest part of the city where the buildings are more than a thousand years old, and we shall have a grand brunch. Then we shall walk to the bridge that crosses the Inn River. I think I would like us to stand there and watch the river as it disappears into the slopes and flows to the Danube. We shall dream and talk of our future together and give thanks."

———·———

Early Sunday morning, Gretchen rose, allowing Peter to continue to sleep, grabbed her robe, and opened the sliding glass doors of the master suite to step onto the balcony. The golden meadows in the foreground gave way to the distant mountains, resplendent with brilliant foliage and snow-capped peaks. The early-morning sunshine had not yet warmed the wooden floor of the balcony, but she did not mind the wintriness on her bare feet. The chill of the morning breeze caressing her hair, she pulled her robe tighter, leaned against the rail, and inhaled deeply the pure air.

Alone in her thoughts, she remembered the modest home in Moss Point where she'd lived for nearly a quarter of a century. It seemed so far away now—a far-ness that could not be measured in miles. It was as though she had held her breath for three decades until she returned to Austria and found Peter. And now she could breathe again but found herself almost breathless from the beauty of it all. From her first step through the garden gate and into the rustic and yet cozy chalet to her first steps onto the balcony this morning, Gretchen had felt at home. The country house was more than comfortable and the setting nothing short of enchanting.

For the next three days, she and Peter hiked the trails hand in hand and picnicked every day. Just as Peter had planned, they stood on the bridge and dreamed about their future, the future they'd thought of for so long was past. They had lovely, candlelit dinners in small restaurants, always sitting near the fireplace fulgent with flaming wood that crackled with age and smelled of the forest.

On Wednesday morning, a beautiful sadness came over her as they left for Linz. But Peter quickly described new adventures in the city and reminded her she would spend a few days with her family before they returned to the chalet. It was the thought of returning that lifted her veil of melancholy.

———•———

Wednesday, October 20, in Linz, Austria

Peter pulled slowly into his parking space in front of the large office building on the banks of the Danube and turned to Gretchen. "We are here." He pointed toward a park area with trees and walkways. "And there is our beautiful river."

"Your office is in this large building right here on the Danube?"

"This large building belongs to me and houses my company. I had the park designed so I could sit and watch the river and dream, and my employees enjoy it for short walks and lunchtime." Even though he had spoken to Gretchen about his business, her stunned expression revealed she'd had no idea of its size or the scope of what he did. "God blessed me with this business opportunity and with trustworthy employees who dream and work with me. You will meet some of them today."

They had barely stepped into the building when Luisa,

his administrative assistant, rushed to greet them. "Oh, Mr. Kornilov, we are glad to see you and to finally meet your Gretchen." Peter, not surprised, watched Luisa embrace Gretchen. "Mrs. Kornilov, Mr. Kornilov has told me about you since your visit last spring. And now you are married, and you are here. We have a small welcoming party for you to celebrate your marriage."

Peter looked into Gretchen's eyes as she turned to him. "I am better at other things than keeping secrets. These people are like my family, and I wanted them to know we were married."

He took her arm, and they followed Luisa into the board room, its perimeter lined with well-dressed, sharp-looking men and women, some young and some older. They all applauded and cheered as Peter and Gretchen entered the room.

Gretchen leaned and whispered. "You could have told me. I would have dressed differently."

"I was better at keeping this secret, and you look absolutely lovely. Now, let us enjoy the celebration."

For the next hour, Peter paraded Gretchen around the room to meet the staff as they balanced glasses of wine and plates of cheese, bread, fruit, and pastries in their hands. As the party slowed, Luisa approached Peter and pulled him aside.

"Sir, I do not wish to diminish your celebration, but I must speak to you privately before you leave today. I have asked Marie to take Mrs. Kornilov on a tour of the offices and a walk down by the river. I am not certain this is something you would like her to know."

Peter did not like the sound of this. He valued Luisa because she was mature, and she was calm in the most riotous of circumstances. This was serious or she would never have approached him. He returned to Gretchen. "My love, I have a few things I must attend to this afternoon while we are here. If I take care of them now, we will have the rest of our time together in Linz for more enjoyable things. I will only be half an hour." He guided her across the room. "I think Marie is counting on giving you on a tour."

That settled, he walked straightway through the corridor to a large, closed door and went in.

Luisa followed him into his office. "Sir, I am so sorry. I did not want to bring these things to your attention while you were in the States and so soon after your wedding."

"What things, Luisa? Do we have some kind of crisis?"

"No, sir. The business is in fine shape. But . . . I have told you in our conversations that Iris Brandhof has called several times and left urgent messages. She has pressed me to know where you are and when she might hear from you."

The exasperation in his voice showed. "Iris. Will she never stop?"

"And sir, this certified letter came for you last Friday."

He took it from her hand. "What is so pressing about a certified letter?"

"I am uncertain, sir. But the return address is from a Mrs. Nicolai Kornilov in Munich. I thought you should see it straightway in case there is some connection with Ms. Brandhof's calls."

Peter was perplexed. "Thank you, Luisa. You may leave me now."

As Luisa walked out of the room, he eased slowly around his desk and sank into his chair as he turned the letter over in his hands. There it was: "Mrs. Nicolai Kornilov," handwritten with a return address.

Nicolai's wife? Why is she writing me? But Iris? What does she know?

He picked up a brass letter opener and slit the edge of the envelope, careful not to mar the return address. He unfolded the pages and started to read.

Dear Peter,

I should call you Mr. Kornilov out of deep respect and because we have never met, but Nicolai has spoken so fondly of you through the years that I feel I know you. It is with deep sadness that I write this letter to inform you of Nicolai's death. He passed away a few days ago after a brief illness. Enclosed is a letter that he had written and asked me to deliver to you after his passing.

Before you read his letter, please know that Nicolai and I have been married for fifteen years, and we have two beautiful sons. Nicolai was honest with me about his past and has lived an exemplary life ever since I have known him. I wish that the two of you could have become brothers again, as I know it would have meant so much to Nicolai.

With so many details to be tended now and not knowing when I might be able to visit you, I thought it more expedient to write than to wait with this news. There was an occurrence earlier this week that made sending this to you more important. I opened the door of our home to a stranger a few days ago. He identified himself as private detective hired to find Nicolai. I told him nothing other than that Nicolai no longer lived here. I thought that you might be the one looking for your brother, and I did not want a private detective to give you the news of his death.

Nicolai was a gentleman, a wonderful husband and father, and he provided well for us. Although the boys and I are grieving deeply because we miss him so much and cannot bear to think of our future without him, we lack for nothing else. I want you to know how he looked up to you and how much it pained him to know you suffered because of his actions. I hope that you will find it in your heart to forgive him after you have read his letter. I would be most happy if you came for a visit to meet your nephews. They look so much like Nicolai.

My heart is heavy to bring you this news in this manner. I thought it best so that you can cease the services of the private detective you engaged. I have enclosed a copy of Nicolai's obituary so that you might know I write the truth.

Sincerely,
Frida Kornilov

Peter placed the letter on his desk and leaned back in his chair. His brother dead. His last living relative gone from the earth. Although Nicolai had been virtually dead to him for so many years, hearing this news was still a jolt. He closed his eyes to let the news settle in his mind, but it would not. There were too many bewildering questions. A private detective . . . Iris's unremitting calls . . .

After a few moments, he picked up the other papers, unfolded them, and began to read. It was as though he read Nicolai's words in slow motion, taking time with each phrase and rereading each paragraph before moving to the next.

My dear brother, Peter,

If you are reading this, then you know that I have passed into heaven. Perhaps you do not feel that I belong there, but I want you to know that while in prison I returned to the early teachings of our parents, and I have experienced God's grace. I only wish I could have found my way earlier to see you again after your last visit with me and confess to you my wrongdoing and beg your forgiveness. I know that my behavior brought shame to our family and put unnecessary burdens upon you.

I had ten years in prison to reflect on my life, what I had done, and what I wanted for my future. It was evil that I grasped in my youth. Evil seemed more appealing when I was young and reckless. I had no thought of how alcohol would consume me as I consumed it, or how my evil acts would damage and impact others. I was willful, arrogant, and thought of only myself. That left you to tend to our parents and to the business. And you bore the shame not only of my behavior but the grief of Gretchen's disappearance and the deaths of our parents.

I do not even know how to begin to say how sorry I am. I have no words, but I pray you can hear the depths of my heart.

God rescued me in prison when a vicar became my friend and confidant. I attended his Bible studies, and he counseled me. When I was released, he mentored me and advised me to begin afresh in a new place. He said that I would know when I should reach out to you. He introduced me to Frida, one of his congregants. Frida is a wonderful woman and knows every sordid thing about my past, yet she found it in her heart to begin a future with me. We have been blessed with two beautiful sons, and I hope one day you will meet them.

I have been ill with liver cancer for a few months now, and it seems that I will be going home to heaven soon. I wish now that I could have reached out to you earlier, but I was afraid of only bringing you more pain. Although I have cut all ties with Iris for obvious reasons, I have written letters of regret to those whom I harmed. I was not bold enough to ask for forgiveness, only to express my deep sorrow for what I did to them. I pray that somehow you will find a way to forgive me for bringing shame to our family and to myself.

I will crawl into heaven on my knees with bowed head and deepest humility but with a grateful heart that God has seen fit to redeem me. I pray that your life is most satisfying to you, Peter. I know that you will be able to enter heaven's gate looking squarely and loving-ly into the face of the One who loves us all because you have chosen to live your life according to His ways. Our parents named you appropriately. You are Peter, the rock of our family. May God bless you, my brother, until we are united again.

Always with love and deepest respect,
Your brother, Nicolai

Peter's tears flowed freely, and his chest heaved from such bottomless emotion. Despair over his brother's death. Frustration that his death came now. Anger that Nicolai had not confessed or asked for forgiveness for what he did to Gretchen. His only consolation was acceptance that Nicolai clearly had no knowledge of what he'd done to Gretchen.

Still so many questions. *Should I reach out to Frida? Should I tell Gretchen? And who had hired a private detective and why? And why all this now?*

He inhaled and exhaled deeply, and his body calmed. He took his handkerchief from his pocket and wiped his face. With eyes closed, his racing thoughts slowed as he folded his arms and leaned forward on his desk.

Yes. I will write to Frida. It is only right that I should. And yes, I will go there someday to meet Nicolai's sons, but not during this trip. I will not have Nicolai's death mar this time for Gretchen and for me. I will tell Gretchen. I will not begin my married life with secrets. We have lived with far too many secrets through the years. She probably has unspoken worries that someday Nicolai may appear again, and in a mysterious way, this will bring peace to her.

And the private detective? Iris. Who could it be but Iris? Luisa must be correct in her thinking that Iris is connected to this. But how? I do not know, and if I want to know, how should I go about it? I will write the letter to Frida, and I will inform Gretchen and share these letters with her, but I have no notion of what to do about Iris. I only know I must deal with her.

---◆---

Chapter Twenty-Two

Decisions on the Danube

Wednesday, October 20, in Linz, Austria

The front door of Peter's sixth-floor apartment opened to a grand space with a wall of sheer-covered windows looking out on the old part of the city. As Gretchen entered, she could see through the sheers and went immediately to the windows. "Peter, this is so lovely and only minutes from your office." She sighed. "And there is the Danube down below."

"Yes. When I moved here years ago, I chose an apartment rather than a cottage. I was uncertain how things would go with my new business. Also, I did not know the city very well, and I did not need the upkeep of a home when I was starting a new business. My requirements were three: an apartment in the old part of the city, a view of the river, and to be near the office."

Gretchen turned slowly, taking in the room. "The building is one of antiquity, and yet the apartment is so modern."

"I had no desire to live across the river where all the

buildings are new and everything is modern. It is as if they landed here from some faraway place. Here, there is a sense of history and stability. I have only two bedrooms and this spacious living area with a small kitchen. It has suited me well. I hope you will find it agreeable, even though the kitchen is not equipped for your baking and you seem to be more at home with cottage living. When we are in Linz, consider yourself on vacation."

Gretchen went to him and embraced him. "Home is where you are, my love, but I am not sure where you have been since we left the office." She pulled away from him. "You are troubled."

She felt his hand slide down her arm and take her hand. Peter led her to the large sofa facing the windows where they sat with her fingers laced in his. "I am so sorry, my love, but I did receive some unsettling news while we were at the office, news that has already changed some lives. I have vowed never to keep secrets from you, so I must tell you."

"Do not fear telling me. Whatever it is, we shall deal with it together."

Peter pulled the letter from his inside coat pocket. "The reason Luisa needed to see me was to give me this letter." He handed it to Gretchen. "It is a letter from Nicolai's wife, now his widow, and a letter that Nicolai penned before he died. I think it best that you just read them. Then we will talk."

Gretchen was startled as she took the letter. *How could one envelope hold so much? How could its contents change the lives of so many? And why such news now?*

She slowly opened the envelope and read Frida's letter first. Silent tears filled her eyes, sorrow for the woman and her sons who loved Nicolai and would now be forced to learn to live life without him. When finished, she folded the papers, laid them in her lap, and picked up Nicolai's letter.

She read it slowly, learning of his deep regret over what he had done and his need for forgiveness. With a breath, she folded it and put it neatly back into the envelope with Frida's letter.

Quietly and serenely, she said, "It is good that Nicolai made peace with God and with his past. Perhaps Frida became an anchor of goodness for him." She fumbled, not knowing how to say or even if to say what she was thinking, so they sat in silence until she spoke again. "Peter, I do not think Nicolai knew that I was the one he accosted on Christmas Eve. I must believe that if he knew, he would have begged for your forgiveness differently."

She felt Peter's arm encircle her shoulders. "I believe you to be right. I do not think he knew. He was spared that added guilt." He paused and cleared his throat. "Gretchen, part of me wishes he had known and that he had suffered the way I have suffered without you all these years, but that is not the better part of me."

Gretchen stroked his hair. "You are right, my love. There is the better part of you that is at peace now, grateful that Nicolai found his own peace with God and had a family. You and I are together now, and we have such a beautiful future ahead of us. We will be grateful that God redeemed Nicolai and that he is in heaven with your parents." She kissed his cheek. "There is nothing we can do, except you must write to Frida. Do you wish to go and see her and meet Nicolai's sons?"

"I will write to her, and maybe someday when we are here again, we will go to Munich and meet them. But I prefer not to go during this trip."

"I understand, and I trust your wisdom, Peter."

She felt him move away and watched him walk to the window and pull the sheer back for a clear view. She knew that somehow the river had always called to him. When they were young, it delighted him. It cleansed his spirit, and it gave him perspective. Even then, he'd determined that they would live in a cottage on the Danube.

She remained silent while the river comforted him. After a few moments, Peter turned to her but kept his distance. "There is one other thing. You must have had the same question I did about the private investigator, but you are too gentle to bring it up. It was Iris. She has been unrelenting in her quest to find Nicolai. Now we must decide what to do."

Gretchen moved to the edge of her seat. "Are you saying that you will contact Iris?"

She saw the resolve in Peter's face. "Yes. I pray the news of Nicolai's death will put an end to her obsession and that she will move on with her life. I would appreciate your counsel on this. Do you think I should call her? Or do you think I should try to see her when we are in Melk?"

She squeezed her hands together as she did when she was stressed. It was her way of holding fast to things she could control. "That is a most interesting question, and how I wish I had an answer. Iris is unpredictable. But if it is true that she hired the detective, perhaps she already knows of Nicolai's death, and that is why she was calling you."

Peter shook his head. "I do not think she knows. I think she wanted money to find him."

"And you do remember she was trying to contact me for some reason, but now I understand that it also could have been her need for money. She told you that there are journalists who were willing to pay money to have information about Bella and me." She waited. "Honestly, Peter, I do not know what learning of Nicolai's death will cause Iris to do next."

Peter sat down in the chair next to the window. "You have lifted a real concern. Perhaps I will call her, give her the news, and inquire about the investigator. I will not tell her of our marriage or that we are in Austria. Maybe that will be enough to quieten her."

He hung his head. "Oh, how I rue the day I ever mentioned money to her."

"I agree with your decision, but must you ask her about the private investigator?"

He lifted his head and looked at Gretchen. "That is wise counsel. Wise, caring, and lovely you are, my Gretchen. You are right. I will keep my conversation to Nicolai's death, and I will tell her where she might read his obituary."

She was relieved to see the gentleness in Peter's face return. "Yes. That will assure her you are telling the truth."

He reached in his pocket for his phone.

"You will call her now?"

"I can think of no better time. My father always taught me to do the hard jobs first. This is not something I look forward to, but it is best to nail this shut as soon as possible. It will not be a shadow over our time together here."

"Would you like me to excuse myself and go out on the balcony or into another room?"

"No. I wish you to be here to support me. I will put her on speaker so that you can hear."

"Then I will be right here."

He took a deep breath and made the call. Iris answered before the second ring. "It is time you returned my calls. Where have you been, and why have you not called me?"

Peter's voice was calm. "I owe you no answers to your questions, Iris. I am calling you now simply as a courtesy to you."

"So now you decide to be courteous? After all these days of my attempts to reach you."

Gretchen heard the anger and brusqueness in Iris's voice. In contrast, Peter words were composed and measured. "I have news that you should know. I have received a letter from Nicolai's wife. She—"

Before he could finish, Iris interrupted. "His wife? Nicolai is married?"

"Yes, Nicolai was married."

After a pause, Iris frantically asked, "What do you mean *was*?"

"Iris, there is no gentle way to tell you this, but Nicolai is dead. His wife wrote to me of his passing a few days ago. It seems he has been ill for some time. I thought it best for you to know."

There was silence.

Gretchen's and Peter's eyes met, both with questioning looks. Peter broke the silence. "Iris?" No response. "Iris, is there someone I can call to be with you?"

Iris's scream shattered her silence. "*No!* No one." Then an abrupt click.

Gretchen went to Peter as he put his phone away. She knelt on the carpeted floor and embraced him. "You have done what was needed. I am here and will stay with you, or if you would like some time alone to mourn, I understand."

"No, my dearest, I need you."

Gretchen held him as he sobbed. They sat together for the next couple of hours in a rhythm of silence and soft whispers. Gretchen's words of solace. Peter's questions. Expressions of sorrow for Nicolai's family. Suspicions of Iris's behavior.

———•———

Later the same evening in Melk

Her thoughts racing, Iris sat in her cottage, the most alone she had ever felt. She had taken Peter's call at the office and then made an excuse to leave early. And now fears of losing her home, of going to prison, of never seeing Nicolai again were her only company. Her thoughts of Nicolai were a whirlwind of sadness, anger, and longing. Her life was a tangled heap of nothing, but she had to find a way through.

Iris realized Peter was her last chance for deliverance out of the mess she had made. A mess that could cost her what was left of her miserable life—more miserable now that Nicolai was dead and her hopes buried with him. The bank had not yet approved her loan. Selling her cottage would take too long to cover her embezzlement. Wurm was history. No more payments to him. As it stood now, Wurm had been an unnecessary, malevolent expense that got her into this mess.

If Peter would not help, she saw no way out.

She called him, hoping with her last strand of hope that he would answer.

He did. "Yes, Iris." Then silence.

"Thank you for answering, Peter." She paused, but he offered no response. "I am in shock that Nicolai is dead. I had such hopes of being reunited with him, but those hopes are ashes now that I looked up the obituary as you suggested. I knew you were speaking truth because that is what you do."

"I thought you would want to know."

"No one ever wants to know such things, but thank you for your call. It was a decent thing to do even though I have been less than decent to you." She shifted in her chair before continuing. "Peter, I have made a mess of my life. I have wasted most of my life waiting on Nicolai to return. I even hired a private investigator to find him."

Peter's voice was cool and his words calculated. "Yes, I am aware. He knocked on the door of Nicolai's grieving widow, causing her even more pain. She thought I had hired the investigator."

Her voice quivered. "I fear and regret that I have made a terrible muddle of things, causing his widow even more pain, and then I have annoyed you with my calls. It was all out of my desperation. Peter, it is worse for me than you know, and I take great risk in telling you what I am about to tell you, but I have no other option." Iris hesitated and her voice broke as she spoke. "I fear I will be going to prison. The private investigator required considerable funds to do the search. I did not have those funds, yet I was desperate to find Nicolai. I did an unspeakable thing. I embezzled money from the hotel, and I fear it will be discovered and I will go to prison. I just thought if I could find Nicolai, together we could make this work. Finding him was worth everything to me."

"Does anyone else know what you have done?"

"No. No one. I have been able to cover it with falsified reports, but soon that will no longer be possible." She hedged on telling him about her robbery plans but decided it would show Peter her despair. "I have become so desperate that I even planned a robbery attempt a few nights ago, but that plan was thwarted before I could go through with it. I have been to the bank to acquire a personal loan, but the loan officer has not yet responded."

"I see. You are asking me to bail you out of your situation so that you will not need bail to get out of prison."

She did not answer right away. "Peter, you asked me before how much would it take for me to just go away, out of your life. I am not asking you for that. If you could only loan me the money, I will repay you over time. I need my job. I have nothing else. I will be out of your life for good."

"How much money are we talking about?"

She knew he had no way of knowing how much except what she told him. She could ask for more. If he was softening, he might give her what she asked. And yet, from some unfamiliar place inside her came a sense that she should tell him the truth. She told him the exact amount she had stolen.

"That is a substantial amount of money, Iris. I will give it some thought and call you tomorrow."

Fear grasped her throat. "Peter, are you planning to turn me in?"

"No, Iris. I have no plans of making your life more miserable than it is. As I said, I will give this some thought and call you tomorrow."

She heard the click. Peter was gone. Now all she could do was wait.

———·———

Later Wednesday evening in Linz

Gretchen and Peter had been on the balcony with a cup of tea when Iris called, and Gretchen had heard Peter's side of the conversation, which was sketchy. She was anxious for him to fill her in on all that Iris had said, but his venting came before his reporting.

"That woman is miserable, and she inflicts her misery on everyone and everything around her like a contagion. I knew weeks ago when I asked her how much it would take for her to go away that I had opened a door she would not close. And I was right."

"Iris is asking for money? Why does she need money?"

"As I thought, Iris hired the private detective. But worse, she stole money from the hotel to pay for it. She thought if she could find Nicolai, all her problems would be solved. Now Nicolai is dead, she has no money to cover her theft, and she fears she will go to prison."

Gretchen reached across the arm of her chair and caressed Peter's hand. "So, my love, what will you do?"

"My first thought is to do nothing and allow her to stew in her own soup. Why should I bail her out? But then I think of how she was also Nicolai's victim and that I should help her." He sighed. "It seems I am stewing in my own soup too."

"Is giving her the money the only way to help her?"

"I believe it is. She says that she only wants a loan and will pay it back, but if I decide to give her the money, I want nothing else to do with her. I do not want a monthly payment to remind me of that woman." He stopped and became silent.

Gretchen was learning his ways, which were not so different from when he was young. So, she waited, giving him time to think, knowing he would speak when he was ready.

"There may be a way to finally be rid of her. Your name was not mentioned, and she does not know we are married, but it is time she knows. And it is time she accepts we will have no further contact with her. I will call my attorney early in the morning and have him draft something that will keep her from ever contacting me again. The issue is to draft something that will not implicate me in her crime."

"Oh, Peter, that sounds so complicated. Would you really feel at peace with yourself for having done that? It sounds almost like blackmail. Would you feel better if you extended grace to her? We could take her the money together while we are in Melk and tell her we are married and living on another continent. Would that not be a more compassionate way to deal with her? Maybe it will make a difference in her life for someone to treat her with compassion. As you said, in a strange way, she is also Nicolai's victim."

Peter squeezed her hand. "Gretchen, you are a kind and

forgiving woman. And wise, I might add. You are correct. There is nothing to be gained by rubbing this in her face. In a way, it would be putting many things to rest. Nicolai's death. Compensating Iris for the misery he caused her. And letting her know that we are married." He paused. "However, I will not spoil our time in Melk with your family by visiting Iris. I will instruct my attorney to pay her and to write a letter on my behalf that will communicate the things we have talked about."

"But there will be no threat?"

"No. I will not threaten her. I will tell him what needs to be said, but she will hear the instruction that she is never to contact you or me again."

"Yes, we will look at all of this as an expensive but peaceful closure, and we will go on with the new springtime in our lives. We have all we need." Gretchen pulled her shawl tighter around her shoulders. "I speak of springtime, but it is a most beautiful autumn evening with the soft breezes from the river. I think I could sit here forever with you, my love."

Chapter Twenty-Three

---◆---

Closures and New Beginnings

Friday morning, October 22, in Melk, Austria

The tree-lined parkway parallel to the Danube took them straight into Melk. Gretchen enjoyed every one of the sixty miles from Linz as Peter drove. "Oh, Peter, I had forgotten how incredibly beautiful the Wachau Valley can be in autumn. It was stunning last spring, but so much more colorful in the fall. Next autumn, would it not be wonderful to bring Caroline and Roderick for a visit?"

"Yes, I always long for October, and we shall return with Caroline and Roderick. I only wish we had time for another river cruise, but we want to make the most of our time with your family before we return to Innsbruck. How quickly our time will pass here."

"Yes. And how quickly I hope our meeting with Iris will pass this morning. I think it wise that you made an appointment rather than sending the letter to her."

Peter pulled into a parking space outside the Hotel zur Post. "Iris has always been unpredictable, but this is our best chance of seeing how she will react. Having Luisa call to make the appointment and to tell her that we were both coming will have given her time to prepare herself for our arrival."

"I am surprised Iris did not call you immediately."

"It surprised me as well. Unpredictable, as I said." Peter opened the car door. "Wait, I will come and open the door for you, my love."

Out of the car, Peter straightened his collar and took Gretchen's hand. They walked into the lobby of the hotel and told the desk clerk of their appointment with Ms. Brandhof. "Yes, Mr. Kornilov. Ms. Brandhof instructed me to bring you to her office as soon as you arrived."

Peter would not do this on her turf. "Please tell Ms. Brandhof that we will be in the restaurant courtyard having coffee." He took Gretchen's hand and walked with intention to the door of the restaurant. They were seated and their coffee had arrived only seconds before Iris joined them. Peter did not rise when she approached the table.

The server immediately returned. Before Iris sat, she said to the server, "These are my guests. Bring them whatever they like, and I will have coffee." She then sat and raised her head to look at them. "Thank you for coming." Her eyes were puffy—the kind of puffy hard crying and lack of sleep brought.

Peter spoke. "Iris, this is not a casual visit. I come with one purpose, and I will make this brief. As my assistant, Luisa, informed you, Gretchen and I are married. We are here to visit her family. My home is with her now in the States."

Before he could go on, Iris contritely said, "I am happy for you that after all these years you found your way back to each other."

Gretchen spoke softly. "Thank you, Iris."

Peter nodded in agreement. "I have given thought to

your request and have talked it over with Gretchen and have sought counsel from my attorney." He took the envelope from his inside jacket pocket. As always with Iris, his words were measured. "This check is in no way associated with what you have done. Consider it a gift, some compensation for the pain my brother Nicolai has caused you. If this check alleviates other problems, then so be it."

Iris took the envelope and almost whispered. "Thank you, Peter."

Gretchen sat quietly as Peter continued. "There is hope for you, Iris. But it is impossible to focus on your past and focus on your future at the same time. Gretchen and I have chosen to focus on the plans for our future. I advise you to do the same. Nicolai is part of your past. Let him go and move forward. We are leaving our past in Melk behind us. You are part of that past."

Peter stood from his chair and took Gretchen's arm and assisted her to stand. "That is what I came to say, and now we part."

Iris spoke quickly. "But will you not stay for an early lunch?"

"Iris, we have plans," Peter responded. "We are moving on, and so should you."

Gretchen joined him and took his arm. "Iris, I do understand. In a way you have been robbed of the life you desired, and it seems you have chosen to remain a prisoner of your past. Please move forward with your life and not be robbed of another day of joy and God's blessings."

Peter and Gretchen walked silently and resolutely through the courtyard and took the gated entrance to the street. They did not look back and only slowed their steps for Peter to open the picket gate.

Neither of them said anything until they reached the car. Peter spoke first. "It is done. We have been merciful, and now we drive away just as we walked away from Iris back there, without looking back."

Gretchen adjusted her seat belt. "We do not forget the past. We only take what we learned from it and move forward."

Peter, in his effort to lighten the moment and the mood, said, "What would you think of moving forward to our hotel? Luisa has arranged a picnic basket to be delivered." He looked at his watch. "Right about now. We will dress casually and walk the path along the river and find our favorite spot to picnic among the willows."

"Just as we did in our past, but now in the gift of our present, with eyes to our future."

"Beautifully said, my love."

———•———

Gretchen and Peter enjoyed a quiet Friday afternoon before the arrival of her pappá and Elfi and her family. Memories of her childhood had been quietly present with her all afternoon as they walked the familiar lanes near the Danube and as they stopped at their favorite coffeehouse in town. The flowers that had cascaded from the window boxes up and down the narrow, cobble-stoned streets last spring were now but wisps. The blossoms could not stand up to the chilly nights, but they would return next spring. The town was still photograph worthy with the shop windows up and down the streets parading the warm colors of fall.

They waited in the hotel lobby for her family's arrival. When Gretchen's pappá entered, she was there to greet him and Elfi's family. Her memories gave way to the present as she took her pappá's arm and did not let go. They remained in the lobby while Elfi and Yannick and the girls got settled into their rooms. Upon their return, Peter announced that he had made reservations for a family dinner at Rathauskeller, a restaurant known for its wiener schnitzel.

The restaurant menu showcased autumn: pumpkin strudel with garlic dip as an appetizer, creamy pumpkin coconut soup, a tossed salad with roasted pumpkin and pumpkin-seed dressing, and pumpkin risotto. But everyone's choice for dessert was chocolate mousse with the season's last sweet cherries.

Waves of joy washed over Gretchen through the evening. At times as she heard her father's stories and the children's laughter and felt Peter's hand caress hers under the table, she felt as though she were watching a movie of herself. She still found it difficult to believe these moments were real and would not be washing away as a wave rolling back into the sea.

Back at the hotel, after the children and Pappá were settled in bed, Yannick and Elfi came down to Gretchen's suite. Yannick and Peter put on their jackets and sat on the balcony. Gretchen was certain they were enjoying the sights and sounds of Friday night in Melk and that they were talking shop—food, the best cheeses, where to get the best meats.

Gretchen and Elfi found a comfortable spot in the small sitting area of the suite. Their conversation was all about the family. Elfi wanted to hear every detail of the proposal and the wedding. Gretchen shared pictures of the wedding and the photos she had taken when the production team was shooting Bella for her documentary, and pictures of her North Carolina home and Peter's homes in Innsbruck and Linz.

As their chatter became less animated, Gretchen asked, "How is Pappá? Really, how is he? He looks frailer than he did in the springtime.

"I suppose he is. He spends most days quietly in his chair, not making the miniature furniture anymore because of the pain in his hands. He is still there for the girls when they come home from school, but I think Emelia and Annika look after him more than he looks after them."

Gretchen rubbed her hands together. "Will you keep me informed if there are any changes? I would like to be a part of his care if it comes to that. If I cannot be here, I would like to take care of any expenses."

Elfi answered. "Yes, dear sister. I will keep nothing from you, and I am grateful for your offer to help."

"While we are speaking of unpleasant things, there is something I must tell you. We may not have another chance to speak privately." Gretchen told Elfi of Nicolai's death and their morning visit with Iris.

Elfi responded, "Oh, Gretchen, I am sorry you had to learn of all these things on this trip—your honeymoon trip. Iris is a despicable woman. I only hope that this is the last you will see or hear of her."

"I believe it will be. There are more than miles that will separate us now that Peter and I are married and living in the States."

Elfi pulled Gretchen to her and squeezed her. "Sister, it is as though the loose ends of your past have all disappeared and your life is now wrapped in a beautiful package, and on Sunday we will tie it with a lovely ribbon. Pappá is so pleased that you agreed for Pastor Tobias to have a private time with our family and to have a hallowed blessing for your marriage. Jana is preparing a feast. Of course, Yannick and I brought food to help out."

Gretchen was a bit anxious. "That sounds perfect, Elfi. Where will we share our meal?"

"We will feast in the hall at the church. Jana's family will be there, and of course Pastor Tobias and his family."

"More perfection." Then she hesitated. "Although I am enjoying my time here, I do not wish to stumble into Iris. I do not think that will happen at the church."

Elfi snickered. "Iris at church? We are safe."

Just after midnight, Peter and Yannick came back inside. "Elfi," Yannick said, "it has been a long day of travel, and the weather is chilly. I think it is time to retire. I need sleep."

Gretchen responded. "We all do. We have a day of many activities tomorrow."

———◆———

Gretchen's family filled an entire pew at the village church on Sunday morning. There sat the piano Bella had played on the Sunday they were here in April, the Sunday when Peter had slipped in late in the back only to be stunned by Bella's appearance. The autumn light came through the stained-glass windows differently than in the spring but no less vibrant. The center aisle was awash with jewel-toned reflections.

When the service ended, the parishioners who were long-time friends of her pappá came by to speak to him and Elfi and Gretchen. He proudly told them that she and Peter were married and happy and living in the United States. She could hear pleasure in his voice at reporting that she and Peter would be visiting regularly and that he had plans to visit them in North Carolina.

With the parking lot empty, Pastor Tobias gathered the family at the altar, positioning Gretchen and Peter in front of him. Her pappá stood beside her and Elfi beside him. The others stood behind them. The pastor gave a few remarks about the holiness of marriage and then asked Peter and Gretchen to join hands and place them on his open Bible.

He placed his hand on top of theirs and prayed. "Our Father, God of love, we thank You for the union of Peter and Gretchen and for the love You put into their hearts for each other. We pray that their love will always reflect Your love—patient, slow to anger, keeping no record of wrongs, always ready to forgive. May they treat each other with kindness and gentleness. And as Your love is unfailing and sacrificial, may theirs be also. We ask that You help them to serve, to encourage, and to support each other. Father, thank You for restoring to them what they thought was lost. You, O Lord, are the Author of joy and gladness and love. May You surprise them with joy and give them peace and shower them with Your blessings in their new live together. And Father, we ask that You give them many years to love and serve each other as they continue to love and serve You. Through Jesus Christ our Lord, amen."

Several amens echoed the pastor's. He raised his head and looked at Gretchen and Peter. "I almost said, 'And now you may kiss the bride.'" Then he chuckled.

Peter embraced Gretchen and looked at the Pastor Tobias. "I think I shall pretend that you did." He kissed Gretchen sweetly.

They enjoyed their meal, the sharing of stories from her pappá's youth, the laughter, and the family fellowship around a handmade wooden table that was over two centuries old. Gretchen thought that Elfi was right: this was the lovely ribbon to tie their lives together with much-need closures and new beginnings. She only wished Bella, Karina, Caroline, and Roderick could have been there.

After two more days with the family, Gretchen and Peter returned to Innsbruck to relax and enjoy their privacy before boarding the plane for home. As their time there ended, Gretchen's beautiful sadness returned, but her gratitude never waned. Sadness because her anticipated return to Austria was coming to another close; beautiful because she knew they would return; and grateful that her home was with Peter wherever they were.

On takeoff, her tearful eyes were fixed on the airplane window as the plane climbed above the disappearing Alps and headed into clear blue skies.

Chapter Twenty-Four

---◆---

Looking to Springtime

Early November at Rockwater

The early-morning light streaming through window was brighter because the sumac trees were now bare, having said goodbye to the last of their leaves. The beams highlighted the basket of ornamental pumpkins on the breakfast table where Caroline and Lilah sat with their second cups of coffee—Caroline with her calendar and Lilah with all her lists and holiday plans.

Lilah opened her notebook. "You're quiet this morning. Seems like Roderick's meetings and plans and this guest-cottage project have worn you to a frazzle this last week or so. We both know Roderick will always be working on something, but the cottage will be finished in another week and ready for its first guests. So it's high time we get started on holiday plans. That means decorating for Thanksgiving and Christmas and planning meals. It's your first holiday season as mistress of the manor."

Caroline remained quiet.

"Did you hear me? Are you okay?"

"Yes and yes. I was just thinking. We'll get to all that in a moment. I heard Piper Gray sing at church yesterday. His voice was mesmerizing. That young boy is quite gifted, and I guess hearing him made me realize what a responsibility his parents have in giving him the best opportunity to develop his gift. I know there aren't many of those opportunities around here, except maybe in Lexington. And if I'm honest, just hearing him reminded me of how I love to teach."

"Are you saying you're ready to give him lessons?" Lilah asked.

"I think what I'm saying is that it was also a reminder of how much I miss teaching and that perhaps I have some responsibility in helping him."

"Now, we know the student needs a teacher, and now it could be the teacher needs a student. Say the word when you're ready for me to give Harold a call and have him bring Piper to meet you."

Caroline turned in her seat. "Almost ready. And I don't know how long or how much time I can commit to him. I need to have conversation with Roderick, but I've been so busy with the redecorating project and then working on the future projects for Lexington and Moss Point that I've had little time to talk to him about anything else."

"You know that Roderick has no thoughts of your giving up your music if that is your heart's desire. You can always do that and support his work. He can hire someone to help with his projects."

"We're planning to hire someone soon, but right now Celia is handling things and doing a super job as usual. I promised Roderick I'd support our new work, and I will make good on that promise. I just have a few things on my mind. Maybe we'll take a ride this afternoon. Or maybe a walk down to Blue Hole. I'm dying to see the gazebo, but he won't hear of it. But I think I have a way to get him to take me there."

"Girl, I think you're in brooding mode now, and you're looking a little pale. Don't wait too long to talk to Roderick, and a walk or a ride in the afternoon sunshine will do you good. It won't be too long before the winter will set in."

"The winter and then comes spring. I'll talk to him today." She looked up and forced a smile. "Open that notebook, Lilah, and let's get started. Everyone is coming for Thanksgiving. And I mean everyone—my parents, my brothers and their families, Sarah's family, Gretchen's family, Sam and Angel, and the twins. That's like last year's Christmas wedding all over again, only at Thanksgiving. They're coming in on Wednesday afternoon and leaving on Saturday morning. My brothers and their families and Gretchen and her family will stay at the castle. The rest will be here." Caroline paused. "Christmas will be quieter. My side of the family will stay in Ferngrove for Christmas, and Roderick and I will make a quick trip to see them. Just Sarah's family and Sam and Angel, and of course, Ned and Fred if they will accept our invitation. They had no hesitation in saying yes to Thanksgiving. With that, let's talk about plans."

"No Peter and Gretchen and the girls For Christmas? And speaking of Gretchen, are they back from Austria?"

"Yes, I talked to her last night. They're home. They had a great trip, and they practically had another wedding ceremony at the village church with her family. And in God's timing, they had closure on some things that needed closing so they can enjoy this new springtime in their lives." Her thoughts drifted.

"Those two deserve the joy and beauty of springtime in their lives. I'll be happy to see them at Thanksgiving."

"Me too. They gladly accepted our invitation, but they

won't be here for Christmas. Peter is taking all of them back to Innsbruck for Christmas. Can you imagine what Austria would be like at Christmastime, especially the music?"

"Probably something like we don't see or hear around here. But let me tell you, all this family coming and going is like music to my ears. Nothing makes me happier than this old house being full of folks enjoying themselves. And with you and Bella and Karina around, there will be music—beautiful music." Lilah patted Caroline's hand. "Roderick and Sarah needed a family. More than anything, they needed a family, and you have given them one that seems to be growing."

Distracted, Caroline softly repeated Lilah's words. "'One that seems to be growing.'" She caught herself. "Best get busy. I need to run into Lexington to check on a couple of things, and I'd like to be back early afternoon." She looked at Lilah. "Cottage decorating things, you know."

"I see. Now that we know who'll be here when, let's get to work."

They spent the next hour planning the decorating schedule and the Thanksgiving meals and activities.

———·———

Caroline was home by two o'clock. She stopped at Roderick's office door before she entered the kitchen. He was sitting at his desk in front of his computer. "You busy?" she asked softly as though that wouldn't disturb him.

"Always, but not too busy to stop what I'm doing when my wife enters the room."

She went around the desk and leaned to kiss him. His arms went around her waist. "That's good. Because I need help with some bags and boxes. But before that, I need to ask you something."

"I'm listening."

"I know that the gazebo is my Christmas present and you don't want me to see it until then, but my whole family will be here for Thanksgiving. So today, I bought a couple of rocking chairs for the gazebo, and I stopped at the market and bought pumpkins and dried cornstalks and a couple of hay bales. I'd really like it if we could decorate the gazebo for Thanksgiving so that my family can see it."

Roderick was smiling and moving his head from right to left. "You'd do almost anything to see that gazebo, wouldn't you?"

"But I want my family—" He smirked at her, and she decided to come clean. "Fine. Yes, I'd buy cornstalks, fifty pounds of pumpkins, and two wicker rocking chairs to see it. The rocking chairs will be here in about half an hour, but I have the rest in the garage."

He rose from his chair and put his hands on her shoulders. "So, I'm guessing you would like me to put the pumpkins and cornstalks in my truck—oh, and the rocking chairs when they arrive—and drive you down to see your Christmas present in November."

She smiled. "You're always right. And think, if you just do this one thing, you won't be hearing me ask you every day until Christmas if I can see the gazebo."

He chuckled. "That does make it enticing. Hmm . . ." He looked away for a moment, pondering, then faced her again. "You have a deal. Show me the pumpkins."

Within an hour, the white wicker rockers had arrived and the truck was loaded, and they were driving through the meadows to get to the iris garden. Roderick commented. "It would have been a perfect afternoon for a horseback ride. We won't have too many more of those afternoons until springtime."

"The horses don't mind the cold, do they?"

"Not if they're healthy. They tolerate the chill better than we do."

"Good. Then we can still ride in the winter."

"As long as there's no snow on the ground."

Just before the last turn to the oak tree where the gazebo stood, Roderick stopped the truck. "Now, I'm granting you this favor against my better judgment, so you must do as I say. Close your eyes, and promise that you won't open them until I tell you to."

"Done."

He made the turn and drove a couple of hundred yards and parked. "Sit still and keep your eyes closed. I'll come around and get you." He helped her out of the truck and led her to the front entrance of the gazebo. "Now you may open your eyes."

When she opened them, her sudden inhale was audible. "Roderick, it is so much more than I expected. Look! It's perfect and so much like the one Ned and Fred built for the park in Moss Point."

"It's similar, but they built this one just for you. But I'll tell you this now: they will be making one addition when they return for Thanksgiving. They came up with the idea after they left, and they're working on it. It's something just for you."

She walked toward the gazebo and up the steps. "I am so glad you told them to paint it white."

"White paint means periodic maintenance and repainting, but a garden of white and yellow irises and my southern belle of a wife required a white gazebo." He followed her up to the floor of the gazebo. "Ned and Fred did such a good job. And look at the floor. Made from stone right here on the property. Fred's idea. We'll be rocking our grandchildren in this gazebo. Built to last."

"Grandchildren?" She looked out and across the meadow. "Can you imagine how many afternoons we will picnic here? It is truly perfect, Roderick. Thank you." She went to him and kissed his lips and stroked his hair. "You spoil me so."

"Spoiling you is my job."

She laughed. "Right now, your job is to help me get those pumpkins placed on each side of the steps. Then we'll figure out what to do with the cornstalks and bales of hay. When it's all finished, then we'll get the rocking chairs."

Placing a few pumpkins and cornstalks did not take long. "Roderick, let's put the bales of hay right over there." Caroline pointed to a grassy area. "Maybe on another afternoon we can gather some more rocks and create a place to build a fire. We could have a hayride at Thanksgiving, come out here for a fire, and sit on the hay bales."

"Yes, we will do that. Only I'll have a couple of the guys build us a fire pit if that would make you happy."

They finished their arranging. Roderick got the chairs and put them in the gazebo.

Caroline stepped away and looked. "You know the wonderful thing about a gazebo is that we can move the chairs to face any direction. We can watch the sun rise or set and enjoy the changing light and views in every season. Or we can sit and enjoy its shade."

"That never came to my mind, but you are right." Roderick brushed the hay from his shirt and pants. "Ready to go?"

She took his hand and led him to the chairs. "Could we sit for just a little while. It's still a couple of hours before sunset." She sat before he could answer.

"I think we deserve a rest. This will be our inaugural visit to the gazebo."

She grinned. "Our inaugural visit? Maybe you should

carve our initials into that post and put the date on it."

"Don't want to have to answer to Ned and Fred for that."

Caroline rocked and gazed into the late-afternoon sky. She was quiet for several moments. "Every season here at Rockwater is so picturesque and enchanting. Seems there's music for every season." She hummed.

Roderick rocked and sighed. "Hmm. Are you about to sing me a song?"

She reached for his hand. "No. No song. Just thinking about next spring. It will be one like we've never seen." She paused and looked at him. "In the springtime when the daffodils blanket those hills in the distance, and when the white and yellow irises cover the ground around the gazebo and under that oak tree that has seen generations of Adairs, we'll be sitting right here. We'll be rocking, and I'll be singing a lullaby."

Roderick stopped rocking. "A lullaby?"

"Yes. The first of the next generation of Adairs will arrive in the springtime."

Roderick rose from his rocking chair, knelt in front of her, and took her hands. His voice broke as he looked directly into her blue eyes and spoke. "You are having our baby? A baby in the spring?"

She caressed his hair and leaned to kiss him. Then she whispered in his ear. "Yes. And what a springtime it will be!"

About the Author

Phyllis Clark Nichols's character-driven Southern fiction explores profound human questions using the imagined residents of small-town communities you just know you've visited before. With a strong faith and a love for nature, art, music, and ordinary people, she tells redemptive tales of loss and recovery, estrangement and connection, longing, and fulfillment . . . often through surprisingly serendipitous events.

Phyllis grew up in the deep shade of magnolia trees in South Georgia. Born during a hurricane, she is no stranger to the winds of change. In addition to her life as a novelist, Phyllis is a seminary graduate, concert pianist, and cofounder of a national cable network with health- and disability-related programming. Regardless of her role, Phyllis brings creativity and compelling storytelling.

She frequently performs half-hour musical monologues that express her faith, joy, and thoughts about life—all with the homespun humor and gentility of a true Southern woman.

Phyllis currently serves on a number of nonprofit boards. She lives in the Texas Hill Country with her portrait-artist, theologian husband.

Website: PhyllisClarkNichols.com
Facebook: facebook.com/Phyllis Clark Nichols
Twitter: twitter.com/PhyllisCNichols

www.ingramcontent.com/pod-product-compliance
Lightning Source LLC
Chambersburg PA
CBHW070057030726
47506CB00002B/495